BEYOND
THE
ROSES

Cover Design: Perfect Pear Creative Covers
Editing: Editing 4 Indies
Formatting: E.M. Tippetts Book Designs

Follow me on:

authormonicajames.com

OTHER BOOKS BY
MONICA JAMES

THE I SURRENDER SERIES

I Surrender

Surrender to Me

Surrendered

White

SOMETHING LIKE NORMAL SERIES

Something like Normal

Something like Redemption

Something like Love

A HARD LOVE ROMANCE

Dirty Dix

Wicked Dix

The Hunt

MEMORIES FROM YESTERDAY DUET

Forgetting You, Forgetting Me

Forgetting You, Remembering Me

SINS OF THE HEART DUET

Absinthe of the Heart

Defiance of the Heart

ALL THE PRETTY THINGS TRILOGY

Bad Saint

Fallen Saint

Forever My Saint

The Devil's Crown-Part One (Spin-Off)

The Devil's Crown-Part Two (Spin-Off)

THE MONSTERS WITHIN DUET

Bullseye

Blowback

STANDALONE

Mr. Write

Chase the Butterflies

Beyond the Roses

DEDICATION

For my father. You're in my heart. Always. I love you.

ONE

Sometimes, I wonder what it would feel like to be somebody else. I have no preference who, just someone other than me. They wouldn't have to be tall, or thin, or even beautiful. In fact, I'd rather they were ordinary, that they'd blend into a crowd because after being extraordinary, all I wish for is…silence.

"Lola? LOLA!"

A mother's role is to protect, teach, and love their kin unconditionally. And most mothers embrace this responsibility. Some even say that having a child changed their life forever. It gave them a purpose. Unfortunately for me, my mother, Camille Van Allen, missed the memo.

Sighing, I lower the newest Dan Brown novel and remove

my earbuds.

There is no questioning my mother's beauty. Her long, chestnut hair is usually styled in a low chignon, just as she wears it now. Her large green eyes would appear alien on anyone else, but her high cheekbones, pink pout, and slim, delicate nose complement her gracious look. She'd never be seen in anything but designer threads, and although I didn't understand it, I accepted it because I never knew my mother being anything but…perfect. And for that, I envied her because…I'm anything but perfect.

"Sorry, what did you say?" I give her my full attention.

"I said, I wish you'd reconsider and come to Europe with us for the summer. Isn't that right, Dermott?" This is all bullshit, however.

My father peers at me through the rearview mirror, his kind blue eyes reflecting his sadness, but he nods since my mother is awaiting his reply. "Yes, that's right, but I know given your… circumstances"—his pause reveals my circumstances can't be swept under the rug as easily for him as it can for my mom— "why you want to do this." Yet another pause. There seem to be a lot of those lately.

I have accepted that normality isn't in the cards for me. I accepted it four years ago. Many days have passed since then, but unfortunately for me, a new day doesn't bring new hope. My future is mapped out before me, and I don't even have a say in how my story ends.

Discreetly wiping away the betrayal tears that slip from the corners of my eyes, I try my best to smile. My mother, on the other hand, is seconds away from slapping the insolence from my father's cheek. But she says nothing.

This is a common occurrence for the Van Allen family. We don't air our dirty laundry. We especially don't discuss matters that would tarnish the family name. Regrettably, I'm a matter that has stained our reputation.

Peering out the window, I press my forehead to the cool glass, wishing I could feel the sunrays on my skin. Breathtaking landscapes of thunderous waterfalls, lush green forests, and untouched rocky plains pass me by. The sight is beautiful. It's nice to get in touch with nature, seeing as my apartment on the Upper East Side encompasses the hustle and bustle that New York is famous for. Where I'm going, I'll be lucky to get cell reception. Not that it matters because who would I call anyway? My heart aches at the thought.

The farther my dad drives, the more remote and isolated things become, but that's the plan. That's what I signed up for.

The GPS spits out directions, the cheerful, robotic voice the only sound filling the stale air. To the outside world, we're the perfect all-American family, and once upon a time, we were, but behind closed doors, my family hasn't been happy for a very long time. It saddens me to think that I'm the reason behind that sorrow.

My father raises his knowledgeable eyes, reading my

heartache instantly. He feels as if he has failed me, but he hasn't. Some people are just born unlucky.

Tall pine trees line the graveled road like regimented soldiers, never wavering from their position of keeping watch over all those who travel down this shaded path. I know we're close; I can feel the sudden shift in the sky.

The navy Mercedes begins its journey down the winding dirt road. The sun has long gone, hidden away, and a chill passes over me, the unexpected cold an omen of things to come, maybe?

But I quash it down and welcome my arrival at Strawberry Fields with a different mindset. I'm energized and enthusiastic because this is the most valuable I've felt in months.

The tires crunch over the gravel as Dad drives the road with care. He takes a sharp left, and up over the hill, I see it—the white Gothic-style mansion.

"Look, they have horses." My dad's animated tone reminds me of when he took me to see the lions at the zoo when I was seven. Life was so simple back then. I'd give anything to get that back. It was a time of innocence when my world wasn't filled with words I didn't understand.

Returning to the present, I realize my father also yearns for that time. He wants his perfect daughter back, but I haven't been perfect for a long while.

My father pulls the car up beside the domed entrance, and both my parents exit the car with enthusiasm. Collecting my belongings, I swing my legs, placing my sneakers onto the rocky ground. Taking a deep breath, I will my body to move. I stand, thankful that no tremors wrack my frame.

A small win for me.

My mom passes me my suitcase from the trunk, turning up her lip when she sees me stand at my full height of five feet three. "Lola, really? Surely you have something nicer to wear." My scuffed Chucks, torn blue jeans, and PETA tee are not Camille Van Allen approved. Once upon a time, I wore the cocktail dresses and fancy jewels, but that isn't me anymore.

"You look like a homeless person," she says, adding insult to injury.

My last tether snaps. "I hardly think I can get away with wearing heels, *Mother*." My tone drips with venom. I suddenly wish I caught a cab instead of asking them to drive me.

Thankfully, a vibrant voice sounds across the grounds, interrupting a no doubt nasty moment. "Welcome, you must be Lola."

When the middle-aged woman comes to a stop in front of me, her compassion shines through with no obvious ulterior motives. She's here out of the goodness of her heart, and I instantly like her.

"Yes, that's me."

"Hello, Lola. I'm Ms. Carrington, but you can call me June. I'm the administrator here." I like her even more because I recognize her name from the welcome packet I received.

"Hello, June. I can't wait to start. Just point me in the right direction." As June looks at me closely, I have no doubt she's read over my application and everything I disclosed.

Peering up at the enormous manor, I suddenly have a premonition that once I leave, I'll be a different person. I don't know why or how. I just know that once I walk through those doors, my life will change.

"Bye, Dad." I shuffle over, giving him a tight hug.

"Goodbye. I'm proud of you." He squeezes me harder.

I pull from his embrace and smile. "Make sure you eat lots of gelato for me."

His eyes crinkle as he laughs. "You got it." I don't hear the sound too often, but I guess there isn't much left for him to laugh about.

Standing off to the side, my mother waits for some emotional farewell, but she's all for show. I look into her green eyes, eyes so similar to mine. Mine may be hidden behind thick black frames, but there is no doubt I inherited my looks from her. But unlike her, my looks will fade. They already have.

"Bye, Mom. Have a safe flight." I amble over, feeling awkward as I give her a loose hug.

"We will, honey."

Taking one last look at them, I draw the difference between past and future. My future is waiting just past those doors. With that mindset, June and I walk toward the entrance. Life is too short for delays.

Peering up, I stop a few feet away, masking the sun with a cupped hand over my brow. The air is fresh, the sun warm. The sense of discovery still surrounds me, so with a skip to my usual heavy step, I follow June.

The moment I set foot inside the foyer, I'm hit with the elegance Strawberry Fields encompasses. High decorated ceilings, pristine white walls, and polished marble floors are just the start of what is set out before me. I look around in awe; not because I haven't seen such luxuries before, but because there is a tenderness I'm unfamiliar with.

A gentle Bach piece soothes and welcomes all of those who are on the same expedition as me. Regardless of our extravagant surroundings, there is no denying why we are here. The thought weighs heavily like a manacle around my heart, shadowing my newfound excitement with melancholy. Shaking my head to dispel such thoughts, I quicken my step to catch up to June.

"This is your room," June informs me over her shoulder, just before stopping in front of a wooden door.

"Take your time getting settled. There are a few more volunteers yet to arrive. You being here means so much to us."

I can't help but smile at her kindness. "Thank you."

June may be one of the only people who can understand what I'm going through because, sadly for her, she sees it every day.

She doesn't linger.

I clutch the cool door handle, but a voice behind me stops

me from entering. "Hi! I'm Zoe. Fellow volunteer."

Turning, I see a woman of similar age to me standing mere feet away. Her dark hair is short, only a few inches in length. It seems to emphasize the clarity of her blue eyes. She extends her slender hand, which I shake. Her warmth thaws my chill.

"Hi, I'm Lola."

"Nice to meet you." Without pause, she takes the suitcase from my hand and wanders into my room, dragging it behind her.

I follow suit, and the first thing that captures my attention is the two wide windows directly in front of me. They are fitted with sheets of Tiffany glass. The stunning stained image is spread across both windows. The scene is of a pink weeping willow. The petals litter the side panel and extend along the top; the vibrant colors highlighted as the sun breaks through.

Once I tear my eyes away from the magnificence, I admire the room's generous size. A stunning sky-blue duvet covers the bed, and matching throw pillows rest quaintly against one another.

The plush carpet feels soft beneath my feet as I turn in a small circle, absorbing the quiet.

"You weren't expecting this?" Zoe asks, leaving my suitcase at the foot of the bed as she flops onto the mattress, stomach first. I stifle a giggle behind my hand.

"I don't know what I was expecting," I confess honestly. "I thought it was going to be a little more... rustic." I didn't look at any photos online because I didn't care what my housing looked like. That's not the reason I decided to come.

Zoe sits up, her intelligent eyes focusing on me. "So…why are you here?" I wheeze in a strangled breath, surprised by her flippant attitude. I push my glasses up the bridge of my nose, swallowing loudly.

"Ah, c'mon, life is short…we both know that. There's no point in being coy. This is my third year here, and in my experience, we all come here for a reason. Mine is my little sister passed away from cancer three years ago."

The spectacular walls, ones I once admired, are now closing in on me as I'm finding it harder to breathe. I bend at the waist and wrap my arms around my middle, wishing I'd paid more attention to Dr. Carter when he detailed ways for me to deal with stress.

"Lola, all those drugs you're on…they're to help you."

"Help me how?" I was so angry. I still am. Why did this happen? What did I do to deserve such a punishment? What did *she* do to deserve such injustice?

"If you don't take them, you'll—"

No.

Why is life so cruel?

I slam my hands over my ears, needing to block out the voices in my head. But the more desperate I become to escape my future, the louder things become.

"…they're trial drugs for a high-grade glioblastoma, also

known as grade four astrocytoma, which is growing on the right side of your brain." Tears prick my eyes because no matter how fast I run, I can never outrun fate.

"Lola, are you all right?" Zoe's voice portrays concern, but her sympathy only makes me feel worse.

Hidden beneath the pretty pastels, the comforting calmness, and the soothing works of Bach is the epicenter of what this place is. The superficial ruse can't mask the truth. Strawberry Fields is a sanctuary, a summer camp where terminally ill children come to forget and just be kids.

And the reason I'm here—I'm here to volunteer because those children are me.

My name is Lola Van Allen. There's no easy way to say it, but…I'm dying.

TWO

"**L**ola, can you hear me?" Zoe's words fade in and out of focus, but I'm familiar with the muted voices. It started when I was twenty-one.

I did what every socialite my age did—I shopped, partied. I didn't have a care in the world. But when I began hearing voices no one else heard, I thought I was going crazy. And when the voices came with debilitating headaches, I went to the best doctors in New York because I knew something wasn't right. They ran endless tests, and that was when they found it—a black blob inside my head.

It turns out, the blob was a glioblastoma, also known as grade four astrocytoma, which was devouring the right side of my brain. In layman's terms, I had an inoperable brain tumor.

However, I refused to accept my fate, adamant there was some mistake. This didn't happen to people like me. How naïve I was because no matter who I saw, the prognosis was always the same.

The symptoms amplified weeks later. I was a car wreck. Not only did I have blurred vision, occasional blackouts, and spoke with a stutter, but I also walked with a slight limp. It goes without saying the supposedly best years of my life ended up being my worst.

All of my so-called friends hit the road when things got serious, proving to me just how superficial and shallow my life really was.

My mother couldn't deal with everyone looking at her differently because word spread the Van Allen name was tarnished. That's how smallminded the social circle my mother belonged to was—the circle *I* once belonged to.

But I made the most out of my shitty situation. For the first time in my life, I opened a book and studied. I became the master of my own disease; educating myself, I was determined to find a cure. I exhausted every drug my doctors gave me, but to no avail. The chemotherapy drugs may as well have been aspirin.

It took me a long while, but finally, my perseverance paid off. A doctor in Germany claimed to have found a drug that broke down the protein in the tumor I had, thus reducing the size. Trials were taking place in Germany, and I wanted in.

I phoned my doctor, Dr. Carter, who was aware of the trials. He said I didn't have anything to lose, and I was put on the wait list.

Three weeks later, I was taking every color of drug known to mankind four times a day for the next year. The side effects were hideous, but so was having the sword of Damocles hanging over my head. I was constantly sick with flu-like symptoms as the drugs depleted my immune system. My hair fell out completely, which was fine, as it was thinning from the chemo anyway. But to my mother, I highlighted the fact that her perfect life wasn't so perfect after all. She preferred me the spoiled brat I once was as opposed to the sick young woman I became.

But I continued because, after the first quarter of the trial, my tumor had shrunk. It was now roughly the size of a small lemon.

Dr. Carter told me not to get my hopes up, but I was thrilled. I was convinced I would beat this. I was beating the odds as it was for surviving for as long as I had, but it was all in vain. Regardless, for the first time in a long time, I had hope. And that hope was thanks to someone who changed my life forever.

Georgia Faye was my one and only true friend. All my socialite friends had long forgotten about me, and our "friendship" presented itself for what it truly was—superficial, just like the world I once lived and thrived in.

I met Georgia while she too was receiving the trial drugs. We would chat daily, and it was nice to have someone who understood just how hard life was. Soon, we grew inseparable, as our dire circumstances bound us together.

We decided we wouldn't let this disease beat us without a fight. Georgia's tumor was slightly larger and more aggressive than mine was, but that only inspired her to fight harder. Georgia was the most positive and inspirational person I knew.

We joined a gym, grew strong, and obliterated the stigma that came with being sick. We drank disgusting potions believed to keep the brain healthy, but we downed that gunk like it was going out of fashion. Everything was better back then because Georgia was by my side.

When our results came back as showing improvement, we felt like the luckiest girls alive.

Both our muscle masses had grown thanks to our strenuous workouts, so my limp was gone. Georgia helped me with my stutter while I helped her with her blackouts by teaching her some meditation I learned in yoga.

Life was good. Well, as good as good can be for two women, such as Georgia and me.

Georgia and I were friends for a year, and it was the best year of my life. But life can be cruel, and it showed me just how unforgiving it could be. To celebrate her twenty-fifth birthday, we were going to go out to a bar.

I was applying my favorite shade of lipstick when my cell rang. There was a bounce to my step, but it was the last I ever had. On the other end of the line was Georgia's mom—she was sobbing, inconsolable, her words a blubbering mess. She informed me that Georgia had passed in her sleep. She had succumbed to the disease we were certain we would beat.

The funeral was beautiful. Georgia would have loved it. It was colorful and vivacious, just like Georgia. But my best friend would be none of those things ever again. After Georgia's death, I lost all hope. It felt as if my heart was ripped from my chest. I stopped doing all the things Georgia and I used to do as the memories were too painful to bear alone.

If the strongest person I knew couldn't beat this, then how could I?

Dr. Carter said a new trial drug had just become available, and that I was the perfect candidate. It was stronger than the previous drugs, and because of my positive test results, he thought I had a good shot at making my inoperable tumor operable. The previous drugs had reduced the size of my tumor, but it was still inoperable. He had hope. But me, I didn't. Once upon a time, I had hope, but all it did was give me a false sense of normalcy. So I stopped taking any drugs and accepted that I would eventually end up in a hole in the ground, just like the only person I ever loved, and who had loved me back in return.

Wiping away the torrent of tears, I force myself to return to the now. Since Georgia's death, it's been too easy to slip back into the darkness.

"S-sorry, Zoe, I didn't m-mean to scare y-you." I stand slowly, the world constantly spinning. When I meet her wide, concerned eyes, my stomach drops.

"It's completely okay. Please don't apologize. Are you all right?"

"I'll be okay." Zoe doesn't buy it, but she doesn't press.

"Can I help you unpack?"

"I can unpack later. I'd love to take a look around."

"I'd be happy to show you."

"Sure, thank you."

A grin lights up her face. "Would you mind if I go to my room first? I need to grab a sweater."

"Of course, no problem." She's out the door, promising to be back in five minutes.

Deciding to go barefoot, I sit on the edge of the bed and untie my laces. As I kick off my shoes, a flesh of red from inside my backpack catches my eye. I know without looking what it is.

This red bandana I packed with care belonged to Georgia.

She used to wear it around her pale head with pride. Deciding to honor my friend, I reach for it, fingering the soft material between my fingers. "I miss you," I whisper, wishing she was here with me.

Suppressing my sadness, I wobble as I walk over to the wall mirror. I hate that my limp comes and goes because I know that I can be strong again. But there's no point.

My reflection stares back at me in the mirror as I comb my fingers through my chestnut hair. It's grown healthy since I stopped taking the drugs. It's just past my shoulders. I tie the bandana in my hair, styling it like a headband, just how Georgia did. The red draws out the green in my eyes. It also emphasizes the dark circles. I look and feel so much older than twenty-five.

Looking around my room, I appreciate Strawberry Fields for what it is—it's a holiday camp, a summer vacation for the dying. The membership requirements—you must be dying to get in—pun completely intentional.

And that's why I'm here.

The doctors have told me it's only a matter of time before I succumb to my illness, just like Georgia. But until that time comes, I want to help people. I've volunteered for three months because after reading the brochure, no matter how much time I have left, I want to make a difference. I can relate to what these kids are going through because all I ever wanted was for someone to listen to me and to be treated normally. I intend to be here for these kids and let them know they're not alone. I want them to know that even though they've been given a life sentence, that doesn't mean they can't live life to the fullest. I want them to know that it's okay to be different.

This is the first time in so many months I feel like I belong.

A smile is etched on my face as I close my door, thankful I listened to my gut and came here. However, a yelp replaced that smile when I turn without looking and bump straight into something hard.

At first, I'm certain it's the wall, but that's impossible, considering I'm standing in the open corridor. That only leaves one other option. I've just rudely slammed into someone.

"I am so…" The words die in a gargled mess when I peer up, and up, and see the striking face of a man who emanates sheer masculinity. The first thing that catches my attention is the vibrancy of his blue-gray eyes. They are crystal clear, mesmerizing beneath his black, horn-rimmed glasses. His dark brown hair is slicked back with short sides.

His face is complete perfection, and I'm staring like a total creep.

Mortified, I look down, which is a bad idea because I see that perfect face is attached to a perfect body. I now understand why I believed I bumped into a wall—a brick wall, that is—because he has muscles where I didn't even know muscles existed.

"Sorry," I choke out, finishing my sentence spoken a lifetime ago.

"No problem," he replies a moment later. His voice is deep, honeyed. I suddenly wonder why my arms feel like they're on fire. Peering down, I see his strong fingers are wrapped around my biceps. The gesture was to stop me from falling, which I'm grateful for because I'm certain I'm about to collapse in a messy heap.

He is the most handsome man I have ever seen. I can't help but wonder who he is.

Zoe answers the question for me. "Hello, Dr. Archibald."

Her voice seems to snap us from whatever bubble we're

in because he smoothly removes his hands while I physically shake my head, hoping to knock some sense into it.

He clears his throat before turning to look at her. "Hi, Zoe. Keeping out of mischief, I hope?"

She chuckles, and I'm thankful I can breathe again. "Shh, I have a reputation to uphold."

He's a *doctor*? I suddenly feel beyond mortified for slobbering all over myself.

"Okay. Your secret is safe with me." There is a weighty silence before Dr. Archibald spins slowly. I hold my breath. "I'm sorry I didn't introduce myself. I'm Dr. Archibald. I'm one of the many doctors who work here."

"Hello, Dr. Archibald. It's nice to meet you. I'm Lola. Lola Van Allen." I give him a small wave, thankful I managed to spit out my sentence in one attempt.

"Likewise." He places his hands into his pressed pants pockets. "Did you just arrive?"

His innocent comment snaps me from my hormone-fueled episode, and I nod. "Yes. Zoe was just about to show me around."

A dimple kisses his right whiskered cheek. "Well, you're in good hands. I'll see you around, Lola." I nod, incapable of speech.

He lingers for a moment, clearly sizing me up. He gives me a once-over before those stunning blue eyes rest on the bandana in my hair. Can he see the significance? How I tied it with love and care.

He appears to want to say something else but changes his mind at the last minute. The air shifts.

A second later, he walks off before I can question my temporary insanity further.

A small giggle has me turning over my shoulder, raising a brow. "What?" I'm surprised I can speak.

Zoe shrugs mischievously. "Nothing," she replies, dragging out the G.

"Spit it out." I'm curious to know what's going on.

"Oh nothing, other than the fact you've just been infected with the Dr. Roman Archibald love bug."

"The what?" I scrunch up my nose.

She bursts into fits of laughter. "You've got a lot to learn." She wraps her arm around me playfully. "What do you want to see first?"

"I want to see it all." And for the first time in a long time, I mean it.

Zoe shows me the gardens first as the sun is too beautiful to waste. The earth feels liberating beneath my toes; so much so, Zoe also kicks off her sandals halfway through the tour.

The luscious greens extend as far as the eye can see. Numerous water activities take place on the lake as the still waters run along the edge of the entire property. Many rowboats are tied to the docks.

Zoe details the multiple activities that take place on different days. Water polo, canoeing, volleyball, golf, and horseback riding are just the start of what's on hand. A handful of kids are sitting under the trees and reading while most are splashing water in the lake.

Zoe is chatting about how Strawberry Fields caters for thirty kids when I stop, needing to catch my breath. She doesn't realize until she turns and sees me leaning against a tree for support. "Oh, my god! Am I walking too fast? I'm so sorry." She runs over, concerned.

"It's okay. I just…my leg. It hurts sometimes." My limp has returned since I stopped taking the drugs. Not as bad as before, but when I overdo it, it reminds me that it's winning at life.

Seeing as Zoe and I will most likely be working together over the next three months, and I don't have anything to hide, I see no point in being evasive. "So the answer to your question as to why I'm here…I have a brain tumor. Inoperable. I've tried many different drugs. Nothing worked except a trial drug, but that too ended up being bullshit." I can't help but be bitter. "The doctors said I could go at any time, but no one knows their fate."

When Zoe blinks once, I quickly backtrack. "Sorry. That wasn't incredibly depressing or anything. I just wanted to be honest."

She wets her lips, shaking her head. "No, it's not depressing.

It's uplifting and inspirational that you want to come here and share your experience with kids who could really use your strength. What you're doing…you're making a difference, and these kids will appreciate it, even if they don't show it half the time."

A baseball flies past our heads while she grins.

I've never been ashamed of my illness, which is why I decided to come here. Getting through to children who don't understand why they've been dealt such a bad hand can be tough, and I've seen it with my own two eyes. But being able to relate to them by telling my story—I can only hope I'll be there for them like Georgia was for me.

Zoe is clearly interested in what I just said, and I'm happy to tell her whatever she wants to know. "So you don't take any pills? No chemo drugs?"

"No. I don't see the point. They give me false hope. I'm on medication to control my seizures and migraines. They wanted me to take a mood stabilizer, but I'm not interested in living the rest of my short life as a zombie. But as far as drugs to help my condition, there aren't any. I've tried them all. The limp comes and goes because the tumor is pressing against my frontal lobe, affecting my movement. And just for fun, my temporal lobe is also affected, and that's why I s-stutter occasionally." It kicks in right on cue.

Zoe is quiet, which is a first for her.

"I need a drink," I say out loud, needing to lighten the

mood. I didn't come here for me. I came here to *help* others *like* me.

Zoe sniffs, before letting out a strangled laugh. "Me too." The mood settles as we walk to the house.

"Zoe, I've been looking for you," says a sweet voice. Up ahead, I see a slender girl in a wheelchair veer her way over to us.

"Cassandra." Zoe smiles and throws her arms around her neck. "I want you to meet my new friend, Lola Van Allen."

"It's nice to meet you, Cassandra." I bend forward and shake her limp hand, which is curled by her side. Cassandra is almost completely paralyzed from the chest down. She controls her motorized wheelchair by a joystick with her left hand.

I don't let that stop me from reaching out and touching her because she's not a leper. None of us are.

Cassandra smiles, and the sight is truly beautiful.

"Who's hungry? It's almost time for lunch," Zoe says.

My stomach growls at the mere mention of food. They turn to look at me and burst into fits of laughter. It's nice to laugh. Zoe leads the way.

We enter the dining room, which looks like something out of a movie. A crystal chandelier hangs from the high ceiling. The sunlight drifting in from the copious windows sends mini rainbows across the room as it strikes each dangling gemstone. A vase of roses sits in the center of each table, filling the room with a sweet fragrance.

We follow Cassandra, who zips over to a table in a small alcove. Looking around, I acquaint myself with my fellow volunteers and the children I'll be spending my time with. They're a mixed bunch. Some look unwell while others appear healthy, but the common factor is they're all under fifteen, and they're dying.

"I was homeschooled," I hear the teenage girl at the next table say to her peer. "Yup, I'm *that* freak."

I cluck my tongue.

This is what I came here for. To put an end to this stigma associated with being sick.

Trying this volunteer thing on for size, I approach the table, not wanting to press on my first day. "Hi, I'm Lola." Both girls look at me. "I overheard what you said, and I just want you to know that no, you're not a freak. We're just...different."

The girl looks at me, turning up her lip bitterly. I know what she sees. On the outside, I look like the perfect beacon of health.

Crouching down and dropping to her level, I smile. This is why I'm here. To make a difference. "I have a brain tumor, so if you're a freak, then so am I." Her eyes widen, and I can see it. We're both in the same club no one wants to join, but we're banded by shitty circumstances nonetheless.

"Are you a volunteer here?"

I nod, hoping it's a good thing.

It is.

She beams brightly and reaches for her cell. "I'm going to

text Francis and Ryan. You have to be our buddy. I'm Tash, by the way."

When I read over the welcoming pack, it stated a group of kids are assigned a buddy. A buddy is someone who does activities with their group and is the leader of the pack. It warms me beyond words that Tash wants me as hers.

The smell of ripe tomatoes and golden mozzarella wafts through the air. Volunteers in the green and navy uniform emerge from three entrances off to the sides, carrying silver trays of food.

An older lady walks over to Cassandra and smiles. "Hello, Cassandra. I hope you're hungry. We have lasagna on the menu." Cassandra sighs, and I don't understand why until the volunteer sits beside her and produces an adult bib. She ties it around her neck as Cassandra can't do it herself.

"Welcome to my hell," she quips when she notices Tash looking at her.

Tash quickly averts her gaze. "I'm sorry. I didn't mean to be rude."

"It's okay. Alpers-Huttenlocher syndrome hasn't been kind to me for over ten years. I'm used to people staring."

I've read about Cassandra's condition, as it's a disease that attacks the brain. Cassandra, just like me, would have been healthy and not known better. She walked, talked, and ate on her own, but our stories take the same turn. She would have experienced inexplicable changes, and then as time progressed, she would have watched herself deteriorate before her eyes, helpless to stop it.

Tears sting, but I wipe them away. None of us wants sympathy.

A beautiful woman in a lilac jacket and white pleated pants enters the room. Her white heels add height to her petite frame. Her long dark hair is twisted into a high bun, emphasizing her large green eyes and plump coral-painted lips.

She searches the room, appearing to seek someone out. When her gaze lands on me, I'm surprised to see that someone is me. She waves, and I turn over my shoulder to ensure it *is* me she's addressing. I see it is.

"Hello, Lola." I meet her warm eyes. "I'm Tamara Meriwether, the art teacher." I nod with a smile. "Sorry to interrupt lunch, but I wanted to give you this." She passes me a clear folder as I stand.

"Thank you." I accept and open it up to see a timetable and a long list of activities.

"You're helping out in my art class. I thought you may want it now as we're starting some fun activities after lunch."

"That sounds great. I can't wait."

"Wonderful." She claps her hands together, her Tiffany bracelets twinkling under the bright lights. "All the information is in the folder. The official welcoming happens tonight. But June doesn't like to make a fuss, and instead, we just carry on like normal. That's why we head straight into activities on the first day." I like June even more.

Before coming here, I did an online introduction on what to expect. It was about three hours' worth of study, and even though June may seem casual in her approach, she runs this place with the utmost precision.

"Great. Thank you for this." I hold up the folder.

She nods and opens her mouth, ready to say something, but then abruptly stops and gazes off into the distance over my shoulder. I wait for her to return eye contact, but she doesn't. In fact, her pupils dilate, and she appears flustered.

Curious, I turn to look at what has captured her attention. I need not look far. Standing a few feet away, Dr. Archibald talks to a young girl. He listens, nodding every so often. He's a pillar of support and care.

When he looks our way, a breathy sigh leaves Tamara's parted lips. My first instinct is to look away, but for some unknown reason, I don't. I admire the way Dr. Archibald holds himself with complete confidence and control. He has rolled up the sleeves of his crisp shirt, revealing taut, muscular forearms. He doesn't look like your typical doctor because he's young, around thirty, and he also looks like he belongs on the cover of *Vogue*.

I wonder what brought him here.

When he matches my stare and appears to be as transfixed by me as I am by him, the air sizzles around me. I shyly push my glasses up my nose, feeling an unfamiliar warmth pool within. I'm embarrassed, as I'm certain he can read my strange response to him.

"I'll see you this afternoon." Tamara's voice severs my trance-like state. Zoe was right; I *am* infected by the Dr. Roman Archibald love bug.

"Yes." I clear my hoarse voice. "Yes, I'll see you then."

She scampers past me, headed Dr. Archibald's way. His eyes stay focused on me. However, the look is so intense I feel light-headed. When he finally breaks our eye lock, I can breathe again.

I'm looking forward to Tamara's class.

The timetable seems well mapped out with enough activities to keep everyone busy. When I enter the pastel green room, I admire the inspirational pictures that litter the walls and relish in the soft sprinkle of lavender in the air.

About ten children are seated at desks with bright paints and large sheets of paper spread out in front of them. They all seem excited to get started.

"Hi, I'm Lola." I give a small wave while the kids turn in their seats to give me their undivided attention. "I'll be helping today. So if you have any questions, let me know."

I can't kick my sense of happiness. These children look as excited as I am to be here, confirming that I'm doing the right thing.

Tamara enters, her stylish jacket over her forearm. She appears at ease and comfortable in her natural habitat. "Hello, everyone. Once we're all settled, we will start." She floats over to the docking station and connects her pink iPod.

She then kicks off her heels and places them in the corner of the room. "Today, we're going to do an exercise which requires nothing but a pen and paper." She reaches into her large tote bag. After a moment of riffling around, she produces a stack of journals. "These are yours to keep, and I encourage you to write or draw in them whenever you feel the need." She walks around the room, handing out the books. Her movements are so graceful and agile; a sense of calm surrounds her. She smiles gently when offering me my book.

When everyone has their supplies, she continues. "These journals are for when you don't know what to say." She gazes around the room, connecting with each of us. "There is no judgment here. No rules. No wrong or right. I want you to express everything you feel, no matter what it is. Take your time, and remember, this is a safe place. Begin when you're ready."

There is no doubt Tamara loves what she does.

Just as I'm about to offer my assistance, Tamara gently reaches for my arm. "How about you take a moment to write down why you're here? I do this with all the volunteers. It helps." There is no need for her to explain. Being here takes a toll on everyone.

But I've never been one to write down my feelings even though my doctors encouraged it. I just didn't see the point. Writing down how shitty my life is wouldn't change my circumstances.

I don't see my opinion changing anytime soon, but I open the book, pressing down on the spine in thought. I've always been a reader, as the thought of being a writer is beyond frightening. All those words detailing your feelings, I couldn't think of anything worse. I rub over my chest, my heart squeezing as I know why I'm so afraid. I know who I would write about. She was the only person who listened, really listened, not because she was waiting for her turn to speak, but because she cared about what I had to say.

With that thought in mind, I take the pen and I...let go.

I miss you, G...so much. Every day, I think it's going to get easier, but it doesn't. It gets harder. The thought of doing this alone is scarier than living. I wish I'd gone with you because I have nothing left to live for.

Each night, I wonder if this is the night I won't wake up, if it is finally my time. I hate that a small part of me is disappointed when I bear witness to a new sunrise. I know you'd give anything to have just one more day, and here I am, wishing it was my last. I feel ungrateful. I am.

If I could give you my life to save yours, I would...in a heartbeat.

You're the best thing that ever happened to me. I'm sorry I didn't tell you that more often. I love you, Georgia. Pleasse...com bak.

The last three words appear fuzzy, and my head begins to spin. Something isn't right.

"Lola?" Tamara's sluggish voice sounds as though she's a million miles away.

A splitting pain stabs at my temple, leaving me winded as I clutch my stomach.

No, not again.

Shooting upright, I quickly excuse myself to find the nearest bathroom. Prior to my losing grip on reality, every color of the rainbow flashes before my eyes, and then...everything is replaced with black.

THREE

"She's getting her color back."

"Yes, she is."

"Shall I check her blood pressure again?"

"No, it's fine. I've got it from here."

Hushed voices that aren't really hushed at all float in and out like a radio station trying to tune into its frequency. I have no idea where I am. What's the last thing I remember? I try to recall, but it hurts—it always does.

Running a clammy hand down my face, I scrub over my eyes.

"Ms. Van Allen, can you hear me?"

The deep voice is as smooth as summer cherries. Regardless, I groan, eyes still sealed shut. "It's Lola. Ms. Van Allen is my mother, and I'd rather there was only one of her."

"Oh, c'mon, she can't be that bad."

"She makes Satan look like Mother Theresa."

I'm not trying to be funny, so when I hear a husky chuckle, I crack open an eye. The world is beyond blurry. "My glasses?" I blindly reach out for them and am thankful when they're placed in my palm.

Slipping them onto my face, I slowly take in my unfamiliar surroundings. The only thing I recognize is the man sitting by my bedside. "Dr. Archibald?" It's a statement, intersected with a question.

Shooting upright, I ignore the pain in my head as I gather my bearings. The sterile white walls, beeping machines, and antiseptic smell all point to one place.

"How are you feeling?" he asks, interrupting my thoughts.

My snarled hair feels like straw as I try to tame it. I give up, as it'll take a miracle to tame that beast. "I feel like I've got the world's worst hangover...without the booze."

Again, I'm not attempting to be entertaining, so I'm surprised when I see Dr. Archibald's perfect lips lift at the corner. His delicious exotic fragrance of fresh citrus and woodsy notes of sandalwood overpowers the sterility and has me wanting to take a bigger whiff. But I don't.

"You passed out," he explains, leaning forward in the plastic chair.

"It won't happen again." This is exactly what I was fearful of.

These blackouts are caused by my condition, and although I have them under control on most days, they sneak up on me at times. Like today. I realize I forgot to take my pills this morning. Rookie move on my part.

There is silence for a pregnant moment, those blue eyes hidden beneath clear lenses speaking a language I don't understand. He reaches for the stethoscope around his neck and stands. "I'm just going to check your vitals."

Nodding, I sit taller and lean forward.

He clears his throat before placing the metal disc against my back. "Take a deep breath in," he instructs. I do as he asks. "Good. And out." I exhale, his closeness sending a shiver throughout my entire body.

He moves over to the other side and asks me to do the same thing. This time, he leans in closer, our bodies a hairsbreadth away from touching. "Good." His eyes meet mine when he pulls away. His nearness is almost suffocating.

The neckline of my top is low, allowing Dr. Archibald easy access. He visibly swallows before placing the metal against my skin. I jump as it's cold. "Sorry," he apologizes, peering down at me.

I nod, too afraid to speak.

His huge body shadows mine, his closeness a surprising comfort. He listens to my heart, which is nigh on exploding from my chest. He moves the drum around while listening, his face pensive. My breathing becomes staggered; my heart determined to win an imaginary race. I'm beyond embarrassed as this is the worst time for my body to betray my nerves.

When his fingers brush lightly over my skin, I chew the inside of my cheek to stop my unexpected response to him. I attempt to envision anything other than Dr. Archibald's intoxicating smell. When he lifts the drum and removes the ear tips, I let out the trapped breath I didn't even know I was holding.

"Your heart is fine," he declares, looping the stethoscope around his neck. His comment shatters my blissful bubble.

"It's not my heart that's the problem," I reply honestly.

He frowns, appearing repentant. "Regardless of our ailments, I think the heart is always affected."

I wasn't expecting such a response, but he's right. The vital organ is our epicenter.

"Tamara said you ran out of class. One of the volunteers found you in the bathroom, passed out." He pauses, and I know why. "I had to report it to June, of course, and she told me of your condition."

I'm about ready to lecture him about the invasion of privacy, but I can understand why.

"I've read over your file."

I explained my condition on the application. Dr. Carter gave me the green light to do this as I didn't want management going in blind when they gave me the job.

Lowering my eyes, I tug at a loose thread on the cotton

blanket. "Lucky you."

He ignores my wisecrack. "Are you on any medication?"

"Whatever time I have left, I don't wish to live as a comatose zombie, Dr. Archibald. I want to remember who I was and face death, not hide under a medicated blanket."

I can see I've caught him off guard with my bluntness and am about to apologize but pause when a gravelly rumble sounds loudly within his chest. "Good for you, Ms.—Lola," he hastily corrects. "You're a brave young woman."

"I'm far from brave, but thank you."

His silence is heavy, speaking volumes. But I never expected him to express what he does next. "Never underestimate your impact on the world. You just may be someone's reason for living."

I wonder just whom Dr. Archibald's reason is. I have no doubt he has a long line of admirers and may even be married or have a girlfriend.

"Everything is okay, so you're good to leave whenever you're ready," he says, disturbing my thoughts.

His comment surprises me. "I can stay?"

"Of course. Why would you think otherwise?"

Scratching the back of my neck, I reveal, "I just thought that with passing out on my first day here, I'm not exactly ideal volunteer material."

"June is happy to have you. She thinks you being here will be good for the kids. And so do I."

"You do?" I can't hide my surprise.

"Yes, I do. All anybody ever wants is to be treated normally. You will be able to connect with these kids in a way no one else will. They will confide in you, trust you, and that's something truly priceless."

I meet his eyes, an unreadable look swarming deep within. I don't know what it is about him, but he makes me feel…special. I have had little experience with men, thanks to falling sick in my early twenties, so I blow it off as my hormones reacting to a good-looking, smart man. But a small voice inside me is screaming there's more.

Afraid of that voice, I pull back the blanket and swing my legs. He swoops forward and attempts to help me, but I wave him off. "Thank you."

He appears amused by my stubbornness. "No problem. Take care, Lola."

I nod, holding my breath until he turns and leaves the room. As I exhale, a feeling surfaces that things are about to change. Though I can't help but wonder if they already have.

The rest of the afternoon, I stick to the timetable and join Zoe down at the water, helping the kids canoeing. I decide not to tell her about what happened today because I don't want her to worry.

I had more fun than I've had in forever, and I can't wait to see what tomorrow holds. But now, I'm getting ready for the official meet and greet. I take my pills and make a quick trip to the bathroom to freshen up.

When I walk outside, the humid summer night warms my skin. Countless stars twinkle on the horizon. It's so clear out here, untouched. Manhattan is a concrete jungle; you almost forget another world exists outside.

A large group of people mingles along the dock and around the lake's edge. Some sit with their toes dipped into the still water while others relax under the blossoming trees, chatting with newfound friends. A few kids splash happily in the lake, but everyone is happy to just chill.

Witnessing the kids enjoying themselves comforts me. I know as days turn into weeks, and weeks into months, things will get harder for them. Time isn't on their side, and once the three months is up, I wonder where we will all be.

A young girl who looks no older than thirteen sitting under a large oak tree catches my eye. She's all alone but seems content. When she leans against the trunk and buries her nose farther into the book she's reading, I feel a kinship to her. She's reading a tattered copy of *Treasure Island*.

Taking a deep breath, I walk over to where she sits, hoping not to disturb her. My sneakers crunch over the soft grass, catching her attention. She peers up, her short red hair styled into a pixie cut. Freckles are scattered across her rounded cheeks and small button nose. She nervously tugs at a silver locket around her neck, waiting for me to speak.

"Hi." I wave.

"Hi," she replies in a voice softer than a mouse.

"I love that book. It's my favorite." I point at the tattered copy in her lap.

Her face lights up. There is nothing like finding a fellow book nerd. "Mine too."

"Can I sit?"

"Sure." She shuffles over.

Taking a seat near her, I extend my hand. "I'm Lola."

"I'm Sadie."

"Nice to meet you." We shake, her frail hand feeling skeletal in mine. "How do you like it so far?"

She raises her shoulders. "It seems okay."

Wanting to change the pace, I ask, "Do you have any siblings?"

A sadness overcomes her. I know the look all too well. "No. Just me. You?"

"Same here." A heavy weight submerges me. "I had a sister once," I reveal, not holding back. "We may not have been related by blood, but she was my sister nonetheless."

"What happened to her?" she innocently questions.

Not wanting to lie, I reveal, "She, ah...she passed."

Her hands fly up as she covers her mouth. Her sympathetic eyes fill with tears. "I'm so sorry, Lola."

"It's okay. It's nice to let someone know she existed. It's the only way I can keep her memory alive."

"What was her name?"

Swallowing down my fears, I reply, "Georgia Faye."

"I think I'd like to hear more about Georgia. She sounds like a nice person."

"She was," I reply with conviction. "The best."

"Well, whenever you want to talk, come find me, and we can discuss her." Sadie may be young, but she is far wiser than her years.

"Thank you. I will. And the same applies to me. I'm here any time you need to chat."

Her braces catch the full moon. "Sounds good to me."

"I found a stowaway," Zoe playfully says about Cassandra, who is wearing a pink glitter cowboy hat as they approach us.

Sadie nervously shifts beside me. The instinct to protect her overcomes me.

"Guys, this is Sadie. Sadie, that's Cassandra and Zoe." I point at each person. She nods, waving.

"Hi, Sadie," they say in unison. "Shall we go?"

I nod, looking at Sadie with a smile. "Want to walk with us?"

Her happiness is palpable. "Yes."

We make our way toward the pavilion.

Dusk has taken over the atmosphere, and it won't be long until the stars are twinkling above. The wide, open space has a large white dome branching upward, touching the heavens. A lot of people are already here, most sitting and chatting loudly among themselves. We take our seats and wait for June to speak.

I notice Sadie tugging at her heart-shaped locket again. It must be her security blanket, just how Georgia's bandana is for me.

June rises from a chair in the front row and walks to the white podium—our shepherd standing in front of her flock.

"Seeing this pavilion packed full makes me happy beyond words. I want you to have fun and make friends. The people you see around you are not only your friends but your family as well. Make happy memories and live."

June has a way with words, and I can see each and every one of us is touched.

"Tonight is about getting to know one another, and I welcome anyone who feels comfortable to come up and introduce themselves. I'm June Carrington, and Strawberry Fields is my home…and I welcome you."

As June steps down from the podium, everyone looks around, wondering who has the balls to be the first one to break the ice. I too helplessly gaze around, hoping someone will man up and step up to the plate, but no one does.

Exhaling loudly, I wipe my sweaty palms down my dress before I slowly get to my feet. The movement draws the attention of everyone present, and they all turn, eyes focused on me. I squirm, feeling like a circus sideshow freak. But I'm here to make a difference.

That thought gives me the strength I need, and I make my way to the front. When I'm almost there, my skin tingles with an enigmatic burn. I turn to the left, wondering why. When I see Dr. Archibald leaning against the trunk of an enormous, flourishing elm tree, I know he is the reason. My body is somehow in step to his, scaring and exciting me all in the same breath. His same impassive expression keeps me guessing to his thoughts.

As I continue walking forward, the corner of Dr. Archibald's lips lifts ever so noticeably. I wonder why for all of three seconds until his words come back to haunt me.

"You're a brave young woman."

Breaking our secret exchange, I focus on what's important, and that's remembering why I came here to start with.

"Hi," I mumble into the microphone. Feedback squeals loudly, highlighting my epic failure. However, I pull my shoulders back, hating that Dr. Archibald's words spur me on.

"My name is Lola." I push my glasses up my nose. "And I'm a volunteer here. I really am looking forward to getting to know everyone."

I risk a glance into the crowd and see that I've bored everyone to tears. But I don't blame them. I came here to be real, and although these kids are merely that, they've been introduced to a world that has matured them beyond their years.

Pulling back my shoulders, I smile. "I feel privileged to be here because, just like you, I know how important every moment is. I'm here for you. I promise. I know what you're going through…because I've been there too. I still am there." I swallow, frightened I've shared too much.

But when I see something change in everyone sitting before me, I know that I've shared just enough. "So any time you need me, know that my door is always open. I'm here for the good and the bad." When I witness smiles brightening the faces of those watching me, my heart swells. "So let's celebrate life, and let's…just have fun. Thank you."

As I make my way down the path, I'm speechless when a brunette I've never seen before jumps up and hugs me. I loosely hug her back because I'm taken off guard.

It takes me double the time to get back to Zoe and Sadie because I'm stopped every step of the way. Most want to express their appreciation for what I said while others just want to hug me.

When I finally reach Zoe and Sadie, Zoe stands and throws her arms around me. This time, the affection is welcome.

"What you said was just beautiful."

Sadie stands off to the side as we hug. I gesture with my hand, and she hesitates for a moment before joining the human sandwich.

After a few introductions are made and the crowd disperses, I see Dr. Archibald and Tamara talking awfully close. He is his usual cool, calm, and collected self, keeping his cards close to his chest.

Why does it bother me so much that she's advancing and he's not backing away?

"*Because you like him*," a voice that sounds a lot like Georgia whispers loudly into my ear.

This is a new level of crazy. Maybe I need to see a shrink. To cope with Georgia's death, am I now hearing her like she's my subconscious? I really must lay off the caffeine.

Tamara stands on tippy toes and whispers into Dr. Archibald's ear. He seems to ponder what she just said, then nods. She is elated while my stomach drops. They walk toward the mansion, leaning in close as they talk.

Sighing, I push down whatever this feeling swarming inside me is because it can't lead to anything good.

After twenty minutes of mingling, Sadie yawns, appearing just as tired as me. "I'll walk you to your room?"

She nods.

We make our way toward her room in silence, but I can sense something is playing on Sadie's mind. "Your friend Georgia…" I wait, giving her time to continue. "Do you have the same thing she did?"

When we reach her door, she makes clear she won't enter until I answer her question. "Yes."

The unspoken lingers, but what I said earlier confirms that we're all on borrowed time.

I'm not sure how Sadie will react, but she shows me what a remarkable person she truly is when she wraps her tiny arms around me. "Night, Lola."

"Good night, Sadie." I gently return her warm embrace, and it means more to me than she'll ever know.

She pulls away first and gives me a small wave before entering her room.

I stand outside her door after it's closed, digesting everything that's happened over the few short hours I've been here. I came to Strawberry Fields to help other people who are just like me. But each minute spent here reveals that maybe I was wrong. Maybe we're here to help one *another*.

A light whimper catches on the still night air, interrupting my thoughts. I would have missed it if not for the fact the sound is in concert with my soul. I should turn away and go to my room, but I can't. I feel like I'm now somehow involved.

I follow the sound, tiptoeing down the hallway like a common thief in the night. It gets louder and louder the farther I advance. I round the corner, not sure what I will find. The weeping is now muddled with a jumble of words. I stop just before an open door, knowing the sound comes from within.

This is incredibly rude, and I should let whoever is inside grieve in peace. But curiosity gets the better of me, and I peer around the doorjamb. At first, the darkness shrouds whoever is locked away inside, but a moment later, the full moon shines through the stained-glass window, lighting up the altar and who is contained within. There is no mistaking that long golden hair.

It's June.

Her downturned head and muted sobs touch my heart, and I feel her sorrow. What's made her so sad? She's kneeling at a pew, her hands interlocked as she mumbles, "Why," on a loop.

The small chapel isn't as extravagant as the rest of this place, but it doesn't need to be. The heavy cross which sits on the clothed altar is all the comfort one who comes here needs. One doesn't come here to marvel at the elegance, but to get away from it and just be with their maker. I'm not a religious person; how can I be? I don't understand my sacrifice, but June appears comforted being here and letting her guard down.

I've imposed on her privacy long enough and creep away just as quietly as I arrived.

My mind is plagued because, on the surface, June looks happy—the perfect mainstay of joy—but we all have our demons.

Slipping out of my clothes and climbing into bed, I'm exhausted, and it's only day one. As my eyes slip shut, I can't help but wonder what day two holds.

FOUR

I t's still dark out when I wake.

Reaching for my cell, I see that it's 5:15 a.m. Too worked up to go back to sleep, I decide to take a shower and get an early start on the day.

When I step out, I dry off and stand in front of the mirror. It's fogged up, thanks to my blistering shower, so I swipe my hand down the glass, leaving a slash in its wake. I peer at myself in the shred, half my face and body obscured, but I can see enough.

I've changed so much. Each day robs me of breath. It's like Georgia took a piece of me with her.

A small, bothersome voice whispers in my ear that I've given up too easily. I could call Dr. Carter and ask to trial the new drugs available, but I won't. Since being diagnosed, I've had the choice made for me. I was going to die. But lately, the line has been blurred because I wonder each day if I'm scared of dying…or am I scared to live? Am I afraid that it will work, and therefore, I get to…live? Why am I given such luxuries when Georgia was never given a chance?

I don't bother drying my hair and tie it into a messy ponytail. After sliding into jean shorts and the official volunteer polo, I apply a touch of makeup. When I look semi-human, I slip on my sneakers, take my pills, and then make my way into the hall.

The lights are dimmed, subdued so as not to wake the individuals still sleeping. My first class is art with Tamara, so I decide to go to the art room and set up the supplies. When I pass the chapel, the memory of June's gut-wrenching sobs echoes loudly in my ears. It's a sound I won't ever forget. To express such pain can only mean one thing—she's lost someone she loved. I can feel her pain because I've felt it too, and I've cried her hollow tears.

The distinct sound of someone taking out their raw frustrations can be heard ahead of me. The fitness center is three doors down, so I decide to see who's punishing that punching bag with forceful blows. A long, rectangular window on the door allows a perfect view.

Something red catches my eye, followed by a quick succession of walloping punches. Standing on my tippy toes, I crane my neck to the right and see a punching bag swing from side to side. I can't see who delivers the blows, but whoever it is, is showing no mercy.

I watch, mesmerized, the hint of tanned flesh coming into view for a second before disappearing behind the bag as quickly as it appeared. My nose is inches away from being pressed to the cool glass, desperate to see who this champion is. Just as the bag moves in the right way, I hear a door close and footsteps padding softly along the carpet.

I snap my head to the left and can just make out June coming down the hall. I don't plan to avoid her the entire time I'm here, but after last night, I need to put some distance between us. Her empty cries still etch away at my heart.

I can't turn right, as I'll bump straight into her, and left isn't a better option either as it's a dead end. So with no other choice, I open the door and dive into the sanctuary of the gym. I sidestep away from the door just in case June walks past and sees me standing like a statue in the middle of the room.

The punching doesn't cease, and now that I'm actually inside, I can hear the ferocity and viciousness of the strikes. There is anger behind each punch. Something I can relate to all too well. Stepping forward, I peer around the pole, latching on to it when I see just who the boxer is.

This explains his ripped physique, but who knew Dr. Archibald could pack a punch? He's a dark horse with a secret.

He hasn't seen me as his bare, taut back faces me. His bulging muscles ripple as he delivers each vigorous blow. Beads of sweat coat his glistening flesh, slithering down between his shoulder blades and into his low slung black sweats.

He is truly magnificent, and I watch for minutes, unable to tear my eyes away. He's dominant but tortured all in the same stroke. When he delivers a right hook, his flank catches the light, and a scripted tattoo comes into view. It runs the length of his ribs. I lean forward, still using the pole as my support, curious to see what it says.

Eleanor

I've encroached on a private moment, as I'm sure Dr. Archibald wasn't planning on being shirtless with an audience. This tattoo remains hidden for a reason. It's not for show. It's there for his eyes only as a reminder of someone he cares deeply enough about to have her name permanently inked onto his flesh.

I turn quickly, too quickly, ready to flee, and in my haste, I trip over a rowing machine, performing a lopsided somersault. I tumble onto my ass ungracefully, screeching in shock. The mats break my fall, so I'm not hurt. I'm more embarrassed because the commotion has forewarned Dr. Archibald that he has company.

"Goddamn," I curse under my breath when he turns over his shoulder, slipping off his headphones.

"Lola? Are you all right?" he asks breathlessly when he sees me sprawled out on the floor. I frantically hunt for my glasses. They are nowhere to be seen because I'm searching for them blindly.

"I'm fine." My far from convincing response has me wishing I was a better liar.

"Unless you're fishing for quarters down there, then I dare say you're not." I hear him slip on a T-shirt, then storm over in three huge strides.

"That machine came out of nowhere," I tease, a blanket of nerves holding me tight.

"Are you sure nothing hurts?"

"Other than my pride? I'm fine. Promise."

I'm still rummaging the floor for my glasses, so when Dr. Archibald stretches behind me and places them in my palm, I almost holler in delight.

Once he's done examining me, he nods, appearing satisfied that I sustained no injuries. "What are you doing here?"

I gulp as I can't exactly divulge I was spying. The thought has me remembering the way his strong body moved with forceful strokes. It also is a reminder that his burly body is inches away from me. His signature fragrance is even more refined, and I can't help but take it all in.

Once I slip on my glasses, it's almost impossible to ignore the way his tight T-shirt showcases his body. The neckline is cut low so I can see just a hint of dark hair sprinkled down his chest. He's a lean, mean fighting machine.

I should stop with the visual devouring, but I can't help myself. Focusing on the tattoo—although now covered—I admire not only the beauty of it but also the canvas beneath.

Standing, he offers me his hand, a lifeline I'm desperate to take. We're standing chest to chest, and I suddenly feel so small, dwarfed by his huge frame. We stay unmoving, my hand still enfolded in his. His touch is unlike anything I've ever felt before. I feel charged. I feel alive. He opens his mouth, appearing to want to say something, but he changes his mind at the last minute. He drops my hand and turns his back, searching for his water bottle.

Once he's well hydrated, I can see he's hesitant to turn around to look at me. Why? He unravels the tape from his hands, taking his time, then rubs a towel through his dark hair, tousling it further.

"Will you take a drive with me?" he asks coolly as he turns, and I don't hide my surprise.

"I want to show you something. I won't bite. Promise," he avows when I raise a suspicious brow.

"Where are we going?"

"You'll just have to trust me. Meet me in the parking lot after you're done with your morning class?"

"Fine."

He appears pleased that I didn't refuse.

I have the afternoon free, so I suppose I can entertain him. And besides, whatever he wants to show me, I can't shake the feeling it has the potential to change my life forever.

Dr. Archibald didn't specify where exactly in the parking lot I was supposed to meet him, so I decide to take a seat on a tree stump, which provides a very comfortable waiting spot.

As I wait, my thoughts drift to June. It's clear she runs Strawberry Fields with the utmost care, but I can't help but wonder what transpired for her to start an organization such as this one. Her harrowing cries resonate loudly, unveiling something heart-rending hidden beneath the surface.

I don't have time to think about it further because Dr. Archibald bounces down the steps looking casual in blue jeans and a gray crew neck T-shirt. Black sunglasses sit fashionably on his face. I stand, rubbing my sweaty palms on my shorts.

What does he want to show me?

"I didn't know if you'd be here or hitchhiking down the road." I smile, fond of his dry humor. He comes to a stop a few feet away, running a hand through his damp hair. "You're wearing that?"

I peer down at my jean shorts and "Wear pink, not mink" tank, raising a brow. "I didn't realize there was a dress code," I reply, a touch offended.

Dr. Archibald has the audacity to laugh. He offers no explanation to his random question but instead turns and heads for a cluster of cars over to the left. I presume I'm to follow.

I feel self-conscious as I didn't realize wherever he's taking me requires me to dress up. Is he embarrassed to be seen with me? If so, why bother asking me to accompany him in the first place?

My head begins to throb, and this time, it's not from the usual headaches, but rather me overthinking this entire thing. Just as I'm about to turn back around, Dr. Archibald comes to a stop. He fishes into his back pocket and produces a set of keys.

My eyes widen, and I point at the vehicle he stands near. "What's that?"

"That?" he asks, feigning horror. "*She* is a 1968 low rider chopper. I rebuilt her myself." The way he runs his palm over the black paintwork and shiny silver thingamajigs, I can see it's true love.

"That's a really nice story, but why are we standing near it… her?" I correct when he looks like he's about to cry.

"Don't listen to her, baby," he coos to the bike. A smile touches my lips. "This is my vehicle; although, she's so much more." He fetches two helmets, which are resting on the handlebars. When he passes me a red one, I know he's serious.

"We're *riding* that thing now?"

This time, he doesn't correct my oversight. "Yes, we are, and you're going to love it. Unless…"

"Unless what?"

He runs a hand through his hair. "Are you okay to ride? I mean yesterday…"

"Yesterday, I fainted. No big deal. Now give me that helmet." I thrust out my hand.

I understand his reservations, but I'm fine. And I refuse to be treated any other way.

When he passes me the helmet, I now understand why he asked about my clothes. There's nothing to protect my skin from peeling off when I go flying through the air like Evel Knievel. But regardless, this is happening.

I watch as he mounts the bike with ease, looking like a complete badass settling back against the black leather seat. No wonder he's wearing those motorcycle boots.

When he places the key into the ignition, he turns to look at me. I clutch the helmet with both hands, gulping. "Where do I sit?"

He points at a small incline behind him. I laugh, but abruptly stop when I see that thing he's gesturing to is a pathetic excuse for a seat. "You're not serious?" I shake my head, backing away.

"I'm very serious." He grips the handles, waiting for me to get on.

The helmet feels like it weighs a thousand pounds, and I'm seconds away from handing it back to him and telling him thanks, but no thanks, I like my head where it is.

But that small, bothersome voice, a voice which has been with me since I first arrived, has suddenly become a smidge louder. It's telling me to stop being a chickenshit and…live.

Funny, I've heard that voice before. It's Georgia's.

The voices in my head are no longer nameless. That fact gives me a sense of comfort, and it also gives me the courage I need. Taking a deep breath, I put on the helmet and hope to god I'm not making a terrible mistake.

"If we leave now, we might make it by Christmas." He looks down at his imaginary watch with a dimpled smirk.

I clutch my sides, laughing sarcastically. "When did you get your license?"

His lips move from side to side as if contemplating his response. "Yesterday."

He's joking and trying to make me feel at ease, but I'm still scared. "What if I fall?"

Suddenly turning serious, he offers me his hand. "I promise I won't let you fall." The sincerity behind his pledge has me stepping forward. "But if you're afraid…"

What he's doing is blatantly obvious, but still, I take the bait as I slap his hand away. "I'm not afraid." I fumble with the strap under my chin, and after three attempts, it's buckled tight. Now I must attempt to get on the bike without falling on my face.

I'm mercifully no longer blinded by fear, but when I see how closely I'll be pressed up to Dr. Archibald, a different sort of fear arises. There isn't a seat belt in sight, so to stop myself from face-planting, I'll have to hold him, and tight.

I gulp.

Hoping I don't fall on my ass, I lift my leg and mount the bike just like Dr. Archibald did. All those horse-riding lessons come in handy as I clench my thighs and apprehensively wrap my arms around his firm waist. His body is warm and feels exactly how I envisioned it to feel—divine.

Once I'm settled into place, he revs the engine before we launch off with an ear-splitting whoosh. I scream and tighten my hold around him, pressing my chest to his back. I feel his stomach ripple as he laughs at my response.

He maneuvers the bike with skill, hinting he's ridden for a long while, and before I know it, we're past the pines and out the double steel gates.

The wind whips at my cheeks, breathing a new lease of life into me. The landscape flashes before me, but I absorb enough to appreciate its beauty. Dr. Archibald zigs and zags, taking me on a surprisingly cathartic journey. It's just me and this big, open space, and for the first time in a long time, I want to embrace freedom.

We drive the backroads, and not another soul is in sight. It's nice to imagine that it's just us out here in the wilderness. About ten minutes in, I slacken my vise-like grip and relax my shoulders. If only Georgia could see me now. She'd be so proud.

Peering up into the clear, untouched sky, I think that maybe she is. She was the reason I got on this motorcycle in the first place. She encouraged me to let go and live. Tears sting my eyes, and for once, I don't wipe them away.

The rest of the journey continues in silence, which is ironic, considering the engine rumbles with a deafening shrill. The stillness is inside my head, which hasn't happened for a long time.

Dr. Archibald turns left and pulls into a small country town. There aren't a lot of stores along this strip, but enough to have tourists stopping in to buy souvenirs or grab a bite to eat.

Dr. Archibald parks in a space, backing up the bike with complete skill. Once he kills the engine, I'm surprised my body still vibrates from the ride. My arms are still linked around him, and I regret having to let go. He gently squeezes my hand with his, rubbing over my wrist with his thumb before he dismounts.

I attempt to remove my helmet, but the strap seems jammed. Just as I'm about to accept the certainty I will die wearing this headdress, Dr. Archibald leans forward and lends a hand. His touch surprises me, but I try my best to appear unaffected.

His eyes are still veiled beneath his dark glasses, but I'm almost certain his fingers tremble as he unbuckles the strap below my chin.

Once it snaps open, he clears his throat and quickly lowers his hands.

My arms feel heavy as I slip off the helmet, but it feels good not to have my head confined. I shake out my hair, almost certain I have helmet hair. When I think I'm in the clear, I'm about to ask Dr. Archibald what happens next but hastily seal my lips when I see him watching me closely. His eyes may be cloaked, but I can *feel* him. I suddenly feel like I'm on fire.

"S-so where are we g-going?" My stutter this time isn't from my condition, but rather my sudden nerves.

My voice seems to snap him from his thoughts. His cool demeanor returns, and he smirks. "Follow me."

He turns around, giving me a spectacular view of his firm butt. I scold myself for thinking such inappropriate thoughts, but a laugh, *Georgia's* magical laugh, cackles loudly inside my head. It's official—I've finally gone mad.

The delectable smell of burgers and fries floats on the breeze, resulting in my stomach growling. It somersaults in delight when Dr. Archibald opens a heavy glass door, the bell above it chiming, and gestures for me to enter.

Looking at the old-fashioned red logo on the storefront window, I see that the diner we're standing in front of is called Peggy Lee's. This is where that lip-smacking smell is coming from. He doesn't have to ask me twice, and I walk past him with a smile on my face.

The moment I step inside, I've been transported back to the '50s. The polished floor is the traditional black and white checker, complementing long laminate countertops and red barstools.

A waitress in a mint green retro diner dress greets us with menus in hand. "Hello, Dr. Archibald."

I raise an eyebrow. It appears he's a regular. "Afternoon, Anita. How are you?"

"I'm fine, thanks. Busy as usual. Would a booth in the back be okay?"

"Of course. That'll be fine."

Anita leads the way while Dr. Archibald courteously gestures with his hand that I'm to go first. I nod my thanks and follow, eager to sit because I'm suddenly ravenous. I can feel the stares of everyone surrounding me, stopping mid-bite as I hobble down the aisle. The stint on the motorcycle was fun, but my sore legs are now paying the price. I'm familiar with people staring, so I continue with my head held high.

When we finally reach the booth, I slide into the seat, thankful to be sitting. Dr. Archibald sits across from me, accepting the menus from Anita. "I'll bring you some coffee."

"Thank you," he says with a smile.

He doesn't seem embarrassed to be seen in public with a cripple, but I suppose he's seen it all. It's his job, after all. Pushing my glasses up my nose, I peer around, uncertain what to say. I need a conversation starter, something to break the ice. But what?

Dr. Archibald leans back into his seat, cool as a cucumber. "Have you always had your limp?" Well, this wasn't the breaking of ice I had in mind.

I squirm. Have I repulsed him somehow? "It comes and goes," I confess, reaching for a sugar packet and turning it over between my trembling fingers.

"When did it go away?"

"When I went to the gym. And when I was participating in the clinical trials." There is no need to elaborate on what comprised those trials.

He rearranges the sunglasses on his head, mussing his hair up further. "If your limp improved, the drugs must have had a positive effect then?"

"I suppose."

He smirks, appearing amused by my evasiveness. "Yet you chose to cease the trials. Why?"

"What is this, twenty questions?" I snap, folding my arms over my chest. "You're a doctor. I'm sure you have access to my files. All the info you require is in there."

"I *have* read your files."

My mouth falls open very ungracefully. "You? What? *Why*?" It's all I can manage to spit out.

"Just answer the question," he says lightheartedly.

I huff, blowing a stray piece of hair off my brow. "I'd rather we discuss anything other than this."

"I'm just making conversation, Lola."

His response isn't snarky or invasive, but this is a very sensitive topic for me. I can't casually discuss this decision over coffee like I'm talking about the weather. Anita returns with our coffee, breaking the sudden stale mood.

I bury my head into the menu, hoping Dr. Archibald will stop with the questions. He doesn't. "So how long was the trial?"

"The triple cheeseburger with extra onions sounds amazing," I reply, ignoring his question with my face still obscured by the menu.

My sanctuary only lasts for a second because the menu is lowered slowly by two stubborn fingers. Raising my eyes, I meet the amused baby blues of the annoying doctor.

"How long?" he presses, revealing he won't let the matter drop.

Surrendering, I drop the menu with a sigh. "A year."

He nods, deep in thought. "You do know that the trial was a success, correct?"

"Yes, and…?" If he has a point, I hope he makes it soon.

"And I wanted to know why you chose to stop." He leans back into the booth, never breaking eye contact with me.

"Because life's a bitch, Dr. Archibald." A lot more venom laces my sentence than I intended. I instantly feel terrible for snapping, but why is he pressing my buttons?

Reaching for his coffee, he appears quite pensive once again, which makes me nervous. If I knew where the hell we were, I'd flag down a cab and escape a conversation sure to end in tears. "How about you call me Roman, and we cut the bullshit, Lola?"

My mouth hinges open as I was not expecting that response. "I don't know what you want from me."

"I want you to be honest with me and yourself. We're just two friends out for coffee."

"I don't dabble in make believe, *Dr. Archibald*," I snap, his name never sounding so dirty. I really must calm down, but he's pissing me off.

My bravado, however, seems to please Roman…Dr.

Archibald. His mouth curves into that bold, trademark grin. "You really have no idea just how special you are." I almost choke on thin air. "And stubborn…"

"Am not," I oppose, but quickly shut up when I've just proved his point.

He continues. "You're also a fighter. I've seen it. Last night you stood up before anyone else. And today, you had no qualms about riding my bike."

"Have you been testing me?" I don't see the point in being coy. We're well past that.

"What if I have?" he replies, steepling his fingers under his chin as he places both elbows on the table.

I eye my cup, wondering what a scalding hot coffee facial would feel like if I threw the contents into his smug face. He reads my thoughts instantly and laughs hoarsely.

"What are you trying to achieve with your guerrilla tactics?" I ask. Leaning forward, I'm not the slightest bit intimidated. "If this is your idea of a pep talk, then I suggest you rethink your approach because it fucking sucks. Death is looking more appealing by the second."

He continues laughing, not at all offended. Well, screw him.

"I'd know that laugh anywhere."

The sweet voice has both of us turning.

"Erin." Dr. Archibald stands, giving the young woman wearing an identical uniform as Anita a hug. She hugs him back tightly. My eyes narrow on their own accord. Who is this woman? She is attractive with large brown eyes and plump pink lips. An elegant green silk scarf is wrapped stylishly around her head. It's a good idea to keep the hair from her eyes.

I mustn't have a very good poker face because she pulls away apologetically. "How rude of me. I'm Erin." She extends her hand, which I shake lightly. "Don't let this guy give you any trouble. If he does, just tell him you saw a bigger bike than his." When she winks, I smile. Any joke at the doctor's expense is just fine by me.

Dr. Archibald clutches at his chest, staging distress. Erin giggles. "I'll be right back to take your order." She rubs his arm affectionately before leaving our table.

As he watches her fondly, a surge of suspicion overwhelms me. Why the hell did he bring me here? "So who's Erin?"

With his gaze still pinned to her, he reveals, "She's someone remarkable."

I put two and two together and roll my eyes. Did he bring me here to rub my face in his happiness? Or maybe he brought me along to make her jealous? Or maybe she's his girlfriend? There are too many maybes in this equation, and I don't like it.

"Well, I'm happy for you both," I say, reaching for my coffee, hoping to drown my sorrows.

Anyone would think Dr. Archibald is sucking on a lemon when he turns to look at me. His nose and forehead are scrunched up tight. "We're not a…thing," he clarifies, gesturing back and forth between them with two fingers.

"So why did you bring me here? Doctor—Roman?" It feels beyond strange to call him by his first name, but this is the only way he'll tell me the truth.

He gestures with his chin to Erin, who is laughing and chatting with customers. "What do you see when you look at Erin?"

"Excuse me?"

"You heard me. What do you see?" When I hesitate, he adds, "This isn't a trick question."

Fed up with his games, I look at Erin and shrug. "A pretty young woman."

"And?"

"And what? I doubt she's a real blonde. What do you want from me?" I snap, throwing my hands out to the side.

"You're missing the most vital point. Think. What is the difference between you and her?" He rounds the table and lowers his face inches from mine. I hold my breath because he is absolutely, infuriatingly beautiful.

I know what he wants me to say, but why? Surely, he wouldn't be so cruel. But he is. "Does she walk with a limp? Or talk with a stutter? Is her life going to be cut incredibly short?"

The tears I've tried to keep at bay break the surface because his malice hurts more than I thought it would. "Why would you say that?" I whisper, my lower lip trembling. "Why would you compare me to someone like her? She's…perfect."

I don't wait for him to explain because no reason can

excuse such spite. I shoot up, shoving past him, not caring that the entire diner is now staring. I storm past them all; none, including Dr. Archibald, mean anything.

The fresh air isn't sufficient to ease my impending breakdown. Nothing will. No one has ever been this cruel, not even my mother. I feel a fool for thinking Dr. Archibald was different.

"Lola!"

"Go away," I affirm, sniffing back my tears as I charge away from him. "What did I ever do to you?"

"Lola, listen to me. I'm sorry I made you cry." The breeze carries his apparent remorse, but I won't listen.

"I'm not crying," I stubbornly argue as I'll be damned if he sees my tears.

"Stop, please." But it's too late.

I break into a sprint, surprised what adrenaline can do. My victory is short-lived, however, because I'm swathed in his arms, and I reproach my body for relishing in the contact.

"Let me go!" My sadness is steadily replaced with rage as I fight to break his hold. "If you wanted to humiliate me and make me feel like utter shit, mission accomplished."

His strong arms lift me off the ground to stop me from squirming. "The answer to your question is—"

"I don't care what the answer is. The only answer I want to know is where I am so I can get the hell away from you, you asshole!"

Roman ignores me and storms down a small alley with me kicking and screaming. When we're out of sight from curious passersby, he releases me but pushes my back against the brick wall. I try to bounce off it, but he presses his chest to mine, pinning me down.

"Because...she was you." He's breathless as he slams his arm above my head, trapping me.

"Who was?" I spit, fruitlessly shoving against him. It won't break his hold.

"Erin was you. She was you."

His winded admission freezes me in place, as I'm beyond confused. He reads my uncertainty, and his face, the face I knew was lingering under the surface all along, shines through.

"Erin was my patient. She had a high-grade glioblastoma, a grade four astrocytoma." His eyes turn soft, searching every plane of my face.

"That's not possible," I whisper, shaking my head animatedly.

"It's very possible," he refutes. His faltering heart beats in frantic sync with mine. He presses us closer together. I almost can't breathe. "She was told by every doctor that her tumor was inoperable, but she refused to accept her life was over. I work at St. Mary's Hospital; that's where I first met Erin. She was in the clinical trials, just like you, and like you, Lola, her tumor reduced in size. But she never gave up, and a year ago, she underwent a new trial, and her tumor shrank down to the size where the doctors could operate."

"No, she's not me," I whisper to myself.

"Yes, she is. I was one of those doctors. She was told she wouldn't live past twenty-five. She's now twenty-nine years old. Her tumor has been completely removed because she took the drugs you refuse to take—the ones that *will* save your life."

I close my eyes, his words a cruel trick. There's no such thing. A magical potion does not exist.

"You can have everything that Erin has, but you choose to live in the dark. You're afraid to live because dying is the easy way out. I don't know why you're refusing treatment, but I can't stand by and watch you die without at least trying. I wanted you to see what you could have. I could tell you, but you're so headstrong, and I know you've heard it all before."

"She's not me," I repeat, my movements slowing.

"Everyone is different, but I've compared your files, your blood work, your clinical trial results, and everything is almost identical. I know that if you take the trial drugs Dr. Carter recommended, you will live. Or at least you would have done everything you possibly could. You've been given a lifeline. Stop being so stubborn! You have a chance to live, take it."

My heart hurts, and the truth spews from me. "I don't deserve it. Why do I get a second chance, and others don't? My best friend, she's dead! Where's her second chance?" I state, forlornly.

He hisses, pained. "I'm sorry she's dead, but that doesn't mean you have to be too. Stop with the survivor's guilt!" His frustration and sadness can be heard behind his voice. The sentiment touches my heart, but I don't understand why he cares.

"Why does it matter to you whether I live or die?" I open my eyes gradually, the thick, heavy tears sticking to my lashes.

My question catches him off guard. He turns his cheek, his jaw clenching. The air is heavy with a stagnant silence.

I now understand why Roman brought me here because he's right. Seeing what I could have, who I could be is more tempting than I could ever imagine. But I'm afraid. Lola Van Allen is a coward. And she's also undeserving. Why do I get a second chance when Georgia didn't?

Once Roman releases me, I sag forward, suddenly fatigued beyond words. He catches me, and I fall willingly, no longer guarded because he knows my dirty secrets, and he's still here.

"It's okay," he coos, rubbing my back. "I truly am sorry for making you cry. If I could have done this another way, I would have. Please forgive me."

His sincerity is clear, and the fact he cares enough about my feelings has me burying my face into his neck and hugging him tight. My unguarded, highly inappropriate affection surprises me, but what surprises me more so is that my actions are returned.

"You don't know what it's like, living each day and not knowing if it'll be your last. Being afraid all the time." I'm not ashamed of my fears because even though they linger, I won't allow them to rule me.

Roman's response leaves me baffled. "You'd be surprised."
I'm expecting him to elaborate, but he doesn't.

The mystery continues.

FIVE

"**H**er tumor has been completely removed because she took the drugs you refuse to take—the ones that will save your life."

I tie my laces a little too tightly when thinking of Roman's tactics earlier today. I understand what he was hoping to achieve but talk about an ambush. Regardless of what he thinks, I'm not Erin. I'm also not his lab rat. It may have worked for her, but it won't work for me. Endless doctors have told me that, so the odds are not in his favor.

But it appears he believes that if I were to undergo the new trials, I'd be too stubborn and headstrong not to see it through. I would give it my all, and chances are, if what Roman says is true, I would survive.

Unable to think about this without wanting to throw up, I step out into the hallway, ready to spend the rest of the afternoon with the kids. But when I round the corner, I bump into June. She's holding a cup of coffee, which I thankfully don't spill all over her cream blouse.

"Oh, my god! I am so sorry!" I wipe away the imaginary coffee drops on her arm.

She chuckles, holding her cup out to the side. "That's quite okay, Lola. I'm actually glad I bumped into you. Do you have a moment?"

"Sure." Once I'm satisfied she's blemish-free, I remove my hand.

She glances down the long hallway. Although empty, she hints she'd like to talk in private. "Would you like to chat in my office?"

"Of course." I can't help but wonder why the secrecy, but I follow as she strolls down the hall. Her black high heels sound elegantly against the plush carpet. My heavy, uneven footsteps distinguish our differences.

She steps inside the small but homey office, taking a seat in the high-back leather chair. I close the door behind me, standing with my hands locked behind my back as I look out the large window. A stunning rose garden just beyond the pines boasts a picturesque burst of colors. From this distance, I couldn't even begin to speculate just how many rose bushes sit perfectly erect. Their formation rivals the most scrupulous marching band.

This view is beyond words, and if June spins her chair, she can gaze out into all that she owns and witness the impact she has had on so many.

"Please, take a seat." She points at the leather chair in front of her, disrupting my thoughts.

I do.

As I shift to get comfortable, I notice a decorative frame resting on the heavy oak desk. The photograph is of a young, mousy-haired girl who looks to be no older than ten. The picture captures her standing near the very lake I can see if I peer out the window, holding a huge fish dangling from a fishing pole. She looks happy and carefree.

"That's my daughter," she reveals with a faraway tenor.

"She's adorable."

"She was."

Her use of past tense has my eyebrows shooting up into my hairline. The reality has an ache eating away at my heart. I gently rub over it, pained for June.

"She passed when she was thirteen." She confirms my worst fears. "From a congenital heart defect. A hole in the heart," she clarifies. How ironic, as I'm sure that's what June feels daily.

"I am so"—my voice grows quieter, tears stinging my eyes—"so sorry." The reason for June's harrowing cries has been uncovered.

"Thank you." She dabs at the corner of her wet eye with her index finger. "It was a long time ago."

"But I bet it still feels like yesterday?" I offer as I know this kind of loss is eternal.

"Yes." Running her finger over the glass, she reveals, "That's why Strawberry Fields exists—in honor of my daughter. She was always a sick child, and the frequent hospital visits made her worse. I could see she hated being treated like a sick person, but sadly, back in those days, there were no real options on where she could go. The hospital was the only place she could receive around-the-clock care. It didn't make a difference in the end."

The layers of grief to her voice have me chewing the inside of my cheek to stop me from breaking down.

"So that's why I created this place." She sweeps her arm outward. "I wanted young people, who were just like my daughter, to be able to find comfort in a place that wasn't a sterile hospital room. I wanted them not to miss out on all the things people their age did. Scarlett missed so much." Her longing is clear. "Her days were filled with doctors' appointments and tests when they should have been filled with fresh air and fun. I can't bring her back, but I can make her memory live on through people like you and everyone who walks through these doors." She smiles nostalgically.

When I think I can speak without bawling like a baby, I state, "Strawberry Fields is a beautiful tribute to your daughter. I think she would have loved it here."

"Thank you, Lola." She wipes away a stray tear, embarrassed.

"Anyhow"—she clears her throat— "believe it or not, that's not why I asked you in here." I'm thankful for the change of pace until I hear the topic. "I wanted to discuss your fainting episode."

My back straightens, and all sentiment flies out the window. "I'm so sorry. I completely understand if you want me to leave."

"Leave? Good god, no. I just wanted to make sure you were all right. Can I do anything for you? We have some doctors who could..."

But I wave her off. "Thank you so much for the offer, but I've had enough of doctors." Especially one in particular. "That's not why I came here."

"Of course. But please know how much I appreciate you being here. What you said last night..." She pulls in her lips in an effort not to cry. "It showed everyone just how strong you are. You belong here, and I'm so thankful that you are."

Her admission means so much to me. "Thank you for giving me this opportunity. I know I'm not the ideal candidate for the job."

"You're perfect," she interrupts. "Dr. Archibald also agrees."

"Really?" I raise a brow, intrigued.

"Yes."

"Well, I'm sure Dr. Archibald was pleased someone agreed with him for a change." I chew the inside of my cheek, afraid I've shared too much.

But she reads my body language. "Go easy on him. His

practices may be…unconventional," she settles on, searching for the right word. "But he means well. He has everyone's best interests at heart."

When she sees me mulling over what she just revealed, she shocks me even further by reaching for her coffee. She takes a composing sip and says, "He wants to save the world. That's his problem, Lola."

She doesn't explain what that means, leaving me with more questions than answers. I want to ask her so many things, but I don't because I'm afraid I won't like her reply. Her pink lips form a small frown as she turns her chair and sips her coffee while looking out the window. It's my cue to leave.

"Thanks, June. For everything." She simply nods in response.

I wonder if she has any other children, but the missing happy snaps of another child or even a husband reveals that it's only her—how incredibly sad. That must be the reason she throws herself into work. She has no family, just us, and even then, we leave, some more tragically than others.

June erected this place to pay homage to her daughter. She really loved her. All I can picture is my mother throwing a celebratory party in my honor.

Unable to think about this without getting heartburn, I venture to the happiest place on earth that doesn't involve mouse ears—a library. Two levels with floor-to-ceiling bookcases bursting with books are what I'm faced with.

A few people are tucked away in their own private nooks, entranced in the pages of whatever world they want to get lost in. My fingers itch, excited to uncover a new adventure and lose myself before my volleyball lesson starts in thirty minutes.

I make my way over to the spiral staircase but stop when a computer workstation catches my eye.

"Because he wants to save the world. That's his problem."

What does that mean? Why do I feel there is a hidden message behind her words?

"Only one way to find out," subconscious Georgia says.

Biting my lip, I glimpse at the staircase, then over at the computers. Repeat. I need to keep walking up those stairs and not stalk Roman…said no one ever.

I'm over at the computer and pulling out a chair before I can berate myself for making an impulse decision sure to end badly. No one is around me, so I have all the privacy I need, which is a dangerous, dangerous thing.

Peering over my shoulder to ensure no one is looking, I click on the web browser, the flashing cursor taunting me with each blink. I've come this far, so there's no backing out now, but what exactly do I want to know?

My fingers dither over the keys, knowing this is a mistake. Chickening out, I research something which is just as scary as finding out dirt on Roman. I don't know where to start, so I decide to go back to the basics.

The keys whine in protest as I type the words: *clinical trial results for high-grade glioblastomas.* Pages upon pages load before my eyes, and I get an uncanny sense of déjà vu. This takes me back to sitting in my bedroom in Manhattan, researching methodically until the sun went down and then came back up again.

I skim over the top hits, not wanting to get my hopes up. The chemo drugs Dr. Carter wanted me to take, the same ones Erin took, keep popping up in my feed. I open one page and then another, comparing and analyzing the results. Each case study is different, but the odds for people like me…aren't as bleak as they once were. Out of one hundred case studies, eight individuals were "cured." I'm apprehensive about using that word because cured can be interpreted in many ways.

Two out of that eight were cured, meaning they no longer had a brain tumor because the inoperable became operable. For the other six, their tumors were downgraded to low grade. It doesn't detail what the remaining ninety-two subjects' results were, but I'm suddenly curious.

Eight percent had positive results, and it all comes down to the common denominator—they were all on the same trial drugs Georgia and I were on before they were put on the new experimental medication. Their results were similar to mine, and they then were a candidate for the next stage, the stage I opted out of because I was too chickenshit to try.

Closing fourteen of the fifteen tabs I have open, I take a deep breath, suddenly feeling faint. I can't do this again. I can't have false hope. Needing a distraction, I speedily type into the search engine: *Dr. Roman Archibald.*

Not exactly ethical but a distraction.

I'm swamped with pages of global Roman Archibalds, but nothing on the good doctor. I continue searching, determined to uncover something, no matter how small. As I'm scrolling through page three, I see a match that could be a winner. I click on the link, drumming my fingernails on the desk while waiting for it to load.

Just as I'm about to give up, I almost inhale my tongue when those hypnotic eyes flash onto the screen. It's an article from some medical journal, detailing the doctor's career.

He went to NYU—no surprise there—acing all of his subjects and graduating at the top of his class. It says his current work location is St. Mary's Hospital, specializing in cancer research and treatment. Hobbies include a whole bunch of boring as they've left that question blank, by default, no doubt.

On paper, Dr. Archibald appears the perfect specimen, but something is missing. Steepling my fingers underneath my chin, I wonder what that is. This blueprint is flawed. There is no backstory, and I know from my experience in researching many doctors over the years that most like to brag. Most like to detail every accomplishment linked to their name, and I know for a fact Roman was involved with Erin's case, which I'm sure was something talked about in the medical world.

Something is rotten in Denmark.

I continue scrolling through the pages until I see a Facebook page that has me hovering over the link. Call it woman's intuition, but I click on it and try not to holler in smugness when I see a profile picture of Roman carrying a Golden Retriever like a baby. Both look beyond elated.

I'm disappointed when the profile is private. How can I carry on snooping now?

All I can see apart from his photo is that he grew up in Buffalo, New York, and that holy shit, his birthday is in two weeks. He's turning thirty.

I get lost in those eyes, wondering what secrets he holds, like who took this picture. He looks happy, genuinely happy. It's a side I haven't seen since I met him. Not that I can blame him.

"You know…" The moment I hear those words, I want to thump my head against the desk, hoping to render myself unconscious. "You really shouldn't believe everything you read."

Stupidly, I attempt to close the page, but in my haste, I instead minimize it and open the medical journal findings on brain tumors that have been cured. This website was once my go-to, but now I want it to go to hell.

Both pages are just as bad as the other because both reveal I was thinking about Roman. This really couldn't get any more embarrassing. That is, until a pop-up flashes across my screen, detailing how stalkers.com has found over five hundred hits on my current search—one Dr. Roman Archibald.

I turn the screen in horror, my face blistering a beet red.

He stands behind me. I'm almost suffocated by his smugness. I can handle this one of two ways— I can tell him the truth, or I can lie.

"It was like that when I got here." Watch my nose grow.

To corroborate my story, I spin slower than a snail and give Roman the best guiltless look I can muster. He no doubt sees through my lie but doesn't address my big fat tall tale.

Now that it's out there, I don't see the point in wasting this opportunity. Tapping my chin, I state blankly, "I took you for a cat person." He blinks once before his mouth curves into a sinful smirk. "So, what's his name?"

"Freud."

I cock an eyebrow. "You named your fur baby after a mamma's boy who had an unhealthy obsession with phalluses?"

He runs a hand through his hair, attempting to hide his smile. "It was either that or Dr. Jekyll. But I wasn't interested in a two-for-one deal."

Now I'm the one to smile.

He stands over me with both hands dug deep into his pants pockets while I lean back in my seat, smoldering under his heated stare. "I haven't had a chance to commend you on your public speaking. Your mother would be jealous. You'd completely upstage her."

I know he's talking about my impromptu speech last night because Camille Van Allen is a motivational speaker for women who have hit rock bottom. Her job is to inspire and encourage.

Too bad she's full of shit.

I beam as any jab at my mother makes me happy.

So, he's done his homework—interesting. It looks like we've both exhausted stalkers.com. "Thank you."

He remains stone-faced. "It takes courage, Lola…" He pauses before adding, "But we both know how courageous you are." His double-edged sword has me squirming.

We still haven't addressed the Erin incident, or the fact he's caught me researching the very drugs he believes can save my life. I could ask him about them. I mean, he is a doctor. He has all the information I need. But I don't. I can't. All I can think of are the remaining ninety-two case studies. What happened to them? Are they happy, regretful, or are they pessimistic like me?

June made it clear Roman wants to save the world, but I'm beyond saving.

Tapping my pen against the desk, I wonder if this is how every author feels before penning their most treasured thoughts. These words are not for anyone's eyes but mine, but still, I feel an incredible sense of pressure to get it right.

I've never kept a diary or journal, as I didn't see the point in rereading a past I never want to relive. Life is short. I don't know how long I have left, so maybe leaving a legacy behind isn't so bad. But the legacy I leave is a tribute to my friend, who I refuse to forget. I want her memory to live on long after I'm gone.

So, I let go.

I've met some nice people—Zoe is great. I think you'd like her. I also have met someone else...he's a doctor. I know for a fact that you'd like him. He certainly has tested me. He thinks I can be cured.

I pause, pressing the pen to the paper, but I don't know what else to say. I don't want to document my fears because seeing them on paper will confirm what a big ole scaredy-cat I am.

He is infuriatingly stubborn, but I find myself drawn to him, and I don't know why. He has secrets, and I want to uncover each one because, underneath them, I think, lies the reason he wants to help me.

I wish you were here because you would tell me what to do.

A soft knock sounds at my door. "Lola? It's me, Zoe."

I instantly shove the journal into the desk drawer, shutting it abruptly.

"Coming," I reply, brushing the hair from my brow and

attempting to still my racing heart.

"Hey!" My overzealous greeting makes it obvious something is askew, but thankfully, she doesn't comment and enters.

She sits on the edge of my bed, while I eye my desk drawer, wishing my secrets weren't inches away from her. "So, what's been happening?"

"Happening? With what?" I'm quick to reply as I press my back to the wall, needing something to lean on.

"You know, life in general. How's Dr. Archibald?" She wiggles her eyebrows up and down.

Calming down, I take a breather. "I had an interesting run-in with him today."

"What happened?" she asks, sitting forward, intrigued.

Unable to evade her questioning, I decide to be honest because maybe the saying rings true: the truth might set me free.

"He read over my file." I leave out the part why. "He says new drugs are available that may help me." I nervously pick at the nail polish on my thumb, averting my gaze. When she doesn't comment, I clarify. "Help...cure me."

Silence.

I risk looking up, afraid of what I'll see.

Zoe sits frozen, her mouth agape. There is no guessing what she's thinking, but it's not that simple. This was a bad idea, and I really wish I'd kept quiet. "You have to try them," she whispers, breaking the silence.

"Zoe..."

She shakes her head resolutely. "No, this is a no-brainer. Why are you still here?" She jumps off the bed as though it's on fire and charges over to where I stand, still pressed to the wall. "Where is your suitcase?" When I remain mute, she dashes over to my wardrobe, hunting for my luggage.

"I'm not leaving."

She stops searching, spinning so quickly I cringe. "What do you mean you're not leaving? You have to. This is a simple decision to make."

"No, it's not. I've tried this before. It doesn't work."

"But Dr. Archibald says these new drugs will help cure you," she presses.

I shake my head, pushing back from the wall. "Maybe, not definite."

My answer doesn't placate her, however. "Maybe is better than no. Maybe means there is a chance. I wish my sister had a maybe."

I wrap my arms around my middle, feeling ungrateful. "I lost someone, and that someone was my best friend who died while on the trial drugs. I can't go through that again. I've accepted my fate and made peace with it."

Zoe meets me halfway, folding her arms across her chest. "I'm so sorry about your best friend, I truly am, but that's bullshit. You've been given an opportunity...why won't you take it?"

I blink. "Because…" *I'm scared*, I silently reply. "Because…" But I come up short.

"Because you're afraid of living?" Zoe offers with a bite, attempting to piece together a puzzle with pieces that don't fit.

"No, because I'm afraid of living with hope!" I confess, hating how weak I sound. "I can't live another day with false hope. Georgia was the most optimistic person I knew, but regardless, she still died. Life is cruel, and I don't expect it to make an exception for me."

I hate that I'm shaking. This topic is one that will always end this way—in tears. My lower lip trembles, and I succumb to my fears.

Zoe wraps her arms around me, hugging me as I weep. "I'm sorry. I just…I want you to live."

Her affirmation is so much like what Georgia would say. "Thank you, Zoe."

We stand hugging for minutes, both needing the comfort as I'm sure this conversation has brought up memories of her sister.

Her insistence has me wondering if maybe I should reconsider. Everyone seems so intent on saving me, while I just want to forget.

It's late out, but I can't sleep, so I decide to take a walk.

With no real destination in mind, I roam the hallway, taking the long way to venture outside. It's a god's honest unintentional mistake, but when I come to Roman's office, I curse my infernal subconscious.

I should keep walking, but I don't.

Adrenaline surges through my body, causing my heart to race. After ensuring I'm alone, I tiptoe toward the ajar doorway. Counting to three, I spur myself on because it's too late to back out now. I inhale two short breaths, then push open the door.

This is Roman's most treasured space. A place where he can be himself behind closed doors. I wonder just who that person is. He doesn't wear his heart on his sleeve, yet I can't help but think that buried beneath that hard exterior lies a wounded soul. I remember his tattoo. Whoever she is, I believe she's the reason he bears his scars so close to his heart.

Besides the desk, a bookcase, and a bunch of filing cabinets, nothing in the office shows just who Roman is. I know who Dr. Archibald is, but Roman? I saw that determined, hungry, passionate being in the diner.

Just the thought of him, of his hands on me, has me heating in ways that are most inappropriate. His rugged scent lingers lightly in the air, drawing back all the memories of when I caught a sniff firsthand.

Running my fingertips over the cool leather back of his chair, I imagine him sitting ever so seriously as he contemplates saving the world. Can he save me?

However, all thoughts of being saved are literally put to the test when I hear sharp footsteps headed this way. Squeaking in panic, I frantically look from left to right. I need a hiding place. Unless I'm gifted in the contortionist department, then the closet will have to do.

I yank open the slatted door, thankful nothing is inside except a few coat hangers and an ironing board. Shutting the door, I seal the gasp from my lips when Roman charges into his office, appearing to run away from something.

The slats on the door allow me to see out, but I can only hope he can't see in. He paces the office, visibly distressed. What's left him so breathless and flustered?

When he yanks open the desk drawer, I crane my neck to see which drawer it is. The contents get swiped from side to side as he's obviously hunting for something.

He reveals what a moment later.

The light reflects off an orange medicine bottle as he raises it to his lips and tosses his head back, swallowing deeply. The sight shocks me for so many reasons. At the forefront is that I didn't realize he was on any medication. I wonder what it is and what it's for. He slams the bottle onto the desk, bracing his hands on the edge and bowing his head, obviously attempting to calm down.

His wide back rises and falls, becoming steady as the seconds tick by. When he appears composed, he stands tall, brushing the fallen hair from his brow. He leaves his hand threaded through his snarled locks as he squeezes his eyes shut and breathes heavily through his nose.

His navy tie sits askew, the two top buttons of his shirt undone. What has happened for him to lose his cool this way?

He looks defenseless and poignant, and the sight breaks my heart.

When a set of light footsteps patter down the hall, Roman's eyes pop open. He quickly brushes the pills into his drawer. He adjusts his tie and runs a hand down his face.

"Roman?" The partly open door slowly swings, revealing Tamara as Roman's pursuer. When she sees him standing by his desk, she smiles and shuts the door behind her, sealing us all inside.

He coolly places his hands into his pants pockets, waiting for her to speak. His demeanor differs greatly from what I just witnessed a minute ago.

"Is everything all right? One minute, we were talking about your birthday, and the next, you were running away from me as if I had just asked you to sell me your soul."

He chuckles, but it doesn't sound genuine. "Sorry, Tamara. I just forgot to do something very important."

Stepping forward, she says, "That's okay. If I didn't know better, I'd say you were avoiding talking about your thirtieth. There's nothing to be ashamed of."

"I'm not ashamed. I just don't like celebrating my birthday. You know this," he counters, taking a step backward to every step she advances forward.

She knows this? Do they have a past then?

"I know, and I wish you'd tell me why." Why is his birthday such a touchy topic for him?

She stalks him until he rounds the desk, and his knees hit the chair. He's trapped, yet he stands tall while she slinks over like a tigress hunting her prey. She runs her fingertip along the collar of his shirt.

Instead of covering my eyes, I step forward, intrigued.

"Tamara, I told you I can't give you what you want."

"*You* are what I want," she says, winding her fingers around the back of his neck.

My heart accelerates when I witness her stand on tippy toes and kiss the corner of his curved lips. She moves to the other side, kissing the crease while he remains still.

I should look away, but I can't. The sight is too sinful, and I…I'm hooked. Watching Roman this way does something I have never felt before. A small fire builds within.

"Tamara, no, we can't," he says as she lunges forward, desperately trying to entice him to kiss her. Her hands are everywhere as she tries to hold something solid before he disappears. But he slips from her fingers as he recoils.

She pauses, the hurt evident on her face. "Roman?"

"I'm sorry. I can't do this."

Her chest rises and falls. "Can't do what?"

"You know what. My feelings haven't changed since the last time this happened."

She turns her cheek, appearing as if he slapped her with the truth.

His knuckles are white as he grips the desk, waiting for her to speak. She does a moment later.

Pulling her shoulders back, she straightens out her clothes. "Okay, then. So…" She's clearly upset but trying to act brave.

"So…" he repeats, running a hand through his hair. "I better get going."

She sighs, her façade sullied by his obvious need to get away from her.

She yanks open the door, leaving dust in her wake. Roman sighs, lifting his glasses and pinching the bridge of his nose.

Once he switches off the light and closes the door, I exhale, my lungs thankful for the reprieve. I wait a few minutes before bravely cracking open the door and joining the land of the non-Peeping Toms. The desk lamp is the only light source, but it's bright enough to highlight my exit.

Just as I creep toward the door, I remember what happened seconds before Tamara entered and played the aggressor. I should just leave and forget what I saw, but I can't.

Tiptoeing to his desk, I open the drawer and reach for the lone medicine bottle, which is half full. Turning it in my fingers, I expect to see anything else than what I actually do. The pills rattle against the sides as my hand trembles in confusion.

The name on the label indicates these belong to Roman. But the question is…why is he on an antidepressant? And why did he need it moments before Tamara charged through his door?

SIX

There's no denying I'm attracted to Roman, but after last night, that attraction has led to something…else.

That something else has me desperate to uncover what secrets lay hidden in his past. There is something more, deeper, and I find myself being attracted to every side he presents, which is dangerous. It's also highly inappropriate for so many reasons.

I'm attempting to play football but failing miserably. "I'll sit this one out."

"Aw, Lola. We will go easy on you," says Hayden, a blued-eyed little devil.

I laugh in response because they will do no such thing.

Standing on the sidelines is a far better option. That is until

I hear a voice that sends goose bumps from head to toe. "Not a football fan?"

Shielding the sun from my eyes, I turn and see Roman standing to my left. "I'm not a fan of getting my ass whipped by eight-year-olds," I reply with a nervous smile.

He chuckles lightly. "So, how's this weather?"

"Really?" I can't hide my sarcasm.

He smirks at my quip. "I'm just making conversation."

"No offense, but the last time you 'made conversation'"—I used air quotes—"you showed me what a downright asshole you can be." I slap my hand over my mouth, mortified my mouth filter malfunctioned at the most inappropriate time ever.

He doesn't hide his surprise, but instead of reminding me of my manners, he bursts into a husky fit of laughter. He does that a lot when I'm around. I don't know if that's a good or bad thing.

"Roman, I am so sorry. That was highly—"

"Entertaining," he interrupts, still laughing.

I scrunch up my brow. "I'm not sure if you heard me correctly, but I just insulted you. To your face," I add, just in case he's had a lapse in hearing.

His shoulders lift in a carefree shrug. "I've been called worse."

We're silent for a few minutes, both staring ahead but not really watching the game.

Although the lead-in was awfully rude, it was a lead-in

nonetheless. "Why haven't you mentioned what happened at the diner?"

He raises his shoulders in a carefree manner. "I didn't think you wanted to discuss it."

He's right, I didn't, but I do now. "That's never stopped you in the past."

"Touché." A smirk tugs at his lips.

His coolness is infuriating. "Well, maybe I want to talk about it now." Again, there is silence, indicating I have the floor. "I've been doing some research, and you're right, the new trial drugs seem to have a better success rate than the previous ones I was on." Getting those words out feels like gravel is caught in my throat.

He still doesn't face me but instead watches the game. I know he's listening, though. The clenching of his jaw gives him away.

"So, maybe, I…" I lick my lips nervously. "I want to do more research, but I'm not completely against rethinking my decision."

Roman's holler makes me jolt, as I wasn't expecting that response. Someone just scored a touchdown.

"Are you even listening to me?" I try to keep the bite from my tone but can't. "This is what you wanted, right?"

With the slowest of movements, he turns to face me while I hold my breath. I have no idea what he's thinking, which is nothing new. I wish he'd say something, anything really, because

I suddenly feel stupid for putting my heart on the line.

"No, Lola, this isn't about what I want. It's about what *you* should want." His reply denotes he's been listening all along. He knows how I react when backed into a corner, so this is his way of not smothering me with his beliefs. "Only you can make this decision. I can be here for you, but I can't make a choice for you. That's what free will is all about."

He's right. I want someone to blame if things go wrong, but if I do this and things don't change, then I have no one to blame but myself, and that's scary beyond words.

"Do you r-really think I'm brave?" I whisper, baring my vulnerability.

I've caught him off guard. He blinks once before sighing. He appears to weigh his response, but the reply he gives has me mewling. A strand of hair, which is stuck to my lip gloss, is swept away by his gentle touch. I freeze, unable to mask my surprise and also, my yearning.

Closing the distance between us, he bathes my cheeks with his warm, sweet breath. "I think you're beyond brave. I think you're a truly remarkable woman who has no idea what she's capable of."

My lips tremble because his finger still rests at the crease of my mouth. If I move an inch, my lips will feel and taste that finger, but I can't. I won't. So instead, I remain motionless, amazed at how a single touch can produce an array of emotions.

"I wish I had your strength," he reveals in a hushed tone. He's returning the favor by showing his vulnerability. It's beautiful.

Biting my lip, I hope I don't overstep a line when I confess, "You're th-the strongest person I know." My words draw his finger deeper toward the cavern of my mouth, and my eyes widen when he brushes over the corner seam. The simple touch pulsates throughout my entire body.

"Thank you. But if only that were true." I instantly miss his touch when he drops his hand, disheartened.

His comment reminds me of what I found hidden in his drawer. I want to tell him that it doesn't imply weakness; it signifies strength that he sought out the help to better his situation. But I can't without giving myself away.

Roman clears his throat, and the moment is over.

I want to say so many things to him like it's okay to be vulnerable, but I don't. I simply smile, hoping he can read between the lines.

He does. "I'll see you later. Maybe we can finish our discussion in my office when you're free?"

"Maybe," I reply because I haven't made a choice either way.

Although my response wasn't exactly positive, it wasn't negative either. I'm on the fence, which is a big deal, considering I was on a fence…in Antarctica a few days ago. Roman's smirk has me inching closer and closer to one side. How long until the scales tip, and I decide?

Seven cups of coffee later, I'm seeing double. I skipped dinner because I'm determined to gather as much information as I can before I decide my fate.

So far, the odds are stacked in the drugs' favor. The research I've done all details the same findings. The trials have shown some fantastic results, so why am I not jumping for joy? The reason sits scrunched up in my fist.

Georgia's bandana is like my stress ball. It alleviates the stress when I think I'm moments away from having a breakdown, which happens every thirty seconds.

Every time I read about something positive, Georgia's face flashes before me, and a blanket of guilt is thrown over me. Why wasn't this available when Georgia was alive? Both our results showed great promise, and I know this would have saved her life. But it didn't. On the other hand, it's here now, and it can save mine.

Groaning, I drop my face into my palms as I wish I could make this decision and feel good about whatever I decide.

"Is everything okay?"

Lowering my hands, I see Sadie standing with a paperback copy of *Hamlet* pressed to her chest. She looks beyond concerned.

"Not really." I don't even have the energy to lie.

"Want to talk about it?" There is so much knowledge behind Sadie's youthful eyes that it saddens me.

"I wouldn't want to bore you." She smiles, pulling up a chair beside mine, indicating she's listening.

Clearing my throat, I tap at the computer screen. Clue number one.

Sadie leans forward and reads the heading, her intelligent eyes widening. She spins to look at me, not hiding her surprise. "This is what you have?"

I nod.

She continues reading, scrolling through the article. When she gets to the end, she exhales, appearing to process everything she just read. I know it's a lot to take in, and I shouldn't have burdened her with it. I'm supposed to be *her* support unit, after all.

"You have to do it," she says in a small whisper. A command such as this, coming from such a tiny creature, makes me feel obliged to obey.

"I'm thinking about it," I reveal, reaching for my coffee cup. Looking inside it, I'm disappointed that it's empty.

"Thinking about it? What's there to think about?" Her question isn't malicious or accusing; it's simply honest.

"Remember Georgia?" She nods quickly. "I feel so… undeserving to have this opportunity when she never got the chance. Both our trial results were positive, which means I'm in with half a shot of this drug working for me. It's slim, but it's not hopeless."

"I don't understand then. Why wouldn't you try it?"

"Because Georgia had hope and look at what happened to her. I had hope once, and it sucked the life from me. I'm afraid that if I participate in this trial and get my hopes up, it won't work." Expressing my weaknesses and fears aloud is a hard thing to do, but I want to tell Sadie the truth.

She rolls her chair forward so our knees touch. "It's okay to be frightened. I think it's better to be scared because you'll do everything not to feel that way again. And I think it's better to be scared *while* trying instead of being scared *of* trying."

Is this kid for real?

I couldn't have said it better myself.

Unable to stop myself, I lean forward and hug her with all my might. She is smaller than she looks, which only has me squeezing harder, wanting to protect her with my life.

When put so simply, Sadie is right. Better I die fighting than die without a fight.

Life wouldn't be what it is without fear because fear pushes us to beat our demons and transform those weaknesses into strengths. Georgia teaches me that every day. She may not be here, but her memory lives on, reminding me to fight for what I believe in and love.

"I owe you at least a gallon of Ben & Jerry's."

She giggles into my shoulder, never letting go.

She has no siblings, so she knows what it's like to be alone.

"Remember how I told you Georgia was my sister?"

"Yes, I remember," she whispers, wrapping her arms tighter around my neck and snuggling close.

"Well, she was older than I was. I've always wanted to be an older sister. Maybe, if it's okay with you, I could be yours?"

She freezes in my arms, her tiny frame going rigid. Just when I think I've said the wrong thing, she nods. "I'd like that…a lot." Her voice is heavy with approaching tears. She toys with her locket. "My grandma gave this to me. She said I was to fill it with a picture of something or someone I love."

I nod, giving her my complete attention.

It takes three attempts before her trembling fingers can open the clasp. When she does, my heart breaks. It's empty. It appears we're two birds of a feather.

"Welcome to the family, Sadie. Our family." I know how much that means to someone who hasn't heard it before.

We continue to hug, Sadie never letting go, but that's okay because I owe her a million hugs and so much more.

It's now 12:35 a.m., and I'm wide-awake, pondering everything from the mysteries of life to whether I want a grilled cheese or not. Kicking off the covers, I decide to take a walk to clear my head and settle my churning stomach.

Slipping into a peacock-colored summer dress and Chucks,

I close my door quietly and tiptoe down the hallway in the opposite direction of Roman's office. Most people are fast asleep, unlike me, the insomniac skulking through the night. I have no real desire to go anywhere specific, but the gardens seem to be my go-to place when I feel the need to escape.

The star-kissed sky flashes above me, reminding me that I'm a mere speck in the greater scheme of things. So many tragedies are happening right this second, and I should be thankful for all the good things I have.

I venture over a grassy hill and see the tall pine trees surround me on both sides, prompting me to remember that I've seen this sight before. If I recall correctly, a stunning rose garden should be just up ahead. It was stunning from afar, so I can only imagine how extraordinary it will look up close.

The moon is full, providing all the light I need to navigate past the pines. Just beyond is an amazing spectacle that takes my breath away. Rows upon rows of roses are planted as far as the eye can see. Every color rose is cultivated, the well-ordered effect unlike anything I've ever seen before. All the colors of a rose rainbow.

I wonder why this was positioned here. Why is it so far away from the main building?

A light wind picks up speed, alerting me that a fellow insomniac is close by. The shifting of dirt can be heard quite distinctly, which makes me wonder why someone is gardening at this time of the night.

I decide to find out.

The flowering bushes are thick and lush and well maintained. They are looked after with love and care. As I peer down each procession, the digging gets louder and louder, but after five minutes, I'm certain I'm hearing things and consider turning back.

However, I scream bloody murder when a soft voice sounds behind me.

"Lola?"

"Holy shit!" I spin around, wielding the stick that I picked up along my journey as a weapon.

"Are you planning to stab me?"

"Maybe," I reply breathlessly, attempting to calm down my racing heart. "You almost gave me a heart attack. You do realize this is how every horror movie starts, right?"

Roman runs his forearm over his sweaty brow, leaving a dirty smudge in its wake.

Peering down at his shovel and mud-covered boots, I raise a brow. "So…are you digging a grave?" Hardly appropriate, I know, but why on earth is he out here at one a.m.?

As I'm still waving the stick around like a sword, Roman reaches out and lowers my wrist. The contact shoots fireworks all the way to my toes.

"I'm gardening," he reveals, which doesn't explain why he's out at this ungodly hour.

"And this gardening couldn't wait until the morning? When

it's daylight and a lot less…serial killerish?" I ask, searching for the right word.

No matter how often I'm rewarded with that lopsided smirk, it always feels like the first time. "No rest for the wicked." He accents his comment with a wink.

"S-so what is this place?" I ask, breaking the sudden static in the air.

Roman licks his bottom lip, then glances around with a sigh. "Want me to show you?"

I nod.

He extends his palm. I peer down at it, nervous. "I won't bite."

Pushing my fears aside, I take his hand, relishing in the connection. He threads his fingers through mine and leads the way. He knows his way around and explains all the types of roses.

It takes about forty-five minutes, but by the end, Roman has shown me the complete gardens. The entire time I listened, lost in his voice and his passion for something truly beautiful.

When we stop at what appears to be the first row of roses, he doesn't let my hand go. He circles my palm with his thumb, appearing to be lost in thought.

Something near my feet catches my eye, and I look down, wondering what it is. The moonlight has slipped out from behind a cloud, highlighting a small bronzed plaque. The message inscribed and the small cherub depicted in the top right-hand corner have tears instantly welling in my eyes.

Leave Room in the Garden for the Angels to Dance.

A towering rose bush in a dazzling shade of red grows just behind the plaque. This rose is the leader of the pack. This is the sight June looks upon every day from her office window. Realization of just what this place is hits home, and suddenly, I can't help but feel so alone.

A tear slides down my cheek. "Each rose represents someone who has…died, doesn't it?"

His silence says it all. The crisp smelling air suddenly turns sickly sweet.

There are countless roses, each bush standing in place for a once living, breathing soul. "There are so many of them."

He tightens his hold, squeezing tight.

This commemorative garden is what June sees when she looks out her picture-perfect window—all the people she's lost. The red rose, the centerpiece, I know was the first one planted. It was in honor of her daughter.

"That's for June's daughter?" I gesture with my quivering chin to the prevailing rose.

Roman nods, his head bowed. He looks so unbelievably sad. "June planted that rose with her bare hands and nothing else. She didn't want her daughter to be alone, so that's why this place exists."

"And you tend to it?" He nods once again. "Did you know them?"

His pause is poignant. "Most of them, yes. It's my way of remembering them and never forgetting the impact they had on the world."

By this stage, tears are streaming down my cheeks. The thought is so tragically beautiful.

June loved each and every one, and to show that love, she welcomed them into her family. And for Roman to tend to each plant so lovingly reveals that he loved them too.

Being surrounded by such beauty and knowing what each represents has me expressing something aloud that plagues my heart every day. "P-promise me you'll plant me a red rose." I squeeze my pocket where Georgia's bandana lays. "It was my best friend's favorite color."

Roman hisses a breath through his teeth, his hold on my hand becoming tighter.

"Promise me," I whisper when he doesn't reply.

His chest rises and falls, and his face...the broken look on his face hurts more than the thought of my own death.

"No," he says with only raw emotion.

"No?" I query, not understanding why he would refuse this one final request.

"No, Lola, I won't." His conviction is clear.

Before I question why, he staggers forward, placing his large tremulous hand on my cheek. "I'll plant you a sunflower instead." He rubs his thumb over the apple of my cheek, wiping away my tears.

My eyes widen. "W-why would you do that?"

"Because…" He swallows, taking two steadying breaths. "You're different. You stand out from the crowd, and you deserve that, in this lifetime and the next."

A sob rattles in my chest. No one has ever said something so beautiful to me before. At this moment, I feel treasured, and whatever happens, I'll never forget that feeling for as long as I…live.

Live.

And just like that…my decision has never been clearer. It was hidden beneath murky waters, but now, I can reach it.

I can see it.

I want it.

"Okay," I whisper slowly.

Roman's hand is still pressed to my cheek, so I can feel the tremor pass through his body.

"Okay?" he questions, his eyebrows knitted together.

"I'll do it."

His eyes search every inch of my face. "Do what?" He knows what, but he needs to be sure.

Licking my suddenly dry lips, I reply with sincerity, "Live."

Tension crackles between us, setting me on fire. My decision seems to have unlocked a door for us both, and I feel like we've just unearthed something that will change our lives forever.

"You're sure?"

"No, but someone made me realize something." He cocks his head to the side, waiting for me to explain. "Better I die fighting than die without a fight."

He closes his eyes for the briefest of seconds, before allowing me a front row seat into his soul. He looks relieved, but most of all, he looks hopeful.

"I won't go to the hospital, though. I can't do that again."

He nods immediately. "You can do the trials here. I will take care of everything."

"Everything?" I know what I'm asking, but I need to know.

That overwhelming static bounces between us, and I know something is changing. I can taste it in the heavens. He caresses my cheek with a tender touch and corrects hoarsely, "I will take care...of *you*."

And I believe him.

I turn into his touch, closing my eyes, and bask in this stillness. There is no more white noise.

There is nothing left to say because I've made my choice, and I'm sticking to it. Whether I succeed or fail, it doesn't matter. The journey of a thousand miles begins with one step.

I've just taken mine.

SEVEN

"Are you helping Tamara this morning?"

My breakfast bears a resemblance to abstract art as I prod at it with my spoon. Humming under my breath, I scoop outward to construct a beard on my oatmeal Santa.

"Earth to Lola!" *Snap. Snap.*

Zoe's clicking reminds me I have company, and that I have totally spaced.

Shaking my head, I gingerly meet her eyes. "I'm so sorry, Zoe. I'm just a little…distracted."

"I can see that. Want to talk about it?"

"No!" I nearly yell.

My spoon catapults from my grip and skids along the

table. Zoe looks down at it, then up at me. She hands it back as I cringe in my seat. The trials haven't even started, and I'm already buckling under the pressure. I have no idea how I'll keep this a secret.

Last night was intense, the most intense night of my life.

After Roman promised he'd take care of me, I went back to my room, confused and scared. This was a normal response, of course, considering I'd just done a 360 on a decision previously set in stone.

Hope seems to brighten the darkest of spaces, and that's what I have. Hope this will work.

It may be a false sense of security, but having Roman with me every step of the way has changed my outlook. He said he'd organize everything, and we'll start as soon as possible.

We both agreed not to tell a soul as it's best we keep this between us. Although he's qualified and licensed to do the trials, it's not standard protocol to perform them outside a hospital. Not to mention, I'm a volunteer here.

I hate to put him in such a position, but the thought of doing this in a hospital is unbearable.

From the research I've done, the side effects are similar to the first set of trials. I don't expect Roman to be on hand twenty-four seven because things can get ugly, and honestly, I'd rather he wasn't there to witness me puking my guts up. It's not going to be easy, but it never is.

My phone vibrates on the tabletop beside me.

Ready when you are.

My heart hastens because I didn't think Roman could organize everything this quickly. Was he up all night? Either way, this is happening. And it's happening right now.

"Everything all right?" Zoe asks.

"Y-yes, fine. I just have to do something. I'll catch you later?" I hate keeping Zoe in the dark, but it's better this way.

"Sure." We say our goodbyes.

Needing a moment to catch my breath, I peer down at my phone, my fingers wavering over the buttons. This is my last chance to back out. Once I agree, it begins, and there's no turning back. My life from this moment forward changes forever. But I won't know whether it's for the better unless I try.

Roman's message stares back at me, the innocent phrase never seeming more important. Thinking back to standing among the roses and remembering all the lives lost, I let go of my reservations because I'm not ready to be planted among them.

My reply may not be poetic, but it amounts to a thousand words.

I'm ready.

And I am. There is nothing more I can say because, in this circumstance, actions speak louder than words.

With that thought in mind, I pocket my cell and turn, determined to see this through. My willpower diminishes, however, when I see Tamara standing a few feet away.

A brunette is talking to her, but she doesn't appear to listen because her gaze is riveted on me. I hurriedly avert my eyes, giving away my guilt. She knows something is askew.

Using that as my driving force, I go the long way around, avoiding any possibility of bumping into her. I exhale loudly when I make it into the hallway unscathed.

It'll be okay. I give myself a pep talk as I head toward Roman's office.

The moment I knock on his door, he grants me permission to enter. He glances up at me from over his glasses. "Hi."

"Hi." I shut the door behind me and notice he's sitting behind his desk buried beneath a mountain of paperwork. "Are those my files?"

He nods. "Yes. I had Dr. Carter's office courier them overnight."

"All of them?" I ask in awe, pointing at the mass of files. He nods once again. "Wow. Just who are you in the medical world?"

He smiles. "Please, take a seat."

I do as he asks and peer around nervously. It suddenly feels so clinical.

His doctor mask slips into place as he opens a folder and reaches for a pen. "Okay, now, before we start, I'd like to run some blood tests, as it's been a few months since labs were run. I know your vitals are good, so it's really just the blood work we need before we begin."

I nod.

"We can do that this morning if you like? Have you had breakfast?"

I shake my head.

"Good. I know Dr. Carter explained in detail what was expected with the previous trials, and I believe you did your own research since you contacted him originally." Nothing slips past him. "I'd like to briefly give you a rundown of what these trials entail and what you can expect. They're a little different from the previous one," he explains, leaning back in his chair.

I shift in my seat, my palms sweating.

Toying with the pen between his fingers, he never wavers his gaze from mine. "You will be taking six kinds of medication, four times a week. There will also be an injection administered once a week with a higher dose of corticosteroids. There are no potent chemo drugs this time around, so you won't lose your hair. However, the side effects in the reported cases seem to be a little more…" He pauses, searching for the right word.

"Extreme," he settles on, and I'm thankful for his honesty. "Once your time here comes to an end, I can still administer the trial. Nothing will change."

It's so much to take in. "How about we cross that bridge once we get to it?" I don't want to sound like a negative Nancy, but in my case, it's best to be realistic.

"Of course." He sits forward, crossing his arms on the desk. "This isn't going to be easy."

"I didn't expect it to be," I counter quickly.

"And you still want to keep this between us? I'm sure June wouldn't…"

I nod animatedly, cutting him off. "Yes. No one can know. No one."

"You have my word. From what I've read, you will be able to live a relatively normal life during the trial period." I cock a brow, amused. Roman reads my thoughts and amends. "Well, as normal as one can. I will be with you every step of the way. You can ask me anything."

My original question is still scratching away at the surface. Why is he doing this? But that can wait for now.

"Do you have any questions?"

"Nope."

"None at all?"

"Nope," I repeat.

He is clearly surprised; it seems he was expecting twenty questions. "In that case"—he stands, adjusting his cherry red tie—"shall we?"

I gulp for so many reasons.

Pushing aside my nerves, I too rise and nervously head for the door.

We walk down the hallway, headed for the small hospital

room. There is a weighty silence between us. My mind is a million miles away, and all I can think about is how each step I take will change my life forever.

I can only hope that change is for the better, because as ironic as this is, being surrounded by death has made me want to live. So much so, I will even endure the weekly injections.

The horror must show on my face because Roman teases, "I swear, whatever you're thinking, I didn't do it." Turning to look at him, I don't hide my confusion. He smirks. "Whatever thought you were lost in didn't appear to be a happy one."

My mouth forms an O. "Just thinking about all the needles headed my way." I shudder at the thought.

He nods in understanding. "No one likes getting jabbed with a needle. I'll try my best to be gentle."

Peering down at his long fingers, I have no doubt he will. "You must think I'm a big crybaby."

"Nonsense. We all have our phobias."

His comment is my cue, one which I shouldn't, but will take. "What's yours?"

I regret it the moment the words leave my lips because it is not only rude, but the hallway is filled with an immediate sense of uneasiness. I don't have time to apologize, however, because June suddenly emerges from a doorway, perusing the file in her hand.

When Roman sees her, he sighs under his breath, and his footsteps slow a fraction. I don't have time to question his odd behavior because the moment June's inquisitive gaze lands our way, I suddenly feel guilty for being caught.

She has no idea what we're doing, but regardless, her slightly narrowed eyes disclose her interest at seeing us together. My footsteps also slow as I'm in no hurry to get up close and personal with her suspicion.

"Good morning," she addresses us both.

"Morning," Roman replies, coming to a stop a few feet away.

"Morning," I repeat, my voice wavering.

"Where are you two off to?" June's innocent question isn't accusing, but nonetheless, I feel like she's probing.

I look up at Roman, my cover almost certainly blown, but as usual, he's as cool as cool can be. "I was just escorting Lola to the library. She tells me she's most interested in scouring the net for the latest scandal."

I refrain from kicking him in the shin—only just. But his wisecrack eases my nerves.

She smiles, but something is missing behind the gesture.

"We'd best be going." I'm certain he knows it's on the tip of her tongue to ask what we're up to, but he stays true to his word and keeps my secret safe.

I'm caught in the middle of an invisible pull, and I instantly feel guilty for lying, and also for putting Roman in an awkward position. June is Roman's boss, and the fact he is lying to her because of me makes me wonder if maybe I should disclose what I've decided to do. He can get into serious trouble for doing this.

Roman's synchronicity with my thoughts surprises me even though it shouldn't because there has been a pull from day one. "Have a nice day, June."

He latches on to my bicep gently, dismissing June.

However, she stops us. "Roman…" She peers down at his hand secured tightly around me. I attempt to shrink away, but he tightens his hold, causing my cheeks to heat. "Can you see me after you're done?"

I can feel the pulse thrum through his taut body. Does she know something is wrong?

Just as I'm about to divulge it all, guilt eating away at my morals, Roman rubs his thumb over my skin, scoring my flesh with his tenderness.

"Of course." His assurance doesn't go unnoticed by June, whose eyes are watching our every move—evident and masked.

I feel beyond uncomfortable because the unspoken is leaving me with a serious case of paranoia. Roman doesn't seem concerned and steers me around her, deadpanned and unmoved.

We walk in silence, Roman as confident as usual, while I will my heart to calm down. I'm on autopilot as I follow him.

He closes the door softly when we enter the medical room. "It's okay. I won't tell her."

"I'm not worried about that." I massage my temples. "What if you get into trouble? I shouldn't have asked you to do this."

"Lola—"

But I don't allow him to finish. "This was a bad idea. Not to mention, it is completely dishonest keeping this from June. She gave me this opportunity, and I thank her by lying to her."

"Lola—"

"She's been nothing but nice to me and—"

This time, however, it's Roman's turn to interrupt me. Not by words but rather, touch.

He's before me, pressing his huge palms to my cheeks before I can register his hands are on me—again. "Just…stop."

My heart begins a steady staccato.

"It'll be okay…*you'll* be okay. If we're going to do this, you need to trust me. Do you trust me?" I watch the blue in his irises turn a sultry, inky gray.

The pregnant pause is laced with anything but silence. "Yes."

And I do.

The heat of his hands still pressed to my cheeks overthrows my constant chill. He searches every plane of my face, his touch turning softer. "Good. So stop worrying." With a gentle stroke, he runs his thumbs along the apple of my cheeks before dropping his hands.

His presence is almost suffocating as we stand inches apart. I need to put some distance between us before I implode. "Should we get started?"

"Of course. Just take a seat on that bed"—he gestures with

his head toward a curtained area—"and I'll get everything I need."

As he makes his way toward the glass supply closet, I walk over to the white table and boost myself up. Peering around, I see this small room encompasses everything a doctor would need. No one likes hospitals, but June has done a fine job in steering away from the fact that this room is just that.

Thoughts of June make me wonder what she wants to speak to Roman about.

"Honestly, I can hear you thinking from over there." My lips tip on their own accord. "Here's a fun fact. We're the same blood type."

Gingerly meeting his eyes, I appreciate that I can get lost in their blue depths because I need all the distraction I can get from the needle he holds. A cold sweat breaks out across my brow.

Roman places the supplies on the stainless steel side table and slips on a pair of blue latex gloves. "It's okay to be afraid. We all get scared sometimes."

As he reaches for the needle, I press my eyes shut and take shallow breaths through my nose. The alcoholic swab feels cold against the crease of my elbow. I need a diversion.

"What scares you?" His fingers pause from preparing my arm.

My question was very forward, and it was also very

personal. I'm seconds away from apologizing but am surprised when Roman replies. "Not much scares me anymore." His admission isn't arrogant; it's simply honest. "But in saying that, a few things still terrify me."

The moment I feel the tourniquet being secured to my upper arm, I squeeze my eyes together tighter.

"Like what?" I ask through deep breaths.

"Like global warming, and whether or not a copycat One Direction band is waiting in the wings." A wavering laugh escapes me.

He's evasive on purpose, hiding behind his humor. I wonder why.

A small prick penetrates my skin before my arm feels heavy, and heat scores the tips of my ears. I bite my lip and tell myself to calm down.

"The things that scare me...are the invisible kind. What is seemingly harmless to most people is my worst nightmare come true," he suddenly reveals.

His heartfelt admission is what I need to focus on, not the needle currently being jabbed into my arm.

"I can relate to that," I divulge around a small intake of breath. "We all have our demons."

The walls suddenly close in on me, and I'm finding it hard to breathe for another reason other than what's going on in the crease of my elbow. There is silence—only our heavy breathing filling the still room—but the unspoken is deafening.

"The demons," he declares softly, "they're not out there, Lola. They're in here…fighting to be free." I hear two taps over what I'm guessing is his temple.

My eyes pop open, uncaring that I'll see blood, and needles, and more blood.

This is the first time he's confessed that something lurks beneath the surface. "What demons?"

He secures a cotton ball and tape over the small puncture wound, indicating he's finished, which was astonishingly fast. He was right, he was gentle, but my phobia has suddenly taken a back seat because I need to know what he meant.

"Don't you mean *which*?" he counters, snapping off his gloves.

I purse my lips, confused. Are these demons the reason he takes medication? It makes sense. And *which*? That makes me think there is more than one.

Roman is a conundrum.

"All done." He labels two vials, completely composed, while my brain is racing a million miles a minute. "The results should be here in a couple of days. I'll let you know as soon as they arrive." Why the sudden change of pace? Did he reveal something he wishes no one to know?

But I couldn't care less about the results. I want to talk more about him and his demons. "Roman…" He pauses, pen pressed to the white label. "I…if you ever need to talk, I'm here. No judgment. You're doing me a huge favor. The least I can do is return it." I'm extending an olive branch. I can only hope he takes it.

"Thank you." He appears genuine, but I can tell by the hard press of his lips that his secrets will remain under lock and key…for now.

He turns his back and busies himself with cleaning up.

Am I being dismissed?

Just when I thought he was going to share a small piece of himself with me, he withdraws and leaves me wanting more.

I jump down from the table, reading his body language loud and clear. Roman is a closed book, but with each moment we spend together, he reveals a small part of himself. The problem is that the more I see…the more I like.

I want to ask so many questions, but I don't. With his back still turned, I excuse myself.

As I walk toward my sports class, I can't help but wonder what happens when Roman's demons meet mine.

My insides warm.

This can only lead to trouble.

EIGHT

I t's been two days since I last saw Roman, and not a second has ticked by without him in my thoughts. I can't stop thinking about his demons, and if they have anything to do with whomever Eleanor is.

"Good morning."

His hoarse voice makes me forget everything but these inexplicable feelings I'm forming for him.

"Good morning, Dr. Archibald," Zoe singsongs, smirking at my sudden internal dilemma.

He smiles before focusing his attention on Sadie. He turns tender. "How are you feeling today?"

"Better," she replies softly, nervously toying with her Monopoly piece.

Their exchange piques my interest as her reply reveals that she's been unwell—a fact I wasn't even aware of.

"Are you all right?" I ask gently, stroking her arm. She nods but lowers her eyes, giving herself away.

I peer at Roman, who pulls in his lips, also reading her deception loud and clear.

My stomach drops. What's the matter with her?

"Lola, do you have a minute?"

I know what he wants to see me about, making my already frayed nerves snap. "Sure," I reply, my voice heavy, plagued.

Jumping from the stool, I focus my attention on Sadie. "Rain check? Tonight?"

She nods, packing up the board game.

Roman walks ahead of me, all businesslike, while I trail him, wishing he'd wait. I compare our usual strolls to this one. I understand he's so aloof because we're surrounded by people. I wonder what we do look like, though, when no one is around. He doesn't mask his touches when we're alone, and I like that.

I like *him*.

"*Tell him*," subconscious Georgia says, but I'm quick to quash down her suggestion.

He opens his office door, waiting for me to enter first. I press past him, savoring his warm fragrance. Taking a seat, I wait for him to close us inside. Once he does, I exhale, happy we're alone.

As I wait for him to speak, I notice a signed Yankees baseball sitting in a small glass case on his desk. This is new. I wonder where it came from.

"I've got your test results," he leads with.

"Okay." I shuffle in my chair.

My gaze is riveted on him as he rounds the desk and takes a seat in his leather chair. He steeples his long fingers, pressing the pointers to his lips, and watches me with a profound eye. I swallow nervously.

"Everything is perfect. We can start as soon as you're ready."

The words register, but my brain can't seem to accept them as truth. "Wow," I manage to choke out.

A smile touches his lips before he opens his desk drawer. I watch with interest as he produces a sight that is all too familiar. Holding two orange medicine bottles, he reveals my fate in his hands. "You start with two of these yellow tablets." He rattles the contents. "Then two of the red tablets tonight."

My attention is riveted to the bottles. The small pills inside look harmless enough, but I know better. They hold the key to my future. He places the bottles on the desk and slides them toward me.

They sit between us—a monkey on my back.

I'm faced with two choices. I either take them, or I don't.

Leaning forward slowly, I reach for the pills with quivering hands. They feel weightless in my palm.

Unscrewing the lid, I dip a finger inside and pull out a single tablet. It barely covers the pad of my pointer. Holding it between my finger and thumb, I slowly raise it, hypnotized by the sight.

This is the key—the literal key to a new chapter in my life. Either I can unlock it or I can throw it away.

"I understand your reservations, but please know this is your choice. If you don't wish to proceed, then forget this conversation ever took place." Roman's voice hums in the background as my attention remains glued to the pill. It glows. The light illuminates its importance.

I could do that. I could forget this ever happened, that I ever had a second chance. Or I could…

Roman's gasp fills the room as I flick the pill into my mouth, tossing my head back and swallowing it in one smooth movement. It drags down my throat, the chalk taste making me gag, threatening to come back up, but I swallow twice, gulping it down.

My body trembles in a mental reaction to what I just did.

"Well…" Roman's voice is full of pride. "I was going to offer you a glass of water, but it appears you've got it covered."

A laugh catches in my throat.

For the second dose, I take him up on his offer and gulp down a bottle of water.

"So what happens now?" I ask, looking at the bottles in front of me as Roman places them in a white paper bag.

"Now"—he stands, buttoning his navy blazer—"you go enjoy the sunshine with the kids. Go, have fun."

His comment has me wondering when he has the time to do just that. He's always here, attending to someone's problems. Who attends to his?

He rounds the desk, ready to start his day, but an urge overcomes me, and I don't fight it. With the door sealed shut, it's nobody but us. What's one moment, one forbidden touch between two friends?

He stops, cocking an eyebrow, unsure why I'm unmoving. I answer his query when I step forward, almost breast to breast, and peer up into his eyes. His mouth parts, and a breathy exhale leaves his lips. My entire body is a bundle of nerves, but I persevere. I stand on tippy toes and wrap my arms around him.

I press my ear to his chest, his heart beating with a strong but faltering rhythm. At first, he stands still, frozen to the spot, as my forwardness has caught him off guard. But with a sweet surrender, he yields. He wraps his strong arms around me, crushing me to his firm torso. I can scarcely breathe, but I wouldn't have it any other way.

His heartbeat is a sound I want to bottle and keep forever. I snuggle closer, closing my eyes. "Thank you."

"Thank you?" The profound sound resonates through my body. I nod against him, unable to stop myself from rubbing my cheek against the soft cotton of his shirt. "For what?"

"For not giving up on me and believing in my life, even when I didn't."

He inhales deeply. "You just needed a reminder."

He's not taking any credit for his involvement, playing it off, but if it weren't for him, we wouldn't be here, standing in his office, hugging. The moment the thought crosses my mind, I realize that I'm still clinging to him like a baby koala. But what leaves me speechless is that he's holding me just as strongly.

We appear to both need the comfort. But eventually, he loosens his hold, and my body protests the disconnection. I regrettably let go.

I'm not repentant for the hug, but his poker face has me wondering what he's thinking. I suddenly get nervous.

"Sorry for invading your personal bubble. I'm pretty sure I left my shoe inside it," I add, hoping to lighten the mood.

He smiles, but something hides beneath it, making me even jumpier.

I clear my throat, grabbing the bag of pills. "Thank you, Dr. Archibald." I suddenly feel out of sorts calling him Roman.

An exit has never looked more appealing as I move toward it. However, I'm stopped in my tracks. "You didn't."

"Didn't?" It's the only word I squeeze out.

"You didn't invade my space," he clarifies while I lick my suddenly dry lips.

"Good to know," I reply flippantly, playing off his response.

Inside, I'm squirming, but I try my best to keep cool. My back is turned, so I can't see his face, but his deep voice alerts me to his sincerity.

"Yeah. Just for future reference," he adds.

"Okay, duly noted." I yank open the door. I'm afraid if I stay a second longer, I'll say something I might regret.

The cool breeze feels wonderful on my flushed skin as I zip down the hallway, seeking the safety of my room. Once inside, I lean against the door, taking three deep breaths. My heart is racing, the adrenaline punch shooting live currents all the way to my toes.

The bag of pills is the furthest thing from my mind, which is a miracle. I just took my first step toward the unknown, and I don't feel frightened—I feel alive, the reason being Roman. The thought makes me happier than I care to admit.

Pushing off the door, I walk over to my laptop and embrace life with both hands. Waiting for it to fire up, I pull out the bottle of pills and line them up neatly. Turning each label, I examine the medical names, which would leave most people tongue-tied.

Pulling out a notepad and pencil, I begin with the red tablet. Typing it into the search engine, I poise my pencil, ready to learn.

Side effects include:
Nausea, vomiting, loss of appetite
Headache, memory problems, fatigue
Dizziness, weakness, loss of coordination.

Reaching for the yellow tablets I took this morning, I do a

search on that also.

The side effects are similar, but may include:
Itchiness, difficulty breathing, swelling of the mouth, cold sweats.

I instantly feel parched, but I know my mind is just playing tricks on me. All in all, I will be in a medicated hell for the next few weeks. But these side effects aren't any different than I've experienced before. The sickness comes with the territory.

I can do this.

A soft knock on the door interrupts my research.

Sweeping the evidence into my drawer, I slam the laptop closed and dash for the door. Hoping my face doesn't betray my guilt, I open the door, surprised when I see Sadie. Her usually rosy cheeks are now a deathly white, and her eyes are sunken in.

"Sadie? Are you all right?" My high-pitched voice betrays my fears.

"Yes, I'm okay." She bites her dry lip. This is a blatant lie, but I don't press. "I'm just tired. Would it be okay if I stayed here?" She tugs her long sleeves over her tiny hands, toying with the ends nervously.

"Of course." I open the door wider, inviting her in. As she ambles in, it almost appears an effort for her to move.

"Want to have a slumber party?" I ask when she stands timidly near the doorway.

"But it's daytime." She cocks her head in confusion.

"Who says?" I slide the heavy blinds closed, shrouding us in darkness. Her happiness is palpable, which warms my heart.

We both bounce into bed, and five minutes later, Sadie is snoring softly beside me. A contented sigh leaves her when I wrap my arm around her.

It appears we all crave human contact. Sometimes, a single touch is all the medicine we need.

That has my thoughts wandering to Roman and our interaction earlier. He's been there for me even when I didn't want him to be. I want to do the same for him. I suddenly remember the Yankees baseball I saw in his office.

He's stuck here twenty-four seven, so I doubt he's even seen a game this season.

As gently as I can, I reach for my phone off the dresser, not wanting to disturb Sadie. I pull up the Yankees homepage and click on the tickets tab. As I read carefully over the schedule, one date stands out. It's Roman's birthday. It's a home game, and it's also on a Saturday night.

He can stay overnight if he doesn't want to make the commute back here after the game. Or he could make a night of it with a friend. Or someone special.

I grit my teeth at the thought. But I can't be selfish and presume he'll go alone. It's his birthday, for god's sake. No one should spend their birthday alone; regardless of how opposed they are to celebrating it.

Decision made, I allow the webpage to choose the best

seats available and enter my credit card details. Two tickets are emailed to my inbox minutes later.

I feel good about my spontaneity and hope Roman does too.

When Sadie woke, we spent the entire afternoon laughing, taking stupid selfies, and watching movie after movie. It was the best afternoon I've had in a long time. But now, the pain twisting my stomach into knots has me wanting to curl into a ball and die. It's been roughly two hours since Sadie left, and Roman texted me, reminding me to take my next dose. I did, and now I'm feeling the effects tenfold.

It started with sudden dizziness, followed by nausea.

I stand, needing to move as I'm getting motion sickness sitting down. The moment I rise, however, I collapse onto the floor, muting my groan behind my palm. It feels like a thousand knives are marching a circle around my stomach, not satisfied until I'm bled dry.

Curling into a ball, I tuck my arms around myself. A fierce pain tears through my body, and I taste blood as I bite down on my tongue to mute my cries.

I can do this, I repeat endless times. I've lived through worse. That may be true, but my mind has purposely forgotten this level of agony, never wanting to relive such torture.

Sweat coats my body, but I feel like I'm caught naked in a snowstorm. The nausea comes in violent waves, so brutal I almost black out from the pain. I almost wish I would.

Silently dragging myself along the floor, I reach overhead, hoping my fingers will pass over my cell sitting on my dresser. When they do, I squeak in relief.

Squinting, hoping the action will help clear my blurry vision, I hold the phone out in front of me. The screen moves in and out of focus, but the moment it clears, I type the only word I can. The only word he'll understand.

Sunflower.

The phone slips from my palm, and my head hits the carpet as I fold into a heap. It's quiet here, the pain thrumming in the background. Everything is so cluttered—chunks of reality slipping from my palms. I don't know where I am or who I am anymore. But I can't help but think that maybe it's where I was always destined to land.

I don't realize I'm throwing up until my throat screams at me, the burn almost rendering me unconscious once again.

"Don't you dare! Fight, Lola. Stay awake!"

My eyes pop open, his voice the only anchor I need to

slip back into the now. As I blink countless times, my murky brain attempts to decipher where I am. But my surroundings are unfamiliar. I know I'm face-first in a toilet bowl, but whose toilet bowl?

"That's it." I would know that voice from any corner of the globe. Roman rubs my back, the motion surprisingly soothing.

I will my breathing to slow and take a moment to dig through the fog. The last thing I remember is passing out on my bedroom floor.

"Lola, can you hear me?" His troubled voice pulls me closer to this plane, and the fog begins to clear.

I nod, too afraid to speak.

"You're in my house. Actually, you're in my bathroom. I got your text message and found you passed out on your bedroom floor. Do you think you can lift your head? I assure you there are a lot nicer things to see in here."

His quip has me laughing, but groaning a second later when my head feels like it's on the verge of exploding. "Ugh, screw you."

"Sorry." He chuckles, rubbing between my shoulder blades.

When I think I can face the land of the living, I wearily raise my head and almost celebrate when the room stops spinning. My hair hangs limply around my face, and my mouth feels drier than the Sahara Desert.

"Here." Roman passes me a glass of water, and I gulp it down. My stomach gurgles, but I clamp my lips shut, insistent on keeping it down. "Do you want to lie down?"

I nod, positive I can move without throwing up.

Roman gently cups my elbow and helps me stand. My legs feel like jelly, but I don't allow that to discourage me.

We take two small steps before I tremble. "I've got you, and I won't let you go," Roman assures, wrapping his arm around me. His strength pacifies my weakness, and I slouch against him, grateful for his support.

We take baby steps, but eventually, we make it out into the living room.

A thought suddenly occurs. "I am so sorry I dragged you from your b-bed to come rescue my sorry ass." He's in dark gray sweats and a white T-shirt. Odds are I interrupted his sleep.

"Don't even mention it," he quickly replies, tightening his hold around me. "I didn't have far to go."

We can tackle the matter of his address later because the room begins to spin again. "Please don't throw up. I just had the carpets steam cleaned." His humor has my sickness subsiding, and we make it through the room unscathed.

He switches on the light, showcasing a striking bedroom. A huge bed draped with black silk sits dead center with a nightstand on each side. A colorful abstract painting sits above the wooden headboard, giving the elegant room a modern feel.

We sway over to the bed where Roman pulls back the covers with one hand. "Here. Lie down."

I do as he says because those silk sheets look too inviting

not to.

I feel like I'm lying among clouds as I settle on the mattress with a sigh. Roman sits on the edge, watching me. I peer up at him, the reality of where I am sinking in—the material beneath me ingrained with his aroma. I instantly feel a blanket of sleep envelop me.

"Thank you. For everything." If I listed all the things I'm thankful for, we'd be here all night.

Roman nods. "There's no need to thank me. I'm sorry you fell ill."

"Not your fault. It's all part of the d-deal." I suppress a deep breath, wishing I purged up my stammer.

"Get some rest." Roman sweeps the hair from my brow.

When he goes to stand, I latch on to his wrist. "Where are you going?"

"I'm going to crash on the sofa."

Oh, right. Of course, he is. That's what a gentleman does.

I let him go, smiling bashfully. "Not only did I disturb your sleep, but now, I've stolen your bed too. I'll make it up to you. Promise." I yawn, my eyes drooping shut.

Caught between reality and the dream world, I don't know what's real and what's not. So when I hear Roman whisper, "You already have," I can't help but slip into a deeper slumber at total and complete peace.

NINE

I only wake because my stiff muscles protest. I have no idea how long I've been asleep. The fact my eyes aren't stinging is a sure sign I've slept more than three hours.

The bathroom light creeps in through the sliver of the ajar doorway. It takes me a moment to adjust to the near dark, but when I do, I'm faced with a sight that reminds me where I am.

Roman's bare back greets me. He's standing at the foot of the bed, about to slip on a white dress shirt. I've never seen a man dress before. Pressed black slacks sit low on his narrow waist, drawing attention to his rock-hard flank. The muscles in his body coil and curve as he works his arms into the garment.

Once he's tucked his shirt into his pants, he reaches for a tie on the tall dresser in front of him. A mirror is not needed as he loops it around his neck and ties it with precision. It's a chore he's done a thousand times before, but not for me—I can't tear my eyes away. I presume cuff links are the next addition to his routine. Once he's dressed, he opens a drawer and hunts for what I soon realize are socks.

Who would have thought watching a man dress, as opposed to undressing, could be sexy as hell? Maybe my brain really is fried. Or it could be his musky cologne clouding my good judgment.

"Morning."

I squeak in surprise, completely busted. I wonder how long he knew I was watching.

"Morning," I reply, my voice hoarse.

"Sleep okay?"

Shifting upright, I lean against the headboard, drawing the blanket over my chest. "Yes, I did, actually. Best sleep I've had in ages. Must be the silk sheets."

Roman chuckles before turning and almost giving me a near heart attack. His hair is damp, the longer strands tousled. On cue, he runs his fingers through it, combing it back. He hasn't shaved, so his scruff is longer, more rugged.

I remember to close my mouth when a dimple presses into his left cheek. "Do you want anything to eat?"

The notion of food turns my stomach. "No, thanks."

He sits at the foot of the bed, slipping on his socks and shoes. Once he's done, he glances over his shoulder. "I have to go to work."

"Oh, right. Sorry." He wants me to leave, but he's too polite to say. I attempt to push back the blankets but then freeze when Roman places his hand over my lower leg.

"No"—he grins—"I'm not kicking you out. I just meant I have to go, but you're welcome to stay."

"Stay here?" I question in case I'm lost in translation. Today is my day off, so I suppose I could, but I'm torn.

"Yes. You're not confined to the room, however. This isn't a Stephen King novel." I shake my head, smirking. "I'll be back around two thirty."

"Are you sure it's okay to stay here?"

"Of course. I've hidden all valuables and locked the liquor cabinet." I burst into laughter, loving this easiness between us. He squeezes my leg before standing. "And besides, Freud will love having a playmate." On cue, a loud, excited bark sounds at the door. "Make yourself at home. If you need me, just call my cell."

"Okay. Thank you."

Reaching for his blazer off the back of a chair, he pockets his keys, wallet, and phone. "Ready?" he asks with a smile.

"Ready?" I arch a brow.

My question is answered a moment later.

The moment he opens the door, a boisterous Golden Retriever comes charging into the bedroom, jumping onto the bed with one big leap. He has no problem invading my personal space as he falls into my lap, demanding belly rubs.

"Hey, big fella," I coo, scratching under his chin before going to town on his stomach.

Roman hides his smile beneath his palm. "I think he likes you."

"Well, the feeling is most definitely mutual." I continue scratching his belly with both hands, laughing when his big pink tongue droops from the side of his mouth. "Have a good day. Your fur baby is in good hands."

"I can see that. Lucky Freud." He shrugs into his blazer while I feel my cheeks blister. He gives us one final look before he leaves, the front door closing a few seconds later.

When it's just us, I exhale loudly. "Your daddy is something else." Freud yaps in harmony.

I stand, thankful I'm steady on my feet. After last night, I didn't know what to expect.

I peer around the doorjamb, not sure which direction the kitchen is. Freud barks once and pads down the carpeted hallway. With nothing to lose, I follow. As he takes a right, I see that up ahead is the kitchen. Clever dog.

The small but well-stocked kitchen is bright and homey. Two high-backed wooden barstools are lined up beneath the marble counter. A fruit bowl with one banana and a freshly brewed pot of coffee sits close by.

I practically run toward the coffee, my sense of smell doing a somersault in excitement. Once I've poured myself a cup, I cradle it, basking in the bitter yet rich aroma.

I wonder how long Roman has lived here, wherever here is. With that thought in mind, I take a tour. Freud leads the way. The first stop is the living room, where a large black leather sofa curves around an oval glass coffee table. A tall lamp sits off to the right, but the centerpiece of the room is the bookcases lining every wall. Volumes upon volumes of books are stacked high, without a spare shelf in sight. A plasma is mounted on the wall above a fireplace.

Next on the list is Roman's office. It looks very similar to the one at work. There is also a spare room, but it's rather sparse with only an old leather couch and some stacked boxes. I quickly close the door, feeling like I'm encroaching on a space that isn't meant to be seen.

I reenter the kitchen, ready for my second cup of coffee.

Roman's house is humble, but it contains all the things he needs. One major thing is missing, though—photographs. Even in my loveless home, Camille had pictures on display. They were there just for show, but regardless, they were there. This home lacks a personal touch. Has Roman done this on purpose? Or maybe he just doesn't like photographs. That's not a crime, but I can't help but think there's a reason behind the impersonal feel.

Once I finish my coffee, I wash my cup and place it in the dishwasher. The clock on the wall reveals it's just past seven a.m. I really would love a shower, but I have no clean clothes. I'm sure Roman wouldn't mind if I borrowed some of his. The thought of rummaging through his drawers seems like a total invasion of his privacy, however.

But so does parading around naked.

Before hunting through his drawers, I make his bed. I fist pump when I find an old Yankees tee and sweats. I strip on the way to the en suite, leaving a trail of clothes.

The scorching droplets of water feel heavenly against my skin as the showerhead spurts out a downpour of heavy rain. I stand under the spray for twenty minutes, my mind calm.

Once I step out, I reach for a clean towel from a long rectangular shelf. I draw the fluffy material to my nose and take a big whiff. It smells fresh, like laundry detergent, but there is an undertone of Roman's trademark cologne.

I've never felt this way about anyone before. Granted, I haven't really been around the opposite sex, but I have a feeling even if I were, they would all pale compared to Roman. I've fooled around and kissed a few guys, but I'm still a virgin. Getting sick in my prime hardly made me dateable material.

Dressing in Roman's attire, I chuckle at my appearance in the mirror because his clothes hang off my gaunt frame. Picking at the hem of this well-loved shirt, I wonder what the story is behind it. If not for this T-shirt and the baseball in his office, I would have never known about his love for the Yankees.

That has me wondering about the lack of personal effects in not only his office but also his home.

The boxes in the spare room may be filled with his most

prized possessions. Photographs of loved ones. Maybe he's moving, and he's packed everything away.

Deciding to take a walk, I slip into my Chucks and make my way toward the kitchen. The moment I reach for Freud's lead off the hook near the door, he comes charging down the hallway, tongue and tail flailing. Just as I'm about to open the door, the phone rings, startling me half to death. I peer at it on the counter, wondering if Roman's calling to ensure I haven't burned his house down.

The caller reveals who they are a second later when the machine clicks over.

"Hi, you know what to do." Roman's machine voice still has the power to give me goose bumps.

"Hey, man, it's Teddy. I tried your cell, but you're probably already at work. I wanted to let you know all is set for…September first. I have no idea why that date is so imperative, but I've known you long enough to know not to ask any questions. Hit me up when you're free. Let's grab a beer."

The continuous beeps announcing the end of the call resonate against my hammering heart. What's so special about that date? But more importantly, what's happening on that day? A thousand different scenarios flick through my mind, and my pulse suddenly spikes.

Why does a net of trepidation loom over me?

Freud barks, shaking me from my head. "I'm just paranoid," I mumble under my breath to no one in particular. "He could be doing a thousand things, like fumigating his house for bugs or getting a haircut."

However, my reasons fall flat, and I frown.

I wake to a big sloppy lick being delivered to my right cheek. With a yelp, I pop my eyes open, which only encourages Freud to continue lapping at my face. "You're such a goofball."

"But a lovable goofball." I jolt upward, almost winding myself. Roman chuckles, the sound warming my insides.

"When did you get here?" I ask. After my walk, I came back here and collapsed on Roman's couch.

"About an hour ago."

"Why didn't you wake me?" The blush creeps up my neck.

He clucks his tongue. "And interrupt the resonance of nature? I think not. I never knew there were so many sounds a human nose could produce."

The blush transforms into an inferno, and I cover my face, mortified.

Roman chuckles once again.

His touch is warm as his fingers clasp my wrist, drawing my hands downward.

Meeting his eyes, I feel a tad better when a lopsided smirk tugs at his lips.

"So I snore? I've never slept beside anyone before, so

I wouldn't know." My attempt to be sassy has me closing my mouth and pressing my lips together.

Roman reads my discomfort, and in true Roman fashion, he eases the blow. "You also drool…but who's keeping score?"

A laugh escapes me, and this time, instead of hiding, I lash out and playfully slap his arm.

"How was work?"

"It was okay. I was at St. Mary's hospital, not Strawberry Fields."

"How long have you worked there?"

"About four years."

"Between that and Strawberry Fields, when do you get any downtime?"

"I don't," he replies evenly. When my lips dip into a frown, he shakes his head. "I've chosen this life. I wouldn't have it any other way."

"I know, it just sounds so…"

"Boring?"

I avert my gaze. "No, I was going to say lonely."

Silence fills the space between us, and I worry I've overstepped a line.

"Knowing I've helped so many people is all the company I need. And besides, who wants to be tied to someone like me?"

I can't believe my ears.

"I brought over your pills and a change of clothes. But I see you've made other arrangements." Gingerly meeting his eyes,

I breathe a sigh of relief when he doesn't appear angry that I raided his room.

"Your pills are in the bathroom."

I nod and make my way down the hall.

Hunting through the bottles, I tap out two pills and toss them down my throat. Turning on the faucet, I cup a handful of water and drink it down. The sting is still there, but I know that's all in my head.

Just as I pad down the hallway, I hear Roman speaking to someone in a hushed tone.

I pause, midstride, and lean against the wall. I shouldn't eavesdrop, but the temptation is too great, especially when I hear who is at the door.

"Tamara, now isn't a good time."

"Why not? I know you have the afternoon off."

"That I do, which is precisely the reason now isn't a good time. I have errands to run."

"Maybe I could help?" I almost feel sorry for her. The heart wants what the heart wants, and Tamara can't help that, regardless of the brush-offs, she wants Roman.

"Thank you, but I'd rather do it alone."

"Have I done something wrong?" The hurt is clear in her tone.

"No, of course not." The annoyance is clear in his.

"Then why are you giving me the cold shoulder? I understand you're emotionally unavailable, you have been for years, but I thought things would change. You've erected this wall around yourself and won't let anyone in."

"Tamara—"

"No, not this time. It's my turn to talk. I like you. I have for some time. You know this. What more can I do to prove my feelings for you are real?"

Wow, I really am encroaching on a private moment. I should give them the privacy they deserve, but I don't.

"I'm doing this for you. I'm not someone you want to date. Just trust me on this."

"How can you say that? You're incredible. Not only to look at but on the inside too. Roman, you're a great guy. You're the perfect man."

"There's no such thing." The bitterness makes me recoil. "I'm not telling you this because I want you to tell me what a great catch I am, or for you to inflate my ego. I'm telling you this because it's how I feel. It's also the truth. That won't change anytime soon, so for the sake of never having this conversation again, please, just drop it."

Ouch. What a slap to her ego.

Her sniffles reveal his harsh words have sunk in. "Fine, have it your way then. You're going to die a lonely old man."

"One can only hope."

I cock a brow, unsure what he means.

A sniff follows Tamara's exasperated sigh. "Goodbye, Roman." Her heels pound against the front porch and down the wooden stairs.

I don't even know how to process what I just heard. I wanted to get a better insight into Roman's personal life, and now that I have, I'm even more confused. I believe him when he says he's telling her this for her own good. He truly believes he's no good for her, or anyone, in fact. But the thing is, he's not telling her this because he has low self-esteem or needs an ego boost. He's telling her because he's burdened with something he believes makes him an undesirable partner.

What is it?

"You can come out now."

It doesn't surprise me that I'm completely busted. You'd think I'd care, but I don't. I can now address the issues scratching at the surface.

Roman stands in the center of the living room, arms crossed. He waits for me to speak. "So…"

"So…"

"You've got the afternoon off. That's a nice change." I need some warmup time before I endeavor to ask him to unburden his soul. He's obviously not expecting my response because he suddenly bursts into a husky fit of laughter.

I could pester him and ask him to decode what the entire conversation meant, but although he's wedged his way into my life and made me face things I haven't wanted to face, he's always done so within my limits. I have an inkling this is a touchy subject for Roman, and I know what it feels like when someone pushes when you don't want to be pushed.

He has, in a roundabout way, respected my wishes, so I'll do the same. If he wants to tell me about his past, then I want it to be because he wants to share it, not because I asked.

"Seeing as you're free, how about we get some lunch?" Furrow lines gather between his brow. He thinks there's a catch, but there isn't.

When my stance radiates nothing but sincerity, his posture loosens, and his arms drop to his side. "Sure. I know how much you loved riding my bike," he muses. "So lucky for you, I have another means of transportation with four wheels."

Folding my arms across my chest, I defiantly challenge, "Where's the fun in that?"

Roman shakes his head. "You're full of surprises." My bold response catches him off guard.

Deciding this will be the only acknowledgment I'll make about what I just witnessed, I affirm, "We both are."

After lunch, Roman stopped into the grocery store because that one lonely banana in his fruit bowl was the only speck of food in his home.

The distraction of stocking Roman's fridge has taken my mind off things. It's been nice to worry about someone other than me.

"Are you hungry?" His question is simple, but I stand, mute. "Seeing as I have all this food, how about we cook some of it?"

"You want to eat? Here?" I question, ensuring I heard him correctly.

He nods, rubbing the back of his neck. "Unless you have something against food and my house and want to go back?"

"No!" I reply, a little louder than I anticipated. I cringe as I quickly backtrack. "Sure, I could eat. What's on the menu?"

"Do you like pasta?"

"I love pasta," I reply with a little too much enthusiasm.

"Pasta, it is then." A bubble of excitement swells in my belly. I'm overjoyed to be spending the evening here.

Roman brushes past me while I quickly sidestep to get out of the way. However, when he opens a drawer and stands back, scratching his head, I know he has no idea what he's looking for.

"Move out of the way." I bustle in, playfully shoving him to the side with my hip. He goes willingly.

I collect everything I need to make an easy spaghetti Bolognese. Roman takes a seat on a barstool, watching my every move. I'm suddenly nervous, but I try to conceal my nerves.

"So who taught you how to cook? Your mom?"

I can't help but snigger. "Are you kidding me? My mom wouldn't know a spoon from a spatula. I learned early on how to fend for myself."

"She sounds like she won't be in the running for mother of the year anytime soon."

"You got that right."

"How old were you...?"

"When I got sick?" I fill in the blanks as I look up from peeling the garlic. Roman nods. "Twenty-one."

His compassion shines as he shakes his head. "Life really is unfair. Sorry, Lola."

I raise my shoulders. "It is what it is. I still get bitter, but then in some ways, I really have lived the most extraordinary life. Only now am I coming to realize that." I not only surprise Roman with my confession but I also surprise myself.

He runs his fingers over his scruff, appearing to ponder what I just said.

"How about you?" I ask, turning around to reach for a knife from the wooden block.

"How about me what?" He's evasive for a reason, but this time, I don't let it slide.

"Did your mom do all the cooking?" The room drops to an arctic degree as I turn and watch him shift uncomfortably in his seat.

"She"—he clears his throat—"she used to."

I slice the tomatoes, not pressing him to divulge anything he's not comfortable sharing.

"Things changed. My parents divorced when I was fourteen. I bounced from home to home, but I lived with my dad mostly. My mom had depression, so it was easier if I stayed with him. It took the strain off her. My dad remarried, so I liked living with him anyway. My stepmom had four kids of her own. We were a big, happy family."

"And you weren't when your mom and dad were together?"

The room is still. The only sound is the knife slicing through ripened flesh.

"We were once, but things change." He abruptly stands and makes his way over to the fridge.

I refocus my attention on the tomatoes, not wanting to smother him with questions.

The unmistakable sound of a beer bottle being opened alerts me to Roman's actions. His mom had depression. Could her son suffer the same ailment? It explains what I saw in his office.

Lost in tomatoes and conspiracies, I don't feel Roman until the hair at the back of my neck pricks in heightened awareness. He's standing behind me, looking over my shoulder. The act is innocent enough, but I still feel my legs grow weak and my mouth parched.

"Is that why you don't have any photographs around your home?"

Why my mouth filter malfunctioned at this certain point in time, I'll never know, but now that it's out there, I can't take it back.

"Nothing slips past you." My skin breaks out into tiny goose bumps, his breath warm against my neck. "I don't have any photographs because all the memories I have are in here."

He places two fingers against my temple while I stop breathing. "And in here." He then lowers his hand and places a fist over my heart.

His touch is between my breasts, but it isn't at all sordid. It actually brings a tear to my eye.

"I don't need a visual reminder of the good times I've shared because those memories will always remain with me. A photograph can never capture what your mind stows away or what your heart feels. Those moments are priceless, and I'll never forget them."

His words ring true because my memories of Georgia are far better than looking at her photographs and remembering who she was. My memories of her are a moving picture and allow me to remember who she is. In my head and heart, she'll never be gone.

My chest rises and falls, a tear tracing down my cheek.

Roman splays out his fingers and lightly presses the heel of his hand against my thundering heart. "I'm sorry I made you cry."

"You didn't. My memories did." There's no need to explain.

Roman clears his throat before returning to his seat.

Once my hands stop shaking, I continue preparing dinner. I wonder if what just happened will be a memory my mind takes a photograph of.

Sitting at the small dinner table, I pick at my hardly touched meal while Roman devours every last morsel left in his bowl.

Over the course of an hour, that familiar nausea is beginning to rear its ugly head. I haven't said anything to Roman because I'll be damned if I let my sickness rain on my parade. Once he's done, however, I shoot up and collect his plate. I need an excuse to move, hoping it'll help with the nausea.

"I can do that. You cooked, so it's only fair." He goes to stand, but I gently push him back down. He peers up at me in confusion.

"It's fine. I'm happy to do it. Doing normal things like this helps me forget." And it's true. Besides the past hour, I have felt normal, and it's been wonderful.

I rinse off the plates before stacking them in the dishwasher. As I stand from my downward position, a wave of nausea rolls over me, and I think I'm going to be sick. Roman is thankfully distracted when his cell chimes, giving me the out I need.

"I'm just going to use the bathroom." I barely get out the words before dashing down the hallway, both hands covering my mouth to stop from being sick.

I slam the door shut behind me and run over to the toilet, throwing up the contents of my stomach as I cradle the bowl. Tremors wrack my body, and I shudder, unable to stop the vomit. A light sheen of perspiration coats my body, bringing home the cold sweats.

Usually, I would be cursing the choice to do this to my body, but not today. My mindset has changed. I try to place a positive spin on it, hoping that every purge is eliminating my body of the disease which ravages it. Surely, the more I throw up, the better it is? I use this as my reasoning as I heave up everything I ate today.

I feel like utter shit, so when a soft knock sounds on the door, it's expected for my response to be a garbled, "Go away." My wishes are, of course, ignored, and when the door creaks open, I bury my head farther into the toilet bowl.

"Lola?" His concerned voice has me groaning. I feel like a fool. The visual he must have right now has me throwing up again.

"Don't worry"—my voice echoes off the bowl—"I don't think it's contagious." This is hardly the time to be making jokes, but it's either that or I cry myself into a heap.

When his footsteps proceed toward me, I thrust my hand out, requesting he stay put. "No, don't. I'm all icky."

He tsks me, appearing unconcerned by my repulsive state. "Don't be silly. I don't care about that. How long have you been feeling sick?"

I shrug, cradling the bowl like it's my lifeline. "About an hour."

"What?" he admonishes. "Why didn't you say anything?"

"Because…" There are a million reasons, but only one word seems to suffice.

"You're so stubborn." If my head wasn't wedged down a toilet, I'd poke my tongue out at him.

He moves around the room, pushing bottles and god knows what else out of the way. The faucet runs for a few seconds before he turns it off and walks my way. I surrender because I know any attempt to warn him to stay away will just fall on deaf ears.

His huge frame is at my back, and before I can ask what he's doing, a warm cloth is applied to the back of my neck. The sensation appeases my tremors as my body instantly reacts to the warmth.

"That feels n-nice. Th-thank you." I almost hum in relief.

I don't quite trust myself to remove my head from the bowl, so I stay still, enjoying the calm. He turns the cloth over, ensuring I stay heated. After a few minutes, he rises and wets the towel once again.

My stomach soon settles, but I know it's just a ruse. It'll flare up again. It always does. "I'm s-sorry," I stammer. I'm suddenly so cold. "I've ruined a perfect evening."

"Lola." His voice is heavy. "No, you didn't. Believe it or not, today is the best day I've had in a very long time."

I half laugh, half choke. "You really need to get out more then." A wave rolls over me, like a tsunami, poised and ready to drag me under.

"Roman, go." It's all I croak out before I'm violently ill once again. Tears leak from my eyes, and I almost gag from the burn. No food is left in my stomach, but my body wants to purge.

"No, I'm not going anywhere," he argues. And he calls *me* stubborn.

I'm so embarrassed that Roman is here, watching this more than horrifying sight. One wouldn't blame him if he fled from this room and returned with sanitizer and bleach.

I have nothing left, but I can't stop. The nausea laps at my stomach, not content until I'm drained dry.

"Honestly, I'm okay. You can go whenever..." My spiel is short-lived, however.

The entire time I'm throwing up my guts, Roman never leaves my side. He rubs my back and holds back my snarled hair. If I wasn't on the cusp of blacking out, I would thank him for being so nice.

"Lola, don't pass out. Stay awake."

"So tired," I mumble, my eyes slipping shut.

He circles my back before gently encouraging me to lift my head from the bowl. I'm too exhausted to fight him. "You'll be all right."

With eyes still sealed shut, I'm blind, trusting him completely. My head lolls to the side, but Roman places his palm against my cheek for support. I attempt to pull away, but my efforts are futile. I have no strength left.

"Why are you doing this?" It's the second time I've asked

him, but this time, I want the truth.

His touch wavers against my face, the first sign of nerves. "Because it's—"

"If you say it's your job, I swear to god, I'll scream." That's a slight exaggeration, but I've made my point.

When he doesn't speak, I force an eye to half-mast, ensuring he's heard me, and I didn't say those words in my head.

He swallows, a pain slashing at his very core. "I…I lost someone very close to me." If I could gasp, I would have. "Ever since then, I just"—he fumbles over his words—"you remind me of her. That's not the reason I'm helping you, I just…"

I've never seen Roman tongue-tied, but that can wait because just who is this person he lost? Flashes of his tattoo flicker before me. Could it be Eleanor? It makes sense. But the next question is, who is Eleanor?

"I'm so sorry for your loss."

"Thank you." I open my mouth, poised with a thousand other questions, but he stops me. "How are you feeling?" he asks, clearly wanting to drop the topic.

"Better," I confess, pushing the hair from my brow. Roman almost looks relieved.

He stands wearily, and although he wasn't throwing up, he was with me every shudder of the way. Running both hands through his hair, he opens the medicine cabinet. "Want some Pepto-Bismol? It'll help settle your stomach."

I'm happy to take anything if it'll help.

I nod, extending my palm. He passes me the bottle. I'm still a little wobbly, so I don't attempt to rise. I must learn how to crawl before I walk.

Roman brushes his teeth, leaving me to recoup, which I appreciate. I watch with interest as he rinses out his mouth before reaching into the medicine cabinet and shaking out two pills from a bottle. My curiosity is piqued. If I wasn't so fatigued, I'd ask what they're for.

When he's done, he turns, his face a cluster of worry. I feel terrible for placing that concern there. "Just give me a few minutes, and we can go back."

He narrows his eyes. "Go back where?"

"To Strawberry Fields." I'm not expecting to stay another night, as I'm sure I've outstayed my welcome.

"You want to go?"

"No, but I'm pretty sure you want your bed back."

He shakes his head firmly. "Nonsense. You can stay here. You're in no state to travel."

The prospect of staying another night is appealing, but I couldn't allow him to forfeit his bed for another night. "I'll take the couch."

He scoffs, offended. "You'll do no such thing. Your clothes are in the bedroom. I'll grab them for you."

"Thanks." I'm speechless. His kindness knows no bounds.

Once he's out the door, I take a couple of deep breaths and endeavor to stand. After attempt number five, I've risen to semi-full height as I lean slouched against the tiled wall.

Roman reenters, his eyes widening when he sees me struggling. "Let me help you."

"You've done enough." Under this bravado, however, I'm thankful for the assistance as I'm seconds from falling back down. I lean against him, placing my palm to the wall to gain my balance. The room stops spinning after two minutes.

"I'm okay," I affirm, steadying my breathing. He lets me go but has both hands out in front of him, ready if I fall. "I really want to take a shower."

He rubs the back of his neck, clearly uncomfortable. I don't understand why until I realize what I've just said. "Oh my god, no, that was not me hinting for you to help! I think you've seen enough."

"I can help, I mean, I'm a doctor…but I…" He clamps his lips together.

But he what? Finds it weird, too? Why? "It's fine, honestly."

He appears relieved. "Okay. I'll just be outside the door. Call out if you need me."

"Not necessary, but thank you." When he lingers, I shoo him out the door. And even then, he hesitates to leave.

It takes me about ten minutes, but I'm finally naked. I avoid the mirror but look down at my concaved stomach. I look frail and unwell, but here's to hoping that changes soon. I shuffle over to the shower, glancing at the clothes Roman placed on the edge of the basin. I can tell he most likely grabbed handfuls of clothes with his eyes closed, as most items are mismatched, but that's fine. The familiar sight settles my nerves.

Just as I'm about to step into the shower, a flash of red catches my eye. Doing a quick double take, I almost collapse for an entirely different reason. Under my T-shirt sits Georgia's bandana. How did Roman know? As silly as this is, just it being here gives me the strength I need.

This is a sign that things will be okay.

TEN

"Thank you again."

"It's not a problem, really."

Roman's gaze never wavers from the road as he drives us to Strawberry Fields. We've taken his Jeep instead of the bike.

My sensitive stomach feels as if I swallowed a gallon of acid, but it's already feeling better. All in all, the side effects are horrid when they hit, but the aftermath isn't as bad. With the initial trials, Georgia and I would be sick for days.

I finger the red bandana around my neck, smiling at the memory of when she gave it to me. Roman's admission about not needing pictures to recall special events sticks in my mind. I agree with him. I don't have that many photographs of Georgia because neither of us wanted a reminder of how ghastly we looked. We promised that would change once we got well. It might have been wishful thinking, but it gave us something to look forward to.

"Everything okay?"

Roman's concern stirs me from my head, and I nod. "Yes, it really is."

He doesn't address my strange response; he's probably accustomed to my weirdness by now. That has me thinking. "So will you drop me off down the street or something?"

"No. I'll park the car, and then I'll walk you inside," he replies.

I turn to look at him, curling my lip in confusion, but I don't argue.

All this sneaking around could get Roman into serious trouble. I owe him, which reminds me. Lifting my hips, I dig into my back pocket of my jean shorts and fish out my phone.

"What's your email address?"

He averts his eyes from the road, intrigue and curiosity tugging at his lips, but he rattles off his email.

Once I've attached the tickets to the email, I peer at the subject line and think of something witty to write.

Hut! Hut! Hike!

I press send and smile. Roman's phone vibrates in his

pocket. Message sent.

Roman drives around the back to the parking lot.

The sun is pleasantly warm as I exit the car, and I take a moment to feel the balmy rays on my skin.

Closing my eyes, I tip my head back and bask in the sunshine. If the trials were unsuccessful and I was to eventually succumb to my disease, then I think I would miss the little things the most. The sun's rays on my flesh, the lulling sound of rain pounding against a window during a storm, and the stillness of being with someone like Roman Archibald.

Our paths cross with different people for many reasons, and I can't help but think that Roman's and my meeting was fated within the stars. Georgia was a big believer in fate and destiny, and I'm now beginning to believe it too. Whatever happens is mapped out for us, and we're just holding on, hoping for something…better.

Gradually opening my eyes, I take in Roman standing before me. He is an exquisite man, but underneath that beauty lies a broken being. He confessed to me as much last night, and I can't help but wonder who he lost. I remind him of her. Is she the reason he's so closed off to Tamara?

We enter around back, and I lower my face, suddenly feeling like I'm doing the walk of shame. We say our goodbyes, and as I walk to my room, I bump into Sadie.

She looks awful.

Her green dress hangs off her bony body, and her eyes are

sunken into her gaunt cheeks. Her short red hair is sticking up into brittle peaks, appearing as if she gave up mid-brush.

"Hey," she softly says, wringing her hands nervously.

Once I find my voice, I put my game face on. "Hey. Your dress is really pretty."

She smiles, a smidge of color tinting her cheeks. The sight gives me an idea…but can I? Would Georgia be disappointed in me?

"*I won't be mad, Lola. It's time to let go.*"

We hold items because we want to remember, but how can I forget someone who gave me so much to remember them by?

Unfastening the bandana, I toy with the material, recalling the strength it gave me. It's now time to lend that strength to Sadie. I may not be able to save her, but I can hold her hand while trying.

"Georgia…" My profound voice hushes the hallway. "Well, she gave this to me. It was her favorite thing. She would never sit through a treatment without it. She never gave me a reason for why it meant so much to her, but I guess there doesn't have to be one. We find comfort because sometimes, we just need it. I can't tell you how many times this has provided that for me." I turn the bandana over in my fingers.

"But I…I don't need it anymore. I've found my comfort in being your friend." Tears roll down my cheeks, matching the ones streaming down Sadie's cheeks.

"Georgia would have wanted me to pass this on to someone

who needed it more than me. I can never bring her back, but I can share who she was with you. With the world. And let me tell you, she was unbelievable."

I silently ask for permission.

She nods, her large eyes drowning. With the utmost care, I tie the bandana around her head, adjusting it like a headband, just how my Georgia did.

"*You did good, kiddo.*" I snuffle out a laugh. She used to call me that when playing the big sister role.

"Thanks, G," I say aloud, uncaring that I'm talking to the voice inside my head.

"*I love you, Lola.*" I know this will be the last time she speaks to me. I held on to her because I needed her strength, but it's now time I be somebody else's.

"Just one more episode," Sadie says with a yawn, rubbing her heavy eyes.

"Not a chance, kiddo. Time for bed." I gently climb from the sofa. Our day was spent enjoying the sunshine before we came back to the living room and binged on Netflix.

Roman texted me throughout the day. I can't stop my smile when recalling his message.

You really shouldn't have, but thank you.

Just as I was about to reply, a second text came through.

P.S. Hut! Hut! Hike? Really? :P Wrong sport.

My absolute zero knowledge of sports shined through. So much for being clever.

It still has a ball with players in ridiculously tight pants, right? What's the difference? Tomayto, tomahto.

There is a huge difference. Baseball encompasses skill. NFL encompasses concussions.

From what I understood, that's true, but I wouldn't know firsthand.

Bending, I tuck a blanket around Sadie, smiling when I see the bandana securely in her hair. "Sweet dreams," I whisper, not wishing to wake the handful of kids who have passed out around us.

"Night," she replies, settling into the couch cushion. "Thank you."

She catches me off guard. "Thank you?"

She nods. "Thank you for being a reason I can smile again. Back home, I forgot what it felt like. I guess that's because there wasn't a reason to. But that's changed, thanks to you."

My mouth falls open, and my heart swells. This tiny girl is

a godsend and so much more. Sitting on the edge of the sofa, I stroke her cheek with the back of my hand. "Thank you for giving me a reason to make somebody smile again."

Roman instantly comes to mind as he said something similar what feels like a lifetime ago.

"Sisters?" She extends her tiny hand.

I fist bump her with pride. "For life."

"Good night, Lola." Sadie buries herself under the blanket, her eyes slipping shut.

"Good night, Sadie." When her breathing grows shallow, I whisper. "I love you."

I tiptoe through the room, and the moment I reach the doorway, I freeze, tears stinging my eyes.

"I love you, too." She loves me, and it feels so good to be loved.

The dimmed corridor lights indicate it's past eleven, so there isn't much to do at this hour, but I suppose I could watch a movie and hope I fall asleep. But the thought of sleeping in my bed is not as enticing as Roman's silk sheets.

Walking to my room, I realize that my limp isn't as apparent. I also feel stronger. My body is charged. With so much energy to burn, there is only one place I want to go. I dash to my room and change into gear I never thought I'd wear again. Once my laces are tied and I grab a water bottle, I close my door and head for the gym.

As I'm untangling my earbuds, I hear a near muted voice. It's coming from the direction I'm headed. Softening my footsteps, I turn my ear when I hear a voice I'd recognize underwater.

"I just…I just wish you'd reconsider."

"There is nothing to reconsider. It's done. You knew what my decision was from the very beginning."

"I know, Roman, I just…why?" June whispers, her voice saddened.

What are they talking about? And why does June sound like she's seconds away from bursting into tears?

"Can we talk in my office? Please," she almost begs when he remains silent.

After a pregnant pause, he sighs. "Okay, fine."

Their footsteps advance down the plush carpet and away from where I stand, hidden and almost breathless. I don't understand what I just overheard, but it sounded dreadfully grave. What has left June almost in tears?

I want to run after them, press my ear to the door, and finally uncover the skeletons in Roman's closet, but I won't.

Once the coast is clear, I amble down the hallway, unable to clear my mind from June's heartache.

The fitness center is empty, while I'm ready to tackle the treadmill and run myself into fatigue. Powering up my iPod, I select my workout music and press play. The moment the rock music blares through the earbuds, I do some light stretches, not wanting to hurt myself before I've even begun.

Five minutes in, my lungs are screaming at me to slow

down, but I don't. All I can focus on is the weight settled in my stomach; the heavy sensation a premonition of what's to come. I try to shake the feeling, but I can't. Something big is about to happen, I just don't know what.

I continue running, increasing the speed, hoping to run away from my fears. But I doubt I'll ever be able to sprint that fast. The clock reads twenty-two minutes, which is a record for my out-of-shape form.

Once I turn off the treadmill, I guzzle down my water, taking a moment to catch my breath. The red punching bag hangs innocently to my left. The memory of Roman driving into it with feral force is anything but innocent. It was here I saw his tattoo, and the mystery surrounding him began and has only grown.

Deciding to blow off some of my own steam, I make my way over to the bag, marveling at the firm texture as I run my palm across the center. Roman didn't show this bag an ounce of mercy, delivering blows that looked so effortless. But actually standing in front of it and feeling its density, I appreciate just how strong Roman is. I doubt my scrawny arms could make this thing move, but I suppose there's only one way to find out.

Remembering Roman's stance, I place one foot in front of the other and bend my knees. I have no idea how to punch, so I throw all my strength behind it and just hit the thing and hope for the best. Focusing on the center, I curve my arm outward and connect with a brick wall.

"Holy shit!" I cradle my throbbing hand to my chest.

Against my better judgment, I eye the bag, challenging me with its immobile state. Although my hand is aching, it felt mighty good to hit something. Imagine what I could achieve if I threw everything I am behind the next punch, hoping to expunge the years of fury that won't disappear.

This is suddenly the best idea I've had all day.

Every single negative, raw memory, and emotion I can remember comes charging to the surface, armed and ready to explode. I feel like a warrior prepared for battle, but unlike those fighters, my enemies are within. I bend low, engage my core, and just as I'm about to punch the bejesus out of the bag, something, *someone* stops me.

I don't have time to turn to see who it is because that person is suddenly pressed up against my back, his firm grip secured tightly around my poised wrist. His essence is the first thing I notice, and I know without looking who it is.

I attempt to turn around, but Roman doesn't let me.

"Where's the fire, Rocky?"

"No fire. The thing is, this bag looks a little like my mother's head."

He chuckles behind me. "Glad to hear I'm not making a guest appearance in your vision of violence."

"No, you're good. For now."

He releases the hold he has on me, moving his hands low on my hips. A gasp escapes my parted lips. "W-what are you doing?" He's exceptionally close, closer than he's ever been.

"I'm going to teach you how to expend that anger without hurting yourself," he replies into my ear.

"I'm not angry," I pathetically argue, holding back my shiver as his warm breath trickles down the length of my neck.

"I'm sure your bruised hand begs to differ." To accentuate his point, he removes his palm from my waist and runs his thumb along the crease of my pulsating wrist.

"Fine then, show me what you've got."

It's a challenge, one he happily accepts. He tightens the hold around my waist, the heat from his fingers warming the flesh beneath my thin cotton tank. He coaxes me to pivot my body, rotating my hips so I bow backward, leaning into his chest. At the same time, he draws the arm he holds back, so my body is angled and pressed against his.

His heart gallops strongly against my back, the uneven rhythm hinting he's as anxious as I am. My breathing accelerates, and a tremor passes through me.

"Okay"—he squeezes his fingers around my wrist—"you're going to keep your balance and ground your feet when you punch. When you punch, put your entire body behind it. Keep your arm level with your shoulders. Your thumb needs to be on the outside of your fist. Otherwise, you will break it." I automatically adjust my fist and do as he instructs. "Make a tight fist and aim to punch with your first two knuckles, so you don't break your hand."

"Keep my balance. Ground my feet. Make a fist. Don't break anything. Anything else?" I ask, clenching and unclenching my hand to get a feel of my new stance.

"Yes." He leans in close, his lips grazing the shell of my ear. I hold my breath. "Imagine every single thing you loathe, absolutely detest, and all the wrongdoings that have been thrown your way over the years and use that as your ammunition to deliver a punch that will chip away at that anger. That bag is your enemy, and it's your turn to show it who's boss."

His amped-up speech has a fire burning in my belly, and a course of adrenaline sears through me. I begin to shake but for an entirely different reason. My eyes narrow on their own accord as Roman's words invoke a fierce need to drive out this malevolence inside me. The bag suddenly becomes my worst enemy, and all I can see, hear, and taste are bitter memories, ones which fester within and plague me every day.

I see my mom and her apathy toward me. The countless times I was ridiculed for being different. I see the brain tumor eating away at my years. But at the forefront, I see Georgia, lying in her casket, her young life ripped out from under her because life just isn't fair.

I shake in rage as a war cry comes bubbling up from my belly, exploding out of me in a gut-wrenching scream. I barely feel Roman release me as I pull my arm back, ground my feet, and force everything behind my movement and hit the bag. I'm expecting to hear bones break, followed by a blinding pain, but

I don't. All I feel is a release so great that tears sting my eyes.

I pause for a moment before the need to do that again overcomes me, and I give in to my primeval instincts. This time I hold back, afraid that it was a stroke of luck I actually connected with the bag. I also feel stupid, knowing I probably look like a stark raving lunatic.

"C'mon, you're not even trying." Roman appears disappointed by my effort, which infuriates me.

"I am too!" I hit the bag but forget his advice about the positioning of my thumb and wince in pain when I almost break it.

"Seriously? My grandma can hit harder than that…and she's dead. Put some muscle into it, Van Allen!" He's baiting me, and it's working. I scream and punch the bag again, harder this time, but still not hard enough for Roman. "I thought you were a fighter, but maybe I was wrong."

His reverse psychology kick-starts my anger, and I detonate.

I don't know how many times I hit that bag, envisioning all the atrocities that led me here. Tears blind my vision, but I work on impulse and let my bottled-up anger lead me. I wonder how often I have to hit the bag before I feel normal again?

Sweat coats my skin. I'm breathless, and my arms ache, but I continue punching, screaming as I deliver each blow. I don't care that Roman is here, witnessing my meltdown, because didn't I do the same to him? He knows what it feels like to be behind the bag because he's carrying a secret so great, he needs to release it with sheer ferocity, too.

The injustices are no longer sitting so heavily on my chest, and even though I am gasping for breath, I feel like I can breathe. With one last punch, I let go of the regret that led me here and weep in relief. My arms and legs collapse, and I tumble to the ground, exhausted and on the verge of hysteria.

Roman immediately falls to his knees, brushing the hair from my sticky brow. He searches my face, scanning every inch to ensure I didn't break. He's become my anchor, my tether to this place, and I instantly take in air again.

I meet his eyes, those blue depths dragging me under and drowning me in a welcome abyss. We stare at one another, unguarded and raw. The walls he's erected so resolutely around himself unexpectedly come down, and I gasp. A fervent inferno engulfs his irises and burns me from head to toe.

Neither of us dares to say a word. The air is crackling, and I struggle to breathe. Heavy exhalations leave him before he wets his bottom lip with the tip of his tongue. The movement is absolutely intoxicating, and I let out a small whimper. My whimper is matched with a low hum, and it takes me a second to realize the sound is coming from Roman.

Before I know what's happening, he's inching forward, his hand pressed to my cheek, using the touch as guidance to draw my face to his. All thoughts of bottling his perfume are put on hold when his lips are a hairsbreadth away from touching mine.

"Roman…" My lips are trembling, the anticipation soaring

through me.

"Tell me this is a bad idea," he whispers, his eyes dropping to my mouth.

"This is bad…" But I falter, unable to continue.

This is a bad idea for so many reasons, but none of them seem to matter. The only thing that matters is closing this distance between us and forgetting the world exists.

I close my eyes, charged and ready for him, but I feel nothing. The room suddenly fills with a beeping, tearing through my bubble and bringing home the reality of what I was about to do.

Slowly opening my eyes, I see the regret marring Roman. I avert my eyes, embarrassed. "Saved by the bell," I say softly.

"Lola…" I don't want to hear what he has to say because I don't know whether that regret is there because we were interrupted, or because of what we were about to do. The buzzing continues, and with a sigh, he reaches into his pocket and pulls out his pager.

It takes a second, but when he sees who it is, his face turns to stone. His impenetrable mask sends a chill through me. "Roman?" My voice is small, afraid.

"I—" He pauses, his mouth parted as he seems to search for the right words. Roman is never at a loss for words. I wrap my arms around my body, suddenly chilled. "I have to go," he finally says, composing himself.

Before I can ask if everything is okay, he places his palm on my cheek. Searching my face, he beseeches, "Stay here. Promise me."

"What happened?"

"Lola, promise me," he begs, dipping low and pinning me with his stare.

But I can't. I can see it in his eyes. This heartbreak is close to home. My chest begins to ache, and I rub over it, hoping to stop my heart from bleeding from its cage. But nothing can stop that ache.

My feet act before my brain can draw near, and I'm running toward the door, my instinct leading me down the hall. Roman calls my name out behind me, but there's no stopping me. I'm running on pure adrenaline, new and old, as my sneakers pound against the carpet, drawn to the unknown.

Doors open, bystanders curious about the commotion, but I ignore them, powering on until I round the corner and stop dead in my tracks. The first thing I see is Zoe, just a few feet away from the living room. She's leaning against the wall, hands cupped over her mouth, eyes wide. She appears to be in shock. The next thing I see is June dashing down the hallway, a cell pressed to her ear, her silk dressing gown flailing behind her.

I try to call out to Zoe, but my mouth has gone dry. But she seems in sync with me and turns in slow motion. Her movements may not be quick, but nothing seems real anymore as the walls begin closing in on me. I find the strength to say the only word that matters—the only word which will make everything all right again.

"Sadie?"

She just bursts into tears.

"No. *No.*" A surge electrocutes me, and I charge forward, desperate to uncover the lie she tells. I don't get far because determined arms wrap around my middle and press me into the safety net of his chest. "Let me go!" I kick my legs out, but he doesn't budge.

"Please, don't look. Don't remember her like this." His words are filled with loss and sadness.

"No!" I sob, a rattle vibrating within my chest. "Let me go, please. I have to go. She needs me." Roman tightens his hold, a column of strength as I crumple around him.

"I'm sorry. Oh god, I'm so sorry." Those words confirm what I knew to be true the moment he tried to protect me from our reality. Our unforgiving, cruel reality that takes and takes, forgetting how to give.

My outburst has caused a scene, cluing fellow volunteers into what's going on. The entire time, Roman doesn't let me go. He is my strength, my champion as I sag against him, sobbing a cry so guttural my throat feels raw. He stands behind me, never letting me go, and if I were thinking straight, I would grieve elsewhere. Anyone looking can see our connection stems far past professional. But I don't care because I need him. I'm afraid I'll never crawl back from yet another loss without him.

June watches us from just outside the doorway. Her face

shows no emotion, but I know she sees it. A doctor in a white coat pushes past us, suspending June from dissecting what's happening between Roman and me any further. He stops by her side, and she gestures to the bedroom, shaking her head with a blank stare.

He nods before entering.

I want to go in with him, but I know I can't—I can't because I can't move. All I can think about is Sadie's last words to me. "*I love you, too.*"

Did she know those whispered words would be the last she ever spoke?

Roman never wavers from holding me. Back to chest is how we stand and how we stay when Tamara comes around the corner, stopping abruptly when she sees us. Her shock is evident, but she quickly composes herself.

"I came as soon as I heard," she says in a tender voice, approaching Zoe.

Zoe appears to be in shock. She wears a vacant look as she nods.

The somber-faced doctor emerges. He peruses the crowd before his laser stare focuses on Roman. Roman tenses behind me, but a moment later, he slowly loosens his hold. He leans over my shoulder, whispering, "I have to go in. I won't be a minute."

"I-I want to go with you." Before he has a chance to argue, as I know he's bound to, I press, "Please, I have to say goodbye."

I can feel him weighing the pros and cons, but he eventually gives in. I slowly turn, facing him.

Peering up into his plagued eyes, I nod, a silent gesture that I'll be okay.

He exhales heavily, still trying to protect me from seeing one of the hardest sights of my life. But he can't protect me forever.

The moment I set foot inside the room, I'm hit with many incredible memories of the time we spent together. We may not have known one another for years, but it felt like we did. We utilized every second, not knowing when it would be our last.

Sadie looks as if she's sleeping, but I'm not lucky enough for that lie to stick. I know she's gone.

I stand frozen, stuck in the middle of the room as I wrap my arms around my middle, hoping to keep the cold at bay. Roman walks past me, touching my shoulder tenderly before making his way to where Sadie lays. I watch as he feels for a pulse. He tries in vain, and after three attempts, a pained sigh leaves him.

He gently covers her lifeless body with the same blanket I tucked around her. The red bandana disappears from my view. In an inexplicable way, the sight comforts me, knowing Georgia will be there standing at the pearly gates to welcome Sadie home.

"Lola?"

Glancing up, Roman is standing before me, waiting for me

to process what's just happened.

I nod, indicating that regardless of her state, I want to say goodbye. He simply skims his fingertips down my cheek before leaving me alone.

Sniffing back my tears, I stagger to where she lies, taking my time because I don't want to let her go. I stand motionless, my brain unable to process this horrifying truth.

"I'm sorry I wasn't here. I should have been. I should have held your hand until the very end." I wipe away my sadness with the back of my hand. "I hope that wherever you go, you're happy, and there's no more pain. Georgia will look after you now. I know she will. My two sisters together. That thought makes this a little easier to accept."

Reaching out, I gently lift the blanket from her cherub face as a torrent of tears blurs my vision. "Take care, k-kiddo. I'll see you s-soon." Bending forward, I lay a tender kiss to her forehead. A tear splashes onto her cheek, but I don't wipe it away.

Taking one last look at her, I replace the blanket, saying a final goodbye to both Sadie and Georgia. Is this what letting go feels like? Funny, I feel numb.

Once I'm in the hallway, I innately seek out Roman. I don't have far to look. He pushes off the wall, his lips turned downward. Everyone is staring at me, at us, but neither of us seems to care. "I'm going to my room."

He nods, the hands by his side restless, appearing as if he

wants to console me. But he doesn't. "Of course. If you need me, you know where to find me."

I appreciate his kindness and wish like anything to be lost in his arms, but with Tamara and June mere feet away, I know that is not an option.

Just as I turn, June stops me. "Lola?"

I hold my breath. "Can you come with me to my office?"

I don't have the energy to fight her because I knew this moment would come sooner or later. "Okay."

Roman advances, ready to follow, but June sternly shakes her head. "This will only take a minute."

The conflict behind Roman's eyes is clear, but he eventually nods.

June leads the way, and I follow, nodding to Roman that I'll be okay. And I will. I'm thankful he gives me the space I need.

The moment we enter June's office, she rounds her desk and opens a drawer. "I'm so sorry for your loss. I know how close you and Sadie were." Just the mention of her name stabs at my heart.

She appears just as broken as I am. I can't imagine how she'd feel experiencing this loss time and time again. Does every death remind her of her daughter? What a heartbreaking thought.

"How do you do it? How do you make the pain go away?" My voice is laced with despair. When she remains quiet, I realize I'm being rude and insensitive. "I'm sorry. I didn't mean you're not hurting. I just meant…you're so strong to be able to do this."

"I'm far from strong," she confesses. "I still cry and grieve for each life lost. But I think I would be far more saddened if I didn't offer this place to people who needed it." She takes a deep breath. "I do it because I know my daughter would have wanted me to. She was always looking out for others, such a selfless little thing. If I appear strong"—she peers out into the distance—"it's her strength that allows me to get through the day with a smile on my face."

Tears well in my eyes. "Your daughter would have been proud of you, June."

"You think?" she whispers in a faraway tone.

Her question surprises me. "I know she would. You've done so much for so many people. You're our leader, and we look at you as our beacon of hope."

She sniffs, turning to me with a small smile. "Thank you. That means so much to me. After I lost Scarlett, my will to live died with her. It took me years to get to a place where I could accept that she was gone. I still don't fully believe it. I still expect her to come bouncing down the hallway, a dimpled smile pressed to her rosy cheeks. We used to come here over the summer as a family when she was younger. She loved it here."

I want to ask if she had any siblings. And if her father is still alive. But I don't. This is June's story to tell, and I will listen because sometimes, all we want is for someone to listen.

"My family is very wealthy, but I never wanted a dime of their riches. I married young, hoping to escape my mother's clutches." No wonder she was so nice from the beginning. "But I've made some mistakes over the years, ones I'm not proud of. I'm trying hard to make amends and earn back people's love and trust."

"We all make mistakes. We're human," I kindly offer, hating her admonishing view toward herself.

"This home has been in my family for decades, and although it cost me everything I had to purchase the deed from my brother, I did, because there is no price on happiness, especially for people who don't see it too often."

"You're a good person."

My words seem to touch her because she pulls backward, moved. "Thank you."

Underneath her resolute exterior lies a grieving woman. It may get easier, but she'll never forget. Maybe that's the key to coping. Never forget, but rather accept. Accept that some days may be harder than others, but cherish the memories, instead of the tears. Accept that what will be, will be.

"Sadie asked me to give you this."

Before I can question what, June presents me with a bright pink envelope. I stare at the stationery like it is the most priceless gem in the entire world. And in a way, it is. With quivering fingers, I reach for it.

"She was very specific about what she wanted. She may

have been young, but she was far from naïve. She didn't want a memorial in her honor. All she wanted was for me to give you that." My grip tightens around the bright pink envelope, its importance even more significant now.

This reveals that Sadie knew her end was near. "Thank you for minding it for her."

"It really was an honor."

I turn the envelope, fingering each corner as if the action will reveal what's hidden inside. I'm not ready to open it just yet. I don't know when I will be.

Glancing up, I observe her weighing up what to say. "Dr. Archibald seems to have taken you under his wing."

I try not to panic. She's only making conversation.

"I'm glad you and Roman have connected. He's usually very shut off, so to see him let his guard down is a nice change." I don't know what to say, afraid of saying the wrong thing. "It appears you're both helping one another."

"I don't know how much help I am to him. I'm probably more of a hindrance."

June smiles, and the sight is truly magical. "I'm sure he couldn't disagree more."

I hope she doesn't want to discuss Roman in any more detail because I will eventually fold. "Remember, my door is always open."

I almost breathe a sigh of relief. "Thank you. I really appreciate it."

I tuck the envelope into my pocket, not wanting to read it just now. I'd like to be alone because I'm certain ugly tears will be shed. But when my phone chimes, I know my tears can wait.

Sunflower.

I know what it represents, a symbolic message spoken in a language only we understand. I quicken my footsteps and charge out the back door. The moon is buried behind a cluster of clouds, setting an ominous backdrop for this evening's activity. Hurrying down the hill, I breathe a sigh of relief when I see the infamous pines.

The night isn't cold by any means, but I suddenly get a chill. The closer I get, the more subdued things become. I know what I'm walking into; the weight in my back pocket a reminder of what's to come. But I'm not afraid, and the reason is standing a few feet away.

Roman's downturned face and slumped shoulders indicate how he's feeling. It's an anthem we all march to. He doesn't turn even though I'm certain he can hear me.

The rose garden is beyond words. The sights and smells are magical, and even though it represents great loss, it also lets the world know these lives lost were people who lived and were loved.

"Hey." Roman exhales when he hears me, but he still doesn't turn.

"Thanks for the text. I really appreciate it. I want to be here for this."

Roman nods slowly before finally spinning around. The moment our eyes lock, the gravity of our situation hits home, and the weight that has settled in the pit of my stomach gets heavier. There is no easy way to do this. There aren't any words, either. The only thing we can do is dig.

Roman picks up the shovel at his feet, then reaches for a beautiful pink rose bush, the velvety petals regal and proud. It's perfect. Sadie would have loved it.

His expression is vacant, but it's clear he's finding it harder and harder each time he comes out here to bury a new life.

We walk for minutes, the gentle rustle of wind the only sound between us. There are so many things I want to say, but where do I start?

Roman comes to a stop.

Opening up my palm as I extend my arm, Roman doesn't argue and passes me the shovel.

With each mound of dirt I shift, the closer my tears threaten to break free, but I'm trying my hardest to keep them at bay. Sadie wouldn't have wanted me to be sad. We both knew that sooner or later, it would come to this. But being the one left standing time and time again doesn't make you feel lucky or relieved. It's just a reminder of where you'll eventually end up. We all die—some sooner than others.

I continue digging, the thought plaguing me until I struggle for breath.

"Don't feel guilty. You're allowed to live." Roman can read my inner turmoil. "Sadie, Georgia, everyone you love, and everyone who loves you..." His faltering voice matches my erratic heartbeat. "Wants you to live. And that's the greatest gift you can give them."

Raising my eyes, I meet his. Something hides behind them.

"Every breath you take is honoring them, honoring their spirit because they know that your thoughts are never far from them."

Those tears I tried so hard to keep away have no chance at remaining under lock and key. Roman's avowal is beautiful.

He takes the shovel from my hands and finishes what I started.

I watch in silence as he gently removes the rose from the pot, shaking out the dirt and fingering out the roots. He's crouched down on one knee, but his gaze flicks upward. "I think she'd want you to do this."

I nod, sniffing back my tears as I reach for the stem.

I'm careful of the thorns as I wrap my fingers around the length, picturing Sadie's bright smile and contagious laughter. Different memories crash into me as I fall to my knees and immortalize Sadie the only way I know how.

I clutch at the mounds of rich dirt, dragging it with my fingers as I cover the hole in the ground. I only wish I could do the same to the one in my chest because saying goodbye hurts.

"I'll n-never forget you," I whisper, choking on my tears, fisting handfuls of soil. "I think that if I were to join you, then I would be okay with that." And I mean every word. "But I promise, while I'm still here, to tell the world about you. I don't know when I'll see you again, but until then, tell Georgia I said hello. I love you both so v-very m-much." A sob escapes me, and it helps let out this pain.

I don't realize I've finished planting her rose until Roman's cold hand overlaps mine. He's usually so warm, so I jolt at the contact.

"Lola…"

Through clouded vision, I see our fingers slowly intertwine. The sight stirs something in me.

I never want to let him go.

Our hands are muddy, but there is something gritty, almost primeval about it. We are united, and that promise opens a door I never knew could open. I think…I'm falling in love with Roman. I don't know when this happened, but the feelings I have for him seem to continue to grow.

With our hands locked, kneeling before one another, and covered in Sadie's earth, I don't fail to see the significance of that thought. Like Sadie's rose, I want what Roman and I have to flourish. It'll need water, and sunlight, and constant care, but I'll suddenly do anything to see it bloom.

Out here in the partial darkness, I can almost forget the world exists outside this moment. There are no rules, no judgment. Sadie's strength pulses through me, and I grip his fingers, expressing how much he means to me.

A whisper of regret passes over him, but that's soon forgotten as he clenches my hand, his need thrumming through him and burning all the way through my body. I'm breathless as I anticipate his next move.

"Lola…"

I don't allow him to speak; instead, I throw myself into his arms and hum when he catches me.

We wrap our arms around the other, needing to soothe one another's demons. Roman once told me he has many demons, but at this moment, I've come to understand we are all searching for someone whose demons play well with ours.

"Roman," I whisper, not knowing what I want to say.

"I know."

He knows we've just crossed the line of no return. But neither of us seems to care as he sits, encouraging me to straddle his lap. I never let go, tightening my folded arms around his neck and burying myself into the column of his neck. His arms rest low around my waist as he rests his head against my shoulder. I close my eyes and memorize the beating of his heart pounding against mine.

Lub-dub.

Lub-dub.

The sound is strong, powerful, which makes me smile. He is healthy, and hopefully, I will be too.

We stay tangled as one for minutes, neither of us wanting to move.

After countless moments, Roman's hand wanders lower. "What's this?"

When his fingertips pass over my back pocket, I remember Sadie's letter. "It's a letter from Sadie. June gave it to me."

With haste, he removes his hand. "Oh, I'm sorry."

"Don't be. I'd like to read it now. And I'd like to read it to you. If you want to hear it, of course," I add. I promised I'd share her with the world. What better way to start?

Regrettably untangling myself from his arms, I pull backward so our faces, our lips are inches apart. He is a virile man, and I can't help but wet my bottom lip as my mouth has suddenly gone dry. Ignoring the overwhelming need to close the small distance between us, I reach behind me and retrieve the letter.

My fingers tremble as the pink envelope sits innocently in my hands. Roman keeps his arms linked around my middle, which gives me the strength to turn the paper over and slip my pointer under the seal.

The flap falls open, and inside sits a folded piece of matching pink paper. Not seeing the point in prolonging this any further, I draw it out and unfold the crease with care. Her childlike, swirly handwriting makes me smile.

However, when I see what that handwriting details, I fall silent, pensive.

You gave me a piece of your heart…so here is mine.

I could feel a gentle weight in the envelope, but I thought it was pages upon pages of Sadie's words. But I was wrong.

Tipping the envelope upside down, I gasp when a silver heart attached to a necklace falls into my open palm. I instantly recognize Sadie's locket.

My eyes dart up to meet Roman's, who appears baffled by the offering.

The tale behind this keepsake nearly broke my heart, so without a second thought, I open the clasp with anxious fingers. What I see leaves me speechless.

The locket is no longer empty.

Inside the silver border is a photograph of Sadie and me taken during one of our movie marathons. We look happy, caught laughing about something absurd, no doubt. But the candid nature of this picture reveals just how much we cared for one another. The naturalness of it reflects our friendship. Being friends with Sadie was easy. We didn't have to pretend because our friendship was real.

Clutching the locket to my chest, I peer up into the heavens to see a shooting star sweeping across the brightened cosmos.

Smiling so hard it hurts, I whisper, "I love you, too."

ELEVEN

Days have passed since I lost Sadie. Her memory is still ingrained in every corner of this place, and in a way, it's a welcome comfort.

It hurts more than I care to admit, but Roman has been distant. After what happened in the rose garden, I thought he'd at least poke his head in and ensure I was doing okay.

I receive the occasional text message, but they're brief, most times just reminding me to take my medication. I don't need reminding. Sadie's death flipped a switch inside me. If I'm going to do this, I'm going to throw myself into the deep end and hope I remember how to swim.

Death opens your eyes to so many things, and losing Sadie has given me a new perspective on everything. I have done some serious soul-searching this week, and my determination to live has strengthened.

"Almost done." Dr. Tanner's hoarse voice snaps me from my thoughts.

The needle part is surprisingly fine; it's Roman's strange, aloof behavior toward me that has left me scratching my head. He made some excuse for why he couldn't take my blood today, but his good comrade and trusted colleague, Dr. Tanner, would do it and not say a word to anyone.

Roman's weird behavior could be because today is his birthday.

"Okay, all done. I'll pass on the results to Roman."

"Thanks, Dr. Tanner."

As I jump down from the ledge and gather my belongings, Dr. Tanner scoffs. "Please, Dr. Tanner makes me sound so old and responsible." I chuckle as I slip on Sadie's necklace, toying with the locket. "Call me Teddy."

I grip the trinket, feeling my pulse heighten. "You're Te-Teddy?" I ask, fumbling over my words. The same Teddy who left that message on Roman's answering machine I want to add, but don't.

He peers at me with interest, nodding. "Heard of me?"

I need to pull it together because this is my opportunity to gain some intel on Roman.

Gripping the strap of my bag, I smirk. "Maybe." It's a cop-out, but it's the only thing I can say to explain my apparent interest in him. "How do you two know one another again?"

Teddy leans against the wall, shaking his head, smirking. "So typical of Roman to leave out the details. We went to medical school together."

"Oh, that's right." I play along, thinking on my feet. "So you must be good friends then? Go on yearly vacations together? Stuff like that?" I need to know why September first is so important. Why did Roman request that date? And more importantly, what is happening on that day?

Teddy folds his arms, his gray eyes lighting up in humor as he crosses an ankle over the other. "Are you kidding me? Mr. Workaholic hasn't taken a vacation in years. I've tried to persuade him, but I'm sure you know by now, once Roman's mind is made up, there's no changing it. It's one of the many things I respect and admire about him."

"Oh." I can feel the disappointment pouring off me.

I need to ask in a roundabout way what he's organized for Roman. It can't be a surprise, as Roman knows about it. I'm grasping at straws, and I need to go in hard because this is my only shot.

"Maybe you could surprise him? He works so hard. I hear there is an amazing annual jazz festival in Birmingham, Alabama…the first week of September."

The moment those words leave my lips, Teddy goes from relaxed to restless in seconds. His easy demeanor disappears as he unfolds his arms and pushes off the wall, standing rigid.

"Roman isn't a jazz fan."

"I suppose he could always settle for their famous crab cakes then. C'mon, Alabama in September sounds fun. I'd like to do something nice for him. He's gone out of his way for me, and I'd like to surprise him with something special."

Teddy nervously runs a hand through his thick brown hair. "I better get going. I have rounds to do."

He attempts to brush past me, but I quickly sidestep him, blocking his exit. He's clearly confused as to why I'm standing in his way.

I can't let this go because it's the closest I've been to uncovering Roman's secrets. "What's the hurry?"

Teddy exhales and scratches over his full beard. "I know you're trying to be nice. Roman told me he's helping you out, but trust me, just let this go."

"Let what go?" I press, not giving up. "A friend can't do something nice for a friend?"

Teddy has every right to push me aside and leave; he owes me nothing, but it's quite clear that something plagues him. The secret Roman has asked him to keep is one that burdens him. A secret like that is life-changing.

Teddy sighs before stepping in close as if he's about to divulge something so great he needs to say it in a whisper. "Roman..." I hold my breath. This is it—the mystery is about to be solved. "Roman is—"

But my question is never answered. "Roman is wondering

why you're still here? Aren't you late for work?" His voice is dripping with sarcasm.

I redden, embarrassed to be caught.

Teddy instantly recoils, clearing his throat and turning around calmly. "Speaking in the third person now? What would Freud say about that?" He's trying to lighten the sudden sour mood.

However, Roman doesn't appreciate the humor. "He would probably say I need to find better friends."

This is my fault. If I hadn't been so nosy, Teddy wouldn't have to be dealing with Mr. Grumpy Guts. "Thank you for today. I really appreciate everything."

Roman focuses his eyes my way.

Teddy is the meat in this very uncomfortable sandwich, so I don't blame him when he excuses himself and practically runs out the door.

We continue glaring at one another long after the door slams shut.

I can't read the look on Roman's face. It's a mixture of amusement and annoyance. His bad mood is ticking me off. He probably has the birthday blues. It's his party, and he can cry if he wants to. But I will not stand by and let him bring me down.

"What are you doing? Right now?" His question throws me, and it shows. He lets out a deep rumble, amused by my stunned silence.

"I…" Why is he asking me this?

"Do you want to come to the baseball game with me?"

"The baseball game?" I question, thankful to have found my voice.

"Yes." His reply is resolute, and so is his unwavering stare. He's making me nervous. So much is going on behind those soulful eyes.

But I pull my shoulders back, hoping my brave façade sticks. "Wouldn't you prefer to take someone else? Someone a little more knowledgeable about what actually happens?" I leave the unspoken lurking.

"No, I want to go with you." He slips a hand into his pressed pants pocket, watching me closely.

I'm seconds away from combusting under his heated stare, but I pull it together.

Shrugging, hoping to seem aloof, I say, "Don't say I didn't warn you."

"So that's a yes?" He appears hopeful I'll agree.

"Yes."

My response pleases him, which makes me wonder about the sudden change in mood. Earlier, he couldn't wait to put ten feet between us, and now he's asking me to the game...on his birthday nonetheless.

"So are you ready?"

"Oh, you meant right now?"

My naïvety thoroughly entertains him. "Are you done for the day?

"Yes. I was scheduled for this morning's activities only. I just need to swing past my room and change."

"I'll wait for you out front."

I'm surprised by his response. "Out front? You don't want to meet someplace a little less...public?"

He shakes his head. "No."

Something is bugging him, but it appears whatever it is, it has nothing, or everything to do with me. "Sure, out front it is. I'll be down in about twenty minutes."

He's keeping his cards close to his chest, which isn't anything new. But the undercurrent of apathy is something I've not seen before.

I brush past him, ensuring we don't touch, as I have no idea how he's going to respond. I escape unscathed and dash to my room, taking deep breaths to calm down. I have no idea what to wear, so I decide on jean shorts, a slouchy T-shirt, and a sweatshirt just in case the weather cools.

Grabbing a cap, I place it low on my head and adjust the bill, attempting to hide beneath it.

Once I'm satisfied I look semi-inconspicuous, I make my way downstairs. Roman is waiting for me at the bottom of the steps. His back is turned. If this were a fairy tale, I would make a grand entrance, looking regal and beautiful and all princess-like. But the fact I'm in Chucks and my hair is swept beneath a cap ruins that fantasy before it can even begin.

I hold the banister as I descend each step carefully, afraid

I'll face plant if I rush it. Halfway down, Roman turns, and I almost do trip because he is remarkable. Black Ray-Bans hide his eyes, but the hard set of his jawline reveals he's still irritated. The pissed-off look suits him. He's arrogant, almost conceited as a lopsided smirk tugs at his lips. He knows the influence he has over me, and if that smile is anything to go by, he's enjoying every minute.

When I reach the second step above him, his gaze flicks to the hat resting on my head. "The Cubs? Really?"

I descend one more step so I'm hovering above him. "Yeah, it was a gift from my dad. He got it for me when he was traveling for work. The little bear is adorable. I think it's some animal conservation thing." When he does a poor job of concealing his smirk, I place a hand on my hip. "What, you got a thing against bears?"

"No, not at all." His grin reveals otherwise.

"Good, 'cause you sure as hell have acted like one with a sore head this week." I slap my hand over my mouth, mortified. Roman erupts into laughter while I curse my wicked tongue. "Sorry, I didn't mean—"

But he cuts me off, bracing one foot against the step I'm on. "No, you're right. I'm sorry."

His apology surprises me. "It's fine. I hope you're okay?" That's me offering an olive branch, hopeful he'll share why he's been MIA.

He doesn't, but what he does is almost give me a heart

attack. He reaches forward and adjusts the bill of my hat. "I am now."

"I'm glad," I croak out, wetting my dry lips.

"For the record, the Cubs are a baseball team from Chicago, and they're playing the Yankees tonight."

My mouth forms an O. "Well, looks like we're on opposing teams then."

"Looks that way," he replies with a grin. He brushes a stray piece of hair behind my ear before running the back of his pointer along my jawline. I stand motionless, too afraid to breathe. "We better get going before we hit traffic."

All I can do is nod.

When he finally releases me from his invisible spell, I exhale and take a moment to find my feet. He turns and makes his way toward the parking lot. Once I feel confident to move without falling on my face, I follow, a surge of excitement flowing through me.

This is not a date by any means, but I'm excited nonetheless.

We walk to his Jeep in silence, and that silence continues as we leave the gates of Strawberry Fields and head down I-90. A soft rock ballad plays over the speakers, but we both seem too preoccupied to pay attention to the song.

"How'd it go with Teddy?" Roman asks, breaking the stillness.

I shrug, picking at my nail polish. "Fine. He said he'd give you the results."

"Sorry I wasn't there...I had something to take care of." I wait for him to elaborate, but of course that's just wishful thinking. "I'll go over the results as soon as we get back."

"No hurry," I reply.

"You're not curious?" His eyes are focused straight ahead, his hands gripping the steering wheel loosely, but he tightens his hold and breaks his concentration to snap his head my way when he hears my reply.

"It is what it is. Curious or not, that won't change the outcome. Either the trials will work or they won't. I can't change that."

"That sounds like the speech of someone who's given up."

"On the contrary, it's a speech of someone who is finally accepting that what will be, will be. I have thrown myself into this trial harder than I did the first time around. If it doesn't... work"—I swallow—"then at least I can say I did everything I could. I was ready to give up, but I was given a chance at hope thanks to you. Even if that hope is in vain, it's more than I had before I met you."

Roman blinks once, obviously stunned by my honesty. I am too.

He returns his attention to the road, but his white knuckles on the steering wheel give me insight into what's currently going on inside his head.

"This will work," he affirms. "It has to."

"Has to?" I question, sitting taller, never taking my eyes off him. He shifts in his seat.

"Yes, it has to." He stares vacantly ahead. "I won't accept a world where you don't exist."

"Roman," I gasp, touched by his declaration.

A cloud of sadness suddenly shadows him, and all I want to do is hold is hand. "All of this…it isn't for nothing. It can't be. It has to amount to something because what's the point if it doesn't?"

Listening to my heart, I grab his hand, which sits bunched in a fist against his thigh. "Sadie told me something, which now makes complete sense. Better I die fighting than die without a fight." I coax him to unclasp his hold and allow me in. When he finally gives in, the victory leaves me hopeful. "So we'll cross that bridge when we get to it. For now, let's just enjoy today before we worry about tomorrow."

During the entire drive, Roman never releases my hand, and not a word is spoken further. But we don't need words because it's the unspoken that means so much. I allow my mind to wander, getting carried away in a future where I live healthy and grow old. It's something I don't think about too often, not wanting to torture myself with something out of reach. But now hope is lapping at the surface, thanks to the man beside me.

As we pull into a crowded parking lot, a sea of team colors greets us. Roman parks and reaches for a Yankees cap off the back seat. He adjusts it on to his head smugly, while I roll my eyes.

His husky chuckles disband the seriousness because now, it's time to play ball. "Shall we?"

"We shall." I jump from the passenger seat, overwhelmed by what I see as I stand by the open door in awe.

Loyal Yankee and Cub enthusiasts walk toward the stadium, laughing and appearing to forgive their friends for rooting for the opposing team. The vibe is vivacious, each spectator amped and ready for their team to win.

Roman locks the car, smiling from ear to ear. "This place is something else."

He rounds the hood, stopping in front of me. "Regretting your decision?"

I know he's not only referring to the baseball game but also to every decision I've made since coming here. He waits, each second filled with trepidation.

Thinking about all I've achieved, learned, and felt while at Strawberry Fields, I shake my head resolutely. "I don't regret a thing." And I mean it.

Roman doesn't hide his relief. I don't know if it's my honesty or getting lost in the moment, but he offers his hand. Peering down at it, and then at the swarms of people surrounding us, I hesitate for an instant before slipping my palm into his.

The connection sends a tingle through me, and it's not just the physical union, but rather, I become giddy at what it represents. I thought Roman didn't care, that his detachment this week was due to him regretting showing his vulnerability, but I was wrong. He wants to hold my hand in front of all these people, representing we're something a little more than friends.

"What are you smiling about?" he asks as we begin our trek toward the stadium.

"Nothing. I just like…holding your hand." I cringe, realizing how stupid that sounded.

"I like holding yours too," he confesses without pause, making me melt.

This is my cue, my opportunity to fish for something more. "Friends who hold hands." That sounded even more ridiculous aloud than it did in my head. I really need to shut up.

As I'm cursing my inability to talk to men, he draws me to his torso so we're touching shoulders. "We were never friends, Lola," he declares in a confident whisper.

Although the indistinct sounds around us are penetrating, I hear him clearly. I'm glad he's holding me; otherwise, I'd have tripped over my feet. I don't know what to say, so I don't say anything as I allow Roman to guide me through the throngs of people.

He releases me to hunt through his pocket for the tickets. Once we're scanned through, he reaches for my hand once again. The action is so natural, highlighting his earlier comment.

We enter through the steel gates, and if I thought outside was nuts, that's nothing compared to what's going on inside. It's raucous; the excited hollering from fans is humming throughout the air.

Something else thrumming through the air is the smell of pure wickedness.

Roman laughs when I smack my lips together unintentionally. "What is that greasy but completely intoxicating smell?" I snap my head from left to right, hoping to find the source.

"You have a lot to learn." Tugging on my hand, he leads me toward the concessions.

When in line, I openly look at him, unashamed to show him how I feel. He looks down at me, perplexed, but a glimmer of something flashes before his eyes. This moment is beyond words; it is one I will cherish for the rest of my life. The thought gives me an idea.

Regardless of Roman's beliefs, I reach into my back pocket and pull out my phone. Our gaze never wavers, caught in a deadlock, and it's perfect. Positioning my arm above us, I snap a photo, wanting to capture this moment forever.

We don't break eye contact, and I suddenly have an uncontrollable urge to kiss him. The internal war behind his eyes is apparent. He wants to kiss me too, but he knows things will never be the same if he does.

"Next!" The jolting demand shatters my trance-like state.

Roman sighs, nestling the tip of his tongue in the crease of his lips. Frustration palls him, but he also looks to be on cloud nine. Clearing his throat, we step up to the attendant, and Roman orders our food.

I'm embarrassed, but I don't regret a single thing. What I do regret, however, is ordering all this food. The clerk places our mountain of goodies on a tray, sending us away with a look of good luck. I grab the Coke and beer and follow Roman as he maneuvers through the crowd on the hunt to find our seats.

Roman gives directions, allowing me to guide him, which is a nice change. Once we arrive at the elevator, we ride it to our level. Roman takes over as leader and guides us to our seats.

"Some view." I'm impressed that I managed to get such great seats.

"You did good," he replies, passing me my nacho hat. I accept with a teasing sigh. It's going to take me all day to make a dent. As I'm strategizing ways to tackle this mountain of madness, Roman raises his Budweiser. "Let's make a toast."

"To what?" I could suggest the perfect occasion to toast, but I don't. I don't want to ruin a perfect day with birthday talks.

Raising my Coke, I wait for him to speak. "To you."

"To me?" I don't hide my surprise.

"Yes. May a flock of blessings light upon thy back." *Shakespeare.* He knows the way to my heart.

"Cheers." We clink, both taking long sips from our drinks.

As we get settled and the game commences, I think about Roman's toast and how in spite of what's to come, I am already blessed…thanks to him.

Who would have thought I'd be a baseball fan? Nearing the end of the game, I was standing and screaming with all the other enthusiasts, desperate for "my" team to win.

Roman explained the logistics, but all I cared about was the roar when a player hit the ball. The excitement was contagious; so much so that after the fourth inning, I was running to the merchandise store to purchase my foam finger in the Cubs colors.

The game is over and the Cubs won, much to Roman's distaste. "They got lucky," he says, my hand locked in his as we wait for the hordes of people to pass. I bite back my smirk, finding his loyalty toward the Yankees adorable.

The night has turned surprisingly bitter, and a summer storm dallies on the horizon. When the crowd clears, I step out into the aisle, but a huge buffoon across from me charges out at the same time. The beer he's holding splashes all over me, and I yelp, jumping backward. I wipe down my shirt in vain; it's drenched.

"Watch it!" Roman roars from behind me, instantly shoving the guy from over my shoulder. He's unsteady on his feet and almost falls over.

Testosterone swiftly suffocates me, and I sense a fight is brewing. "She'll live," he slurs, half sitting, half standing, his arm draped over the back of a chair. I flinch at his choice of words.

"You spilled your beer all over her!"

"Roman, it's fine." I try to settle him down, but he won't hear it.

"No, it's not fine! Apologize."

"Fuck you!" the guy barks back, finally finding his balance.

He stampedes toward Roman, and Roman does the same to him, but I'm the meat in the sandwich and have no desire to be squished. I've seen Roman pack a punch. This will end ugly.

Thrusting my arms out, I stop the other from moving an inch. "Stop it, you jackass!"

The guy looks down at my scrawny arms and laughs. His humor is short-lived when I smell the distinguishable scent of pot wafting through the air. "Back off, or I'm sure those security guards would love to know what you're hiding in your pockets."

On cue, three guards come dashing up the stairs.

His jaw clenches. "Real tough, having a girl fight your battles." He has to get in the last word as he glares at Roman over my shoulder.

Roman scoffs. "This girl has more balls than you and I do combined. And just like me, she fights for what's hers."

The wind gets knocked from my sails. I'm his, and he's mine?

Even though Roman's chivalry touches me, the buffoon's sexist comment offends me. Dropping my arms, I step into his space, not caring that he's towering over me. "I can kick your ass any day. And for the record, so could he…with his eyes closed…and one arm tied behind his back."

People around us snort at my insult, while he's left standing, speechless, most likely attempting to conjure up a retort, but I'm done. I push past him, hoping Roman follows. He does.

The guards stop us as we attempt to leave, but I set the record straight. "We were just leaving, but that guy"—I point at the meathead who is glaring at me—"spilled his beer all over me. I think his disorientation has to do with the weed he has stashed in his pockets."

The mere mention of the drug has the guards forgetting our involvement and focusing their efforts on the real offender. When I reach the bottom step, I see them grilling him as he's emptying out his pockets.

Roman grabs my hand, and we weave through the masses, ready to leave. He's deadly quiet the entire time, and I get a sense of irritation lapping at the surface.

"I won't break, Roman," I stupidly state, but it only angers him further.

The silence continues as we walk to the parking lot.

He's breathless as we march to his car, and I wonder if he's moments away from exploding. I want to ask if he's okay, but I think I'll just make things worse. He almost tears the door from its hinges as he opens it for me.

Just when I thought this situation couldn't get any more horrible, a sudden drop in temperature has the moon hiding for cover behind a sinister looking storm cloud. Peering up into the once clear sky, I see that things are about to turn nasty.

I jump into the Jeep, jarring when Roman slams the door shut behind me. What is his problem?

I watch as he rounds the hood, fisting both hands through his snarled hair. His bad mood has returned, and just like earlier, I don't understand why.

The moment he dives into the car, I sink low. His mood swings are giving me whiplash.

I sit quiet, turning my cheek to glance out the window. As the night sky ominously hums with a rumble, the dawdling crowd quicken their steps, sensing the calm before the storm. I have my own tempest to deal with.

Just as I spin to ask Roman once and for all what's going on, the Jeep clicks over as he turns the key. Furrow lines crinkle low along his brow as he tries to start the car again. Nothing. He grips the wheel with one hand, while vigorously turning the key with the other. After three failed attempts, it's obvious the car is dead.

"No," Roman exclaims, striking his fist against the wheel in frustration. "Start, goddamn you." A crack of thunder batters down from the heavens, adding to the disorder.

I yelp, startled by the brutality of this act of nature.

A storm is brewing outside, but it's the one inside this car I'm most worried about. The Jeep is forbiddingly silent, and I wonder if the real storm is about to drown us both. "Roman, what the hell is going on?"

He snaps his head my way, his eyes torn. I suddenly regret asking because something is festering within him. "I'm sorry. I'm sorry for everything."

My heart embarks on a rapid staccato, and it's suddenly hard to breathe. "Sorry? For what?" He licks his bottom lip, buying time. But it's time he came clean. "What are you talking about?"

Turning in my seat, I face him, beseeching him to tell me the truth. He throws back his head, blowing out an exasperated sigh. "I have to tell you something." My pulse spikes, but I remain silent, indicating I'm listening. I've been listening this entire time.

His turmoil is palpable, making me all the more nervous.

"Lola, I—"

A downpour of rain suddenly batters down around us, the heavens spilling open and swallowing anyone caught in its way.

The inside of the Jeep echoes with the harsh rain, making it impossible to hear with ease. But I persevere. "What do you have to tell me?" I almost shout to be heard above the downpour. When he shakes his head, I lunge over the console, latching on to his bicep, not caring that my desperation shines. "Tell me."

He lowers his chin, his jaw clenched as he stares at the floor. Just as I'm about to fist his shirt and draw us nose to nose, he exhales, a sound of complete despair. "Today is my thirtieth birthday, but I have a feeling you already knew that."

Now I'm the one to lower my face, ashamed. "Yes, I did."

"Why didn't you say anything?"

"Because I figured if you wanted to tell me, you would. Sometimes, some things are better left unspoken. We all have secrets, and I guessed your secret was the reason you didn't want to celebrate your birthday." I pull at a loose thread on my shorts, worried I've blown it.

But I haven't.

"This has been the best birthday I've had in, well…in a very long time." Lifting my gaze, I wonder why he's confessing this with such sorrow. He explains. "I don't celebrate my birthday. Ever."

"Why?"

This is it. As the thunder and the rain pummel around us, Roman bares his soul.

"I don't celebrate my birthday because…remember how I told you I…lost someone?" I nod, barely breathing. "Well…" Each pause is followed by a shallow breath, giving him the strength to continue. "That person was…" He places the heel of his hand against the wheel; a symbolic gesture that he's wishing someone would meet him halfway. "That person was…my sister. My twin sister."

My heart fills with grief.

"How can I celebrate my birthday when it's a reminder of all I've lost? She was my other half, and celebrating a day which honors us both seems a little heartless when she's not here to celebrate it with me."

I don't believe what I'm hearing.

"I am so sorry for my inexcusable behavior today. I've been so angry with myself because being with you today, yesterday, since we met, has awoken something in me, something I thought long dead. Guilt overwhelms me every time I'm with you because you make me…happy."

I want to say so many things, but where do I start?

"I don't understand what I feel for you. It doesn't make any sense. This wasn't supposed to happen."

He finally meets my eyes, the deep blue depths swirling with fear and confusion. Running a hand through his hair, he implores me to speak.

"Eleanor?"

"*What*?" Roman gasps, his fingers pausing mid-route.

"Your sister, her name was Eleanor?" My voice is no match for the punishing sounds outside, but he hears me, loud and clear.

"How?" Now he's the one left speechless.

I shuffle in my seat, embarrassed to be confessing what I saw. "Before I made a complete fool of myself, I watched you in the fitness center. I saw her name tattooed on you."

"What else did you see?" He's quick to ask, his Adam's apple bobbing as he swallows.

"Nothing. What else was there for me to see?" I ask, puzzled.

He shakes his head. "Nothing. I just…" He pauses as I wet

my dry lips. "Yes, Eleanor was my sister." His voice breaks.

So many thoughts smash into me, but at the forefront are June's words. "*He wants to save the world.*"

I didn't understand what she meant, but now I do.

"That's why you're a doctor? You want to save people because you couldn't save Eleanor," I declare, winded by my revelation. I don't know when he lost his sister, but I think it was long ago, long enough to shape him into the man he is today.

He frowns. "Yes, in part, that's the reason."

In part? There's more. What more could there be?

So many thoughts are rattling inside my head, but suddenly, a thought so heinous overrides any other. "Is that why you want to save me? Because you see her in me?" My stomach fills with dread, threatening to overfill and spill from the seams.

Is he helping me out of sympathy for his dead sister? Maybe what he feels for me is guilt, and when he looks at me, he sees a chance to make amends for his sister's death.

I suddenly can't breathe.

"Roman?" I press. Each silent second is a silent scream.

He turns his cheek, staring at the window. Is his silence all the answer I need?

Every single insecurity I've ever had rolls over me, and I feel a fool for thinking Roman felt something for me. His kindness *was* because he cared, just not in the way I thought, the way I *wanted* him to. He said he doesn't understand what he feels for me. Maybe what we share is a closeness, stirred by the love he has for his sister.

I suddenly can't breathe.

Without a second thought, I yank open the door, uncaring that the heavens are pouring down around me. The heavy rain pounds against my skin, but it feels good to experience something other than this ache in my chest.

Unsure where I'm going, I wrap my arms around my middle, wishing I could wring out this regret in my belly. I'm beyond embarrassed and angry for fabricating something that clearly wasn't there. I'm not out here to be melodramatic. I just need space because everything is so muddled.

"Lola!" Roman shouts to be heard over the storm, but I don't turn. I simply stand still and let the hot tears score my cheeks. "Please get inside the car. I'm sorry." But that's the thing; he has nothing to be sorry for. I'm the one who's sorry for ever believing in fairy tales.

I step forward, lowering my chin and allowing the rain to batter against me. I've never felt this way before. This ache, this heaviness in my heart...is this what a broken heart feels like? I can't stand it, nor can I stand here any longer. I've embarrassed myself long enough.

Before I can act, though, I feel Roman before he speaks. The warmth from this body instantly thaws out my chill, but I scold myself. This needs to stop.

"Lola..." His breath bathes the back of my neck, indicating he's standing close. "Please, turn around and look at me."

The desperation in his voice has me hesitating for a mere second, but that second feels like a lifetime. I would rather cut off my own arm than hear him so miserable ever again. I turn slowly, my chin still downturned, unable to face him.

With the gentlest of touches, Roman places a quivering finger beneath my chin, coaxing me to meet his eyes. When I do, a gasp escapes me because the look reflected in those depths takes my breath away.

Heavy raindrops coat his cheeks, but I'm mesmerized by a single one as it trickles down his temple, over his chiseled cheek, and into his parted, full lips. An urge to lick that raindrop overcomes me, and I grapple with the momentous revelation of wanting to act on that desire.

Roman watches me watching him, and a low hum of approval fills the space between us. The finger under my chin suddenly strokes over my jaw before leaving a hot trail in its wake as he skims it over my trembling bottom lip.

He watches with fire behind his eyes as his finger skates along my ripened flesh. "I'm helping to save you because… you're someone worth saving." The rain pelts down, and we're both soaking wet, but nothing has been more perfect than it is right now.

Roman's confession leaves me speechless, and I part my lips, wanting to say something, but what would I say? We're caught in a deadlock, both knowing that what happens next has the potency to explode.

Roman doesn't let me speak. He runs his finger along my bottom lip one last time, the electricity thrumming through his touch, awakening a molten verve within. I'm terrified but excited all in the same breath, and that breath is stolen from me as Roman swoops forward and replaces his touch with his lips.

At first, I pause, my mind needing a moment to process this miracle as real. This isn't an event my amorous brain conjured up; this is really happening. The softness of his lips, the tenderness of his touch is actually happening, and it's happening to me.

With that as my driver, I open my mouth and allow my body to take over. I surrender, giving all I am to Roman because I am his. And take he does. He wraps his arms around my middle and kisses me with such passion, I see stars. He's everywhere, his gentle touch setting every part of me on fire.

He's dominating my mouth, my body, his tongue cautiously but assertively demanding permission, which I grant as I open myself up to him and get lost in the whirlwind that is Roman Archibald.

He places his palm to my cheek, angling my face so he can govern me and deepen the kiss. Our tongues meet, the warm wetness sending every nerve ending into overdrive. He tightens his hold around my waist, pulling me into him so we're pressed chest to chest. I can feel his heart beating frantically, a frenetic butterfly flapping its wings, demanding to break free from its cage.

He nips my bottom lip, eliciting a moan from me, but it does something to us both, and Roman lets down his guard. He swiftly walks me backward, slamming me up against the hood, our lips never missing a beat. I stand on tippy toes, unable to get enough of him, needing to touch and taste every part of him.

With sheer strength, he lifts me up and my ass crashes onto the hood as he places me on it, sensing my dilemma. The height difference is no longer an issue, and I wrap my arms around his neck, never intending to let go.

We kiss for minutes, Roman moaning into my mouth as he cups the side of my neck, controlling the speed, depth, and passion of our kiss. I prop my feet on the bumper, needing to anchor myself before I melt. This action opens me up to Roman, who nestles between my legs and draws me forward so I slide down the metal. I hook my legs around him, relishing in the connection. I taste him blended with raindrops—it's a flavor I will never forget.

This is what I envisioned our first kiss to be like. I see the proverbial stars and feel the earth move beneath me with each touch, caress, and the unbelievable synchronicity of our bodies. For each push, I pull, needing him just as much as he needs me.

As I toy with the wet strands of hair curling at the nape of his neck, he moans into my mouth before pulling away slowly. I instantly pout, missing our connection far more than I care to admit. He gently draws my bottom lip into his mouth one last time. My eyes roll into the back of my head.

Roman's lips are red and plump, a badge showcasing to the world what we just did, and just how this all started, he runs his pointer along my bottom lip. But this time, a feral look of possession surrounds us both. Raindrops stick to his long lashes as his eyes search every corner of my face.

"Was that your first kiss?"

I know what he means. He's asking if that was my first kiss since I got sick.

I nod, although any kiss before this one is long forgotten.

He closes the distance between us and kisses me again. His lips set me on fire, and as he circles the seam of my mouth with his tongue, I'm certain I've combusted.

The rain pays no heed to us because kissing in a storm is reflective of how I feel. I claw at Roman's wet shirt, tug at the slippery strands of his hair, but most of all, I press my heart against his, obsessed with the beating because that epicenter makes Roman, Roman, and it's what I love most about him.

I've finally uncovered the sheath around his heart, and now that I've seen it, I never want to let go.

TWELVE

After our frenzied, rain-soaked kisses last night, Roman called AAA and we waited, both silent, digesting what just occurred. I fell asleep during my deep meditation, because when I woke, I was in a strange bed, but I wasn't alone. Roman was snoring softly beside me. Looking around, I saw he had checked us in at a hotel. He clearly was too exhausted to drive home.

I don't know if this changes anything for him, but it sure as hell changes everything for me.

I woke this morning with rumpled clothes and snarled hair, but I wouldn't change it for the world.

Last night really happened. It was Roman's thirtieth birthday, and we went to the baseball game and had an incredibly good time. Roman dropped a huge bombshell he had a twin sister, and she's dead. I had a mini freak-out, but Roman put my mind at ease by…kissing me.

My fingers involuntarily rise, brushing over my lips. I can still feel and taste him. I'll never forget just how good he felt.

I can't help but wonder what happens now. I want to explore more, everything he and life has to offer. I suddenly am so eager to see the trials through because if I survive, is Roman my prize? I can't help but grin from ear to ear. That smile only grows as Roman interlaces our fingers.

As we're driving back to Strawberry Fields, I look over my schedule and see that I have a full day of activities ahead. We pull into the parking lot, Roman parking the car and turning off the engine. However, he doesn't jump out right away. He sits, gazing out the windshield.

It appears we're both in a meditative state.

He turns and smiles, stroking the backs of his fingertips down my cheek. My skin breaks out into tiny goose bumps, my body responding to his touch without pause. Pretending will be difficult, because I'm not naïve. I know we can't exactly walk around in public, hand in hand.

The car suddenly fills with the same crackling tension that bounced between us last night. I hold my breath and count to three. I continue counting when Roman runs his finger over my chin and down the slope of my neck. He glides back up, circling over my racing pulse. I can taste his desire. I'm sure he can feel mine.

"I really want to kiss you," he hoarsely confesses, his eyes focused on my mouth.

"I really want you to kiss me."

A smirk tugs at his sinful mouth. I have to look away before I combust.

Reaching for the handle, I'm first to exit as I jump from the Jeep, thankful for the fresh air. Roman's chuckles catch the breeze as he follows.

We walk toward the back staircase, my fingers itching to reach out and touch him, but I don't. As we walk up the stairs, I'm surprised that Roman is a touch breathless beside me. Once we reach the top, he exhales.

Smoothing out my appearance, I'm hoping I can enter and not bump into anyone, as it's obvious I'm still in yesterday's clothes. Roman stands by the door, extending out his hand to allow me to go first. When I brush past him, I smother my moan. It's probably wise we put some distance between us, because if anyone saw us now, we'd be caught red-handed.

As we walk the quiet halls, I focus on Roman's sharp breathing, wondering if he's just as anxious as I am.

"You really need to muzzle your thoughts." I can't help but giggle, as nothing slips past Roman.

That laugh carries down the hallway but dies in my throat when we turn the corner and bump straight into Tamara. "Roman?" She peers at our closeness. My blood turns cold.

"Where have you been?" she asks, crossing her arms over her chest.

"We just went for a walk." It's a pathetic excuse, but it's all I can muster on such short notice.

"That must have been some walk, because I've been waiting for you to come back since yesterday afternoon." She doesn't address me. Only focusing on Roman.

Wringing my hands out behind me, I wish I could think on my feet and make up a plausible excuse. Roman's shadow overlaps mine as he shuffles closer when he senses my anxiety.

To make matters worse, Zoe appears. "Lola? Where have you been? You weren't in your room last night. I was worried."

Tamara pales. She knows. "How could you?" When she finally makes eye contact with me, guilt overcomes me.

"That's enough," Roman snarls, his fierce warning silencing the room. We've drawn the attention of passersby.

"Roman…no." Desperately latching on to his forearm, I shake my head. I can sense what he's about to do. He can't do this. I won't allow it.

"Why?" Tamara questions, her confusion clear.

"Because…" I know he won't tell her the truth. He'll respect my wishes until the bitter end. But I won't allow him to take the fall. He already has.

"Because he's been administering me trial drugs," I confess in a rushed breath. "Drugs I asked him to dispense and keep a secret. There's a chance I could live, and Dr. Archibald has been my savior and strength when I've wanted to give up."

Peering over Zoe's shoulder, I notice June standing by the doorway. I have no idea when she arrived, but her disappointment can only mean one thing—she's heard enough.

Tamara walks over to Roman, who has moved off to the side, not hiding her anger. I really need to talk to him, but I think it's best if we do so in private.

When our eyes lock, a chill passes over me. Something's different about him. Something has changed. He breaks contact, and something inside of me breaks as well.

Tamara stands before him, furiously whispering subdued words while he runs both palms down his face, exhaling. He listens, then nods and follows her out of the room, hands dug deep into his pockets. June is no longer visible.

I scurry down the hallway, never happier to see my door. Once inside my room, I decide to change and get ready for the day ahead.

My mind is going a million miles a minute however. What happens now? What did Tamara say to Roman, but more so, what will June say? I should have never asked him to lie for me. This is my fault, and I should be held accountable. He has every right to be mad at me.

What worries me more than my repercussions is the look Roman gave me before he left. He looked saddened, disappointed, but most of all, he looked defeated.

Once I slip on my sneakers, I'm out the door, on the hunt

for Roman before volleyball starts.

I have no idea where he'll be, so I try his office first. As his ajar door comes into view, I freeze when I hear his hushed voice, followed by a woman's.

June.

"What are you doing with Lola Van Allen?"

The moment I hear my name, I creep forward, stopping a few feet away from the door.

"It's under control."

She exhales loudly. "Roman…" She sounds disappointed. "This will only lead to heartache."

"I know!" he barks. I can picture him pacing the room like a caged tiger. "Did you ever think this was going to end in a happily ever after?"

Silence.

My breathing mounts.

"It won't," he finally concludes. "It never will."

I can't stand to be here a second longer, as I think I'm going to be sick.

Departing as quietly as I arrived, I make a mad dash for the door at the end of the hall. Once outside, I continue my sprint and slump up against a tree.

I never thought Roman and I would live happily ever after with two point three kids and a hybrid car, but I did think that maybe, especially after last night, the possibility of being together wasn't so far-fetched. It appears I was wrong.

She's right. This *will* end in heartache for so many reasons. The biggest elephant in the room is that I might die. Roman is healthy and strong, and me—I don't know what I am anymore.

Am I not good enough for Roman? Is that what June is implying? And Roman? He said he doesn't see us living happily ever after, so why did he kiss me? Did it not mean anything?

Reaching into my pocket, I pull out my cell and send him a text.

I hope you're okay. Sorry about everything.

As far as texts go, it's quite tame. I wait for ten, twenty, thirty minutes, but I never receive a response. When four hours pass and I'm still looking at my screen, I know something is awfully wrong.

Regardless of one's misgivings, the globe will keep on turning. It's a comforting thought knowing that something has structure and reliance in a turbulent world because I still haven't heard from Roman.

After a day of endless activities and still unable to sit still, I end up in the only place that makes sense anymore. This place is my sanctuary. The sweet, floral smell is fused together with earthy undertones, and I instantly take a deep breath. The familiarities calm my raging heart.

Sadie's rose is vibrant, the petals lively and in bloom; just how I like to imagine Sadie is wherever she may be. There is no judgment here, only understanding, and it's times such as these when I need that empathy the most.

Slumped on the ground, I fist a handful of dirt and watch as it slips through my fingers. "I don't know what I'm doing anymore," I whisper my fears aloud. "I thought I was on the right path, but I don't know where that leads. For a split second, I thought I had a chance at being normal, but now, I feel so lost…and alone…again."

Arching my neck, I peer up into the star-filled sky and wish for a sign, an answer to what I should do next. Things with Roman were never easy, but they made sense. In a world of chaos, he was my true north, but now, I'm so far off course I'm afraid I'll never find my way back home.

"I'm scared," I confess, engrossed by each star, hoping one will lead me where I should go. "Please give me a sign of what I should do." None shine brighter than any others, shattering all hope that one has the all-healing answer waiting for me in the cosmos.

Sighing, I toss a fistful of dirt onto the ground, feeling more frustrated and empty than ever before. I'm losing the people I love, but worse still, the person I love is here, but he may as well be gone too.

"I thought I'd find you here."

I inhale sharply, unsure if this is a sign or a curse.

My eyes shoot upward, ensuring my wistful mind isn't conjuring a voice I've been so desperate to hear. But it appears I'm not going crazy because before me stands Roman. It feels like years, not mere hours since I last saw him.

My fingers itch to touch him, but I shun temptation. "You found me," I halfheartedly reply. The question is, now that he's found me, what does he plan to do?

I'm thankful he doesn't dally in pretenses. "I'm sorry."

"Sorry for what?" He needs to be a little more specific.

"For everything."

I gulp. Does everything include our kiss? "Are you a-angry with me?"

"No." His expression turns tender. "Not at all."

"Then why the cold shoulder?" I'm being forward, but he's being evasive.

The atmosphere turns stale.

"It's better this way. We need to put some space between us. It's for the best. Things have gotten out of hand. It's my fault I allowed it to go this far."

My heart throbs. "Why would you say that?"

"Because."

"Because isn't an answer," I snap, angered he won't elaborate. And angered he thinks I wasn't a willing participant.

"It'll have to do." I can see his anguish at saying such a thing, so why is he saying it at all?

Sick of these games, I stand, brushing the dirt from my hands. That's as far as my courage stems. I keep my back turned, unable to face him.

"I know this is all incredibly messed up, and if I could take it back—"

I don't allow him to finish and spin around, enraged. "I'm not interested in hearing about your wrongdoings and then expecting me to absolve you of your sins. I don't understand what is going on. I thought things were going okay, and then you go and do a one-eighty, leaving me wondering who the hell I grew to lo—" I stop myself before I say something I regret.

"I'm not angry with you. I'm angry with myself," he finally confesses, offering a small insight into his thoughts.

"Why?" I press, not caring he wants his space. Charging over, I clutch his bicep, pleading he talk. "Whatever you're thinking, stop it."

"I can't!" he exclaims, lifting his eyes to meet my frightened ones.

A small gasp escapes me.

"Roman…" But he doesn't allow me to finish.

Tearing his arm out from my grip, he chooses his words wisely. "No, Lola…you and me"—he gestures two fingers back and forth between us—"we won't work. We can't."

I step backward, his confession like a slap across my cheek.

"Please try to understand. This is for the best."

"Best for whom?" I fold my arms across my chest, hoping

to keep out the cold.

"For everyone," he clarifies, frowning unhappily. "I never should have kissed you."

A jolt of dejection traps inside my throat. "You r-regret it?"

He smiles, but it's bittersweet. "No…and that's the problem."

"So that's it, then?" He's ending something that never even had a chance.

"There are things you don't understand."

"Then explain them to me and make me understand." It's my final plea.

"I've run out of words."

Tears sting my eyes, and I allow them to fall because this makes it all real. I must accept that this, whatever this was, is really over. It's now time to move on, but move on to what? I'm afraid of what's lurking in the shadows.

"Soon, you won't have to worry about seeing me. You can live, and be strong, and forget you ever met me."

My mouth parts, and a pained breath breaks free. "What's that supposed to mean?" It shouldn't surprise me when I'm greeted with a wall of silence. I'm done with his games. "Roman, you have three seconds to tell me the truth before I walk away, and this, whatever this is"—I throw my hands toward the heavens—"is over."

He presses his lips together, trapping the words within.

"One…two…" I pause, hoping that the floodgates will open by some miracle, but I should know by now that miracles aren't real. "Three," I conclude, wiping away a fallen tear.

Some small part of me believes he will stop me from leaving, but he doesn't. He bows his head and stares at the ground.

I can't stand here and be rejected—twice. Fool me once, shame on you. Fool me twice...

A shard of moonlight illuminates the field of roses, giving me the strength I need. "For the record, you're not someone I can ever forget. The fact you think I can shows me that what I felt for you was clearly not reciprocated." My comment wounds him, but it's too late. I'm done. "Goodbye, Roman."

This is his chance to tell me I'm wrong, but he doesn't. "Goodbye, Lola."

I squeeze my eyes shut. I've always hated goodbyes, but this one tears me in two.

Unable to stand here a second longer, I turn and walk blindly to my room.

Once inside, the walls begin closing in on me, and I can't breathe. I frantically claw at my neck, desperate for air, but in the process, Sadie's necklace falls to the ground, the clasp broken.

"No!" I cry, scrambling on hands and knees to save it. But it's too late. "No!"

Ugly tears I've tried so hard to keep at bay break the floodgates and come gushing from me in a torrent of desolation.

Through heavy tears, I reach for my phone, needing to lean on her more than I ever have before. My fingers shake, and it takes me three attempts to unlock my cell, but when I do, I open my photos, clicking on the folder which I only allow myself to look at in my dire times of need.

I trace over Georgia's heart-shaped cheeks, her forever smiling lips, and remember her words of wisdom. How I miss them. If she were here, she'd tell me what to do, but she's not— no one is.

The thought has me wrapping my fingers around my phone, shaking in saddened rage. Just as I'm about to throw the abomination across the room, another picture flashes across my screen—one too coincidental to ignore.

I asked for a sign, is this it? Is this Georgia and Sadie's divine intervention?

A tidal wave of emotion smashes into me, leaving me winded as I clutch an arm around my middle, my eyes peeled to the screen. It's the only picture I took from the baseball game of Roman and me. This encompasses what our relationship, what Roman meant, means to me—it, *he* matters.

If Roman taught me anything, it was to fight, and that's what I intend to do.

Pocketing Sadie's necklace, I scamper around my room with only one purpose in mind. Before I can question my decision, I power up my laptop and lead with my gut.

Once I have everything I need, I slam the door shut behind me and run down the hallway, not looking back. A cab waits for me as I charge down the front stairs. Although every bone hurts in my battered body, I persevere. The taxi driver punches in the address, and we're speeding down the driveway seconds later.

Everything passes by in a blur, but that's okay because only one thing needs clarity. My foot bounces against the floor as the driver looks at me in the rearview mirror. "Can you wait for me? If I'm not out in five minutes, you can go."

He nods, not asking questions.

This is crazy, I reason with myself, but that self is sick of crying and wondering where she went wrong. Once my destination comes into view, I hurl open the door and toss a fifty at the driver. I don't wait to see if he respects my request.

The weathered front porch steps whine in protest as I charge up them, but the door sputters out a hollowed growl as I bang on it with all my might. Two knocks would probably have been sufficient, but I can't wait a second longer as I'm afraid I'll chicken out.

Darting over to the window, I cup my hand to the cloudy glass. There are no lights on inside, so maybe he's not home. My deflation rises, threatening to catch in my throat. But I refuse to be deterred.

Sprinting around the back, I remember the key I saw underneath the limp potted plant near the back door. It's not technically breaking and entering if I have a key. The door clicks open with ease, and I don't even think twice as I enter the kitchen, searching for the light switch on the wall.

The moment the room lights up, I freeze. The fact I'm

standing in Roman's kitchen uninvited hits home. What am I doing?

But now that I'm here, I'm committed; I'm committed to him. I know Roman is doing this because he thinks he's saving me from heartache. That's all he's ever done since we met. I'm going to demand he tell me what he thinks he's saving me from because I don't give up on the people I love. I plan on telling him that too. And if he still wants me gone, then I'll go with my head held high and no regrets.

I just need him to tell me because I can't live whatever life I live without knowing why.

Freud comes lazily strolling into the kitchen, not at all concerned I'm standing in his house uninvited. I calm my breathing, taking a moment to compose myself in case Roman is moments from bursting through the door.

My composure suddenly alerts me to something different, something missing. Turning in a slow circle, I realize that even though Roman had limited supplies, his kitchen had the standard appliances such as a microwave, toaster, and even a fruit bowl. But now, it appears bare.

Alarm bells sound loudly in my head, a warning that I'm to turn and depart the way I came, but I can't. My hands are unsteady as I madly open each cupboard, drawer and find one thing in common with each—they're all empty.

Leaning against the counter, I cover my gaping mouth, attempting to piece together what is going on. I don't have to look too hard. Roman gave me the final piece; I was just too blind to appreciate what it meant.

"Soon, you won't have to worry about seeing me."

No. He can't. It doesn't end this way.

My good sense is left in the kitchen as my feet are planted in his empty living room, peering around at a gaping emptiness comparable to what I'm feeling right now. All that is left is one wooden chair and his TV.

"No," I weep, running from room to room, only to be confronted by the same sight. Each room is emptier than the one before it. No wonder he checked us into a hotel last night.

When I reach his bedroom, I blink past my tears. The bed that provided me so much comfort in my darkest hours is no longer swathed in silk sheets or a velvety comforter. All that's left is a single mattress in the center of the room, blanketed with a starchy white sheet and crowned with a flat pillow.

This now looks like a squatter's den rather than the house that was my sanctuary when I needed it the most. Closing the door, I only wish I could shut out the utter torment I feel right now. The spare room that was once filled with boxes is now empty, just like the rest of this house.

The only reason I know Roman still lives here is because of Freud, but not for long. He's leaving, and he's leaving without saying goodbye. The vacant space is suddenly like looking into a mirror.

I switch off the lights, each dark room ebbing away at my light. The last room, the kitchen, the room where we shared many laughs, is my last hope. It all seems void, but unlike Roman, I see things through.

This was supposed to represent everything I've gained, but instead, it will highlight all I've lost. Digging into my back pocket, I unfold the picture I printed of Roman and me. The Big Tony's pizza magnet has finally come into use, and I slap it over the picture as I place it dead center on the fridge.

I've just broken Roman's rule of no photos, as all the memories he wishes to store are kept away under lock and key. But seeing as he thought he was easily forgettable, I wanted to show him that what we shared...it was unforgettable.

Staring at the photo, I memorize the pure happiness because I don't know when or if I'll ever feel it again. Roman will be angry that I broke his no photo rule, but it seems fitting, considering he's just broken my heart.

I give Freud one last pat before I switch off the light and lock up. I can't linger. I need to go. Placing the key where I found it, I amble down the steps and walk calmly to the idling cab. The middle-aged driver peers up from his phone, surprised I returned.

Opening the door, I sit silently in the back seat. The driver waits for me to speak, but he doesn't press. I need a moment to process what I just saw.

"Where to, miss?" the driver asks. He seems like a pleasant gentleman, and on any other day, I would make conversation, but not today.

With eyes still lost in the heavens, I numbly reply, "Manhattan. Please take me home."

THIRTEEN

It's been three days since I fled Strawberry Fields in the dead of night.

During the cab ride back to Manhattan, I emailed June, informing her of my decision. I kept it brief. I texted Zoe, begging she forgive me for just taking off without saying goodbye. I promised I'd see her again. I just didn't know when. I emailed Dr. Carter and asked if he would oversee the duration of the trials. He agreed.

I then switched my phone off and did the same thing with my mind.

I only woke when the taxi driver pulled up to the curb, and my home, soaring into the Manhattan skyline, came into view. I thought I would be happy to be home, but coming back here is like admitting defeat.

I made my way into the foyer, thankful Pablo, the front desk manager, gave me a spare key. I then rode the elevator ride to my apartment.

When I finally reached my bedroom, I staggered to my bed and slept like the dead. But I can't sleep forever. Well, not yet anyway.

Once I'm dried and dressed, I brave the mirror above the basin. It's fogged over from the steam of my scorching shower, but I don't need to see clearly. I know what my expression holds.

Here's hoping once I see Dr. Carter tomorrow, that expression can change.

A knock suddenly sounds on the front door. I have no idea who it is.

When I open the door, a whoosh of air leaves me. "Hi, Lola."

I blink, unsure if she's really here. "June?"

She nods, her lips pressed into a thin line. "I'm sorry for turning up announced. May I come in?"

"You want to come inside? My house?" My brain is currently working at half speed.

"Yes, please. If that's okay with you?" She clenches her small hands around something, and when I finally come to, I see she's gripping the handle of my suitcase.

"Oh, my god, yes, of course!" I shake my head, remembering my manners. "I'm so sorry. Please, come in." I step aside, granting her permission to enter, and she doesn't hesitate. She's probably afraid I'll rescind the offer.

As she wheels the suitcase behind her, I quickly shut the door and offer to take it from her. "Thank you for bringing my things. I could have sent for them. I feel awful you came all the way to Manhattan…"

"I didn't just come here for that."

I gulp. "Oh."

"I know I'm being incredibly impolite, but may I trouble you for some coffee?"

Taking a closer look at her, I find her usually composed guise slightly ruffled and heavy with exhaustion. It seems we both could use that coffee.

"It's no trouble." Leaving my belongings in the hallway, I make my way into the kitchen.

Keeping my back turned, I busy myself gathering everything I need. I'm taking twice as long as I usually would to gather the courage to ask why she's here. The barstool slides along the polished tiles, indicating June plans to stay a while.

"I'm sorry things didn't work out for you at Strawberry Fields."

I cradle the cup I've just reached for out of the cupboard, in fear I'll drop it. "It's not your fault, and besides, things did work. It's a truly remarkable place. I just…I needed to get away. I didn't feel right staying there any longer." I don't elaborate on why.

The silence is heavy with our pensive thoughts.

"You needed to get away from Roman?"

The fine bone china cup rattles against the saucer as I place it down on the counter. "I don't know what you know…"

"He told me everything," she reveals, putting my speculation to bed.

"He did?" My brow furrows. "Why would he do that?" I ask, spinning around to look at her.

She suddenly looks so guilty, but I appreciate that she doesn't break eye contact regardless of her shame. "I'm not here to make excuses for him, but there are things about him…"

"Things about him, what?" I press when she pauses, biting her top lip.

She shakes her head. "It's not my story to tell."

"But that's the problem. He won't tell me his story, well, not all of it, anyway. He told me about his…" I leave the sentence hanging, unsure if she knows.

But she does. "About his sister?" she forlornly asks, and I nod. "Poor Roman." I'm left with my mouth hanging open as she buries her face into her cupped palms.

I have no idea what's going on. Her relationship with Roman seems very personal, but I suppose she has a close relationship with many people, considering the circumstances banding them together.

"I went to his house. Everything is packed up. He's leaving?"

June sniffs before removing her hands. It appears she knows more than she has let on. "Yes, he is."

A sharp intake of breath passes through my clenched teeth. "None of this makes any sense." I run a hand through my hair, gripping it lightly by the roots.

Steepling her fingers over her lips, she closes her eyes and takes a deep breath. "Remember I told you Roman wants to save the world? Well, that's what he's doing. You're his world, Lola, and he's doing this to save you."

Her admission is bittersweet. I want to believe her, but how can I? He's leaving. If I were that important to him, he'd tell me where he was going, and he'd say goodbye. "I understand his motives may be chivalrous, but by doing this, he's…tearing out my heart." She flinches, and I instantly wish I'd chosen another phrase. "If he wants to save me, then he needs to tell me the truth."

The coffee is ready. It's the reprieve I need to get my head around what she just said. I pour some coffee, my mind ricocheting and reeling. I'm his world? How does she know? Until a few days ago, she didn't even know we were seeing one another, and I use that term loosely. Unless…she's been privy to Roman's deepest, darkest secrets all along. But why?

I try my best to remain composed as I pass her, her cup. She unexpectedly reaches out and captures my hand. Her touch is a mother's caress. "I'm here because I needed to tell you things aren't always what they seem."

"I really wish someone would give me a straight answer." I sigh, feeling more confused than ever.

"I was hoping Roman would."

"I wouldn't hold your breath. He's most likely long gone by now."

"Don't be so sure." She squeezes my hand before releasing me.

There is an ominous promise behind her words. Once she finishes her coffee, she places the gold-rimmed cup onto the counter and stands. "He's staying at the Hilton."

I can't help but roll my eyes. "Nice to know he's traveling in style." I have no idea why she'd think I'd care. It just cements what a downright jerk he is.

"Room 218."

"Why are you telling me this?"

"Just in case you wanted to seek out the answers you deserve to know."

It takes a few moments, but when I realize the reason, I very unladylike splutter on my coffee. "He's *here*?" I ask, frantically wiping my chin.

June smiles, the first happy gesture I've seen from her all day. "Yes."

"W-why?"

"You know why." I can't speak. I'm too frightened of what I'll say if I do.

She walks over to my frozen form. Placing her hands on the tops of my shoulders, she levels me with her gentle gaze. "Maybe you're the one to save him."

"That seems like a lot of pressure, considering Roman enjoys being a martyr."

She bursts into a low chuckle. "I can see why he likes you so much."

Peering upward, I smile. "Thank you, June. For everything."

"It has been a real honor knowing you, Lola Van Allen. I knew you'd make a difference." She squeezes my shoulders, tears wet in her eyes. I don't know what she means, but it's nice to know I've had a small impact on the world.

Releasing me, she smiles, appearing embarrassed to be caught crying. "Thanks for the coffee."

"Anytime."

With nothing left to say, I walk her to the door, suddenly saddened that this may be the last time I see her. Yet instead of dwelling on the sadness, I rejoice in meeting someone as remarkable as June Carrington. "Goodbye."

A look of nostalgia overcomes her. "Goodbye, Lola." She leaves, and my last memory of her will be leaving with a smile on her face.

Once she's disappeared down the hall, I close the door and lean up against it, processing everything that just happened. June came here to deliver my clothes, but that appeared a ruse to tell me that Roman is in Manhattan. I don't understand why he's here, or why she felt the need to tell me. I never took June for cupid, so why would she do what she did? This seems like a lot of effort for one of her staff members.

I allow my mind to wander, and it wanders to the Hilton and room 218.

How dare he come here and expect...expect what? He obviously doesn't expect anything because he's not knocking down my door, begging for forgiveness.

June hinted he's here because of me, but I don't believe it. What could he possibly want to say he couldn't tell me days ago? I came home to escape this desolation, but it feels worse somehow.

I must figure this out before I can move on. But how am I supposed to do that?

"Room 218."

Groaning, I tip my head backward. "Goddammit." I don't bother changing or untangling my lopsided bun. If I don't go right now, I'll chicken out.

I don't care that Mrs. Dunned is looking at me like I've lost my mind as I run down the hallway without bothering to say hello. All I care about is getting into that elevator and ending this once and for all.

My shoes tear at the carpet, leaving probable footprints in my haste. The elevator doors ding open and I quicken my step, as I'm almost there. Focusing on those doors and nothing else, I bump straight into something, and when I do, I get an uncanny sense of déjà vu.

At first, I'm certain it's the wall, but that's impossible, considering I'm standing in the open corridor. That only leaves one other option. I've just rudely slammed into someone, which is completely my fault.

"I am so…" The words die in a gargled mess when I peer up and see the striking face of a man who emanates sheer masculinity. The first thing that catches my attention is the vibrancy of his blue-gray eyes. However, this time around, those eyes are weighed down with despair.

My brain, the motherboard of my quivering body, suddenly short-circuits, not believing I'm seeing who I'm seeing. This is surely some scam my mind conjured up to help deal with my loss. But when he speaks, his honeyed, smooth voice brings back memories that never, ever faded, and I know this is real.

"Sorry," he states, but I don't know if he's speaking for me, or if he's speaking for himself.

"You're fucking kidding me."

"Well, hello to you too."

I know I'm being rude, but seriously…you're fucking kidding me. "What are you doing here?"

Someone clears their throat, alerting us to the fact we're standing in the middle of the hallway, in front of the elevators, nonetheless. When I turn, I see Mrs. Dunned standing behind us, looking far from impressed. She doesn't mask her disgust as she clearly sizes Roman up. Protection mode kicks in, and I narrow my eyes, a silent warning that if she doesn't remove that scowl, I'll remove it for her…with my palm.

I have no idea why she wouldn't approve of Roman; he

fits into her social circle. However, when I look closely and get over my initial shock of seeing him here, I realize he looks like anyone other than the cocky, vibrant doctor I've grown to love.

His jeans are ripped at the knee, and he's opted for a loose-fitting V neck tee. His tousled hair appears as if he's run his fingers through it, rather than a comb. His scruff is heavier than usual, changing his usual refined look to wayward and angst-ridden.

Roman steps forward, placing his hand against my arm to shift me out of the way. The touch is electric, every nerve ending reverberating in delight. Mrs. Dunned pushes past us, and I have no doubt she'll be texting my mother, informing her of what she just saw, before she hits the lobby.

Not interested in being the topic of gossip over every New York socialite's brunch, I shrug out of Roman's hold. His mouth curves into a bitter smile. This is war.

"What do you want?"

Folding his arms arrogantly over his chest, he radiates pure domination, which ticks me off. How dare he come here unannounced? He ended things, but he's also the one who can't seem to leave me alone. "I thought I was ransacked, but apparently, there was nothing worth stealing."

I arch an apathetic brow. "Is this the last stop on your goodbye tour? If so, I want a refund." This tit for tat is getting us nowhere, but it feels liberating as I'm no longer sad. I'm angry.

"I'm not leaving."

"You're…what?" I scrunch up my nose, confused. "I saw your house, Roman. Unless you suddenly want to slum it, then I dare say you are. And besides, June told me you were. She told me you were in Manhattan." My sassiness is short-lived.

"June told you? She's here?"

"Yes," I reply, my voice small. I hope I haven't gotten her into trouble. "She came to see me earlier."

He seems to ponder my admission before he cocks his head to the side. "Where were you going in such a rush? Were you coming to see me?"

I scoff, attempting to play coy as I push my glasses up my nose. "Please, I have better things to do. I was going for a run." Roman peers down at my ballet flats and summer dress, both brows rising in amused disbelief. "Whatever, it's none of your business where I was going. You gave up the right to know when you turned into a colossal asshole! Goodbye. Have a nice life." I spin around, hating that he can flick my emotions in a blink of an eye.

"Lola, Lola, wait!" He latches on to my wrist, stopping me from fleeing, his desperation clear.

"Wait for what? That's all I've been doing…waiting for you to tell me the truth!"

"I know, and I'm sorry. I thought I was doing the right thing."

"Well, you thought wrong."

It's like staring into a mirror, his pain and frustration

reflecting mine. "I know I don't deserve it, but all I ask for is five minutes. If you still hate me after that, then I promise I will leave you alone for good."

"I don't hate you," I reply, my rage fading. "I should, but I don't. How will five minutes undo all the minutes prior?"

He rubs the back of his neck before sweeping his hand upward, mussing up his hair. "Because this time, each minute will carry the truth. I'm ready to tell you everything. I can only hope you still look at me the same once you've heard it all."

My pulse spikes, and my mouth suddenly becomes dry. He's not being melodramatic. It's evident he means every single word. I'm suddenly terrified, but pushing that fear away, I nod. It's a standoff, and I wonder if anyone will come out of this a winner.

"Will you let me explain?"

I have no other choice. I need to know his secrets. With that as my motivation, I turn and walk to my apartment. His heavy footsteps behind me indicate he's following. I can feel the tension exuding off him, which makes me nervous. He's usually so calm.

My fingers tremble as I attempt to unlock the door, the keys rattling against the love heart keychain. I take a deep breath and steady myself. If I'm going to do this, then I need to keep cool. It takes two attempts, but I manage to open the door without needing to kick it down.

Tossing my keys onto the entryway table, I make my way

into the living room. I fold my arms across my chest, indicating the floor is his. He swallows and begins pacing the room. I survey every rigid step silently, understanding he needs this time to muster the courage to begin.

I want to comfort him, but I don't. I'll give him the time he needs.

The air crackles before he abruptly stops pacing and turns his back. And so, his tale begins. "When I bumped into you that first day, I knew you were going to make a splash, but I never thought you'd cause a tsunami. The more time I spent with you, the more I found myself completely drawn to you. And when apart, I couldn't stop thinking about you.

"I have never met anyone like you before. Your strength is immeasurable, and the most remarkable thing is you don't even realize how incredible you truly are. Your strength, your compassion, but most of all…" He pauses, lowering his head. "Your heart is unlike anything I've ever known before."

I want to thank him for such beautiful words, but I keep still.

"You belong with someone who is young and healthy. Someone who can look after you."

I wet my dry lips. What is he talking about?

"I can't provide that for you…no matter how badly I want to."

"W-why not?"

"I am so sorry. I never meant to hurt you." The regret weighs so heavily I can hear his pain.

"I overheard what you said to June in your office," I confess, watching his shoulders slouch. "What is it about us that makes you think we won't have a happily ever after? Am I not good enough for you? Is that what it is?"

Silence.

I blink back my tears. "The least you can do is face me," I cry, feeling rejected and unwanted by the man I want more than air.

His head hangs low as his hands dig deep into his pockets. "I was trying to put distance between us, Lola, because I was…I am…I have fallen in love with you."

"You…what?" I gasp, drawing a wavering hand to my mouth.

He exhales before confessing, "I love you." Hearts and stars and tears should follow that declaration, but instead, I feel like it's another goodbye.

"Is loving me such a bad thing?" I pose, not understanding any of this.

When he replies, I wish I'd never asked. "Yes. This can never lead to anything. I wasn't being fair to you. I should have just stayed away, but I couldn't. I was addicted to you. I still am. God knows if I was a good man, I wouldn't be here telling you this. I would have left you alone and let you live. But I can't. The thought of you laughing, smiling with another man"—he hisses—"*kissing* another man drives me insane. I can't stand it."

My brain is going a million miles a minute. I should be over the moon, but I'm not. There is an underlying sorrow, and I'm just waiting for the infamous *I love you, but…*

"Why is your house packed up? If you're not leaving, then where are your things?"

Each painful silent second that ticks by just adds to my bewilderment. He has divulged his sins, but I'm missing a vital piece. I'm trying to be patient, but his five minutes are almost up. I'm no closer to uncovering this riddle than I was before he started.

"What was the point to this? What was the point of helping me, trying so hard to save me when you can't even look at me? What was the point of falling in love with you, Roman, if we end in tragedy?" I don't realize what I've said until his head lifts slowly, and a heavy whoosh of air leaves his lungs.

"You love me?"

"Yes. With all my heart."

If not for his shoulders rising and falling steadily, I'd say he was not breathing. I have just confessed my feelings to him, and all he can do is stand unresponsive, adding to my misgivings.

Charging forward, I grip his bicep, forcing him to face me, but he doesn't budge. "Your five minutes are up," I spit, shaking my head, infuriated. "I was stupid to think you could ever love me. I don't fit into your perfect little world; I never did. What was I, some charity case you felt sorry for?" My voice cracks, but I shake out my fears, not shedding a tear for someone who can't even show me the common decency of turning around.

"I'm far from perfect," he finally says. "And I never felt sorry for you."

"Then why did you do this? Why do you want to save me?"

The tension blistering off his taut frame almost burns me, and the room suddenly becomes still. I recoil and watch his demeanor suddenly change. "I want…I want to save you because I'm…beyond saving."

Before I rebuke his claims, he reaches overhead with both hands and yanks the collar of his shirt, pulling it off his body. I stand frozen, barely breathing as I'm faced with his muscular, broad back. I want to ask what he's doing and why he's removing his clothes, but I can't speak. The words catch in my throat.

The T-shirt floats to the ground as he unclasps his fist. "Eleanor was my sister, but that wasn't her real name."

Time stands still. I will remember this moment for as long as I live.

"She was a huge Beatles fan, and 'Eleanor Rigby' was her favorite song. She used to play it on a loop whenever she got sad, which was a lot of the time. It was her escape from living a life no one deserves to live. She was one of the lonely people, and for her entire short life, all she wished to know was where she belonged."

I take one, two steps back, shaking my head, unable to breathe.

"She never found where she belonged; she ran out of time.

But now I like to think she's no longer alone. She's no longer one of the lonely people because she's surrounded by her kind. A field, a *strawberry field* of lonely people surely are no longer alone."

My heart lurches from my chest, and I gasp.

"Her name was...Scarlett." His words are slowed to gibberish, and I cover my ears, shaking my head violently.

But that makes no difference because nothing can prepare my eyes for what I witness next. Roman's head dips before he turns at an excruciatingly slow speed. He doesn't meet my eyes, but even if he did, I can't tear my gaze away from his chest.

The reason is that sitting over his heart, the heart that pounded so soundly beneath my ear, is a long, jagged scar. The angry, red wound is the only answer I ever needed.

Roman could have told me, but like with Erin, he knew showing me would be the only way I would understand.

"So you see"—he places his flat palm over his heart—"not so perfect after all."

The sight of Roman with his head downturned, hand cradled to his scarred heart, will forever be etched into my mind. I don't even understand what I'm seeing.

Afraid that I'm seconds away from fading, I slump onto the sofa, attempting to process what I've just seen and heard. "S-Scarlett is your sister? That was the name of June's daughter who...oh, god..." I cry, unbelieving. There must be some mistake.

But Roman confirms my suspicions as true. "Scarlett was my sister, and June is…my mom." He finally lifts his chin, the sadness pooling in those poignant eyes.

He's watching me closely, sizing up my reaction to what he just confessed. I may appear stoic, but on the inside, every fiber of my being is screaming in sheer horror.

"R-R-Roman…I d-don't…" I place a hand to my mouth, closing my eyes to stop the tears.

Roman's heavy footsteps sound against the soft carpet, getting closer and closer to where I sit. My eyes slip open, unable to focus on anything but the toothed scar. All those times he held me near, I never knew what he was hiding. Buried beneath what I perceived as perfection lay a broken man.

He seems embarrassed and quickly attempts to reach for his shirt. But my hand shoots out, and I snare his wrist. He looks at our connection, then back up at me. "No, don't. You've done enough hiding."

I want to ask him so many questions, but I don't. I simply allow him all the time he needs to share with me something I don't think he's ever shared with anyone before.

He exhales, before telling me his tale. "June told you about Scarlett?" I nod slowly. "She was such a clever kid. It wasn't rare for her to correct her doctors on her condition because no one was better educated than Scarlett. She read every single medical article and book published on her condition. But it didn't make a difference. In the end, the illness claimed her life."

I lower my eyes, feeling a kinship with Scarlett.

"When she…died…" It seems Roman still has a problem saying her outcome aloud. "A piece of my mother died with her. She was never the same, and she never looked at me the same because we were twins…why was I still alive and Scarlett wasn't?

"She slipped into a deep depression and didn't want anything to do with me or my dad. We tried to help her"—the desperation is clear, and I believe every single word—"but she didn't want help. She shut us out.

"I lost my twin, and I lost my mother. I needed her because she was the only person who could understand what it felt like having a piece of your heart ripped out from your chest, and in its place, a gaping void is left, which just got bigger and bigger."

He peers off in the distance, lost in time. "She pushed my father into the arms of her best friend. I know it wasn't intentional, but she just didn't want us around. We were a reminder of everything she once had but lost. I know why she did it, but I have never truly forgiven her."

I want to touch him, but I don't. I sit on my hands, too afraid that if we make contact, I'll disrupt this memory, which is one he's kept buried away.

"A kid can only take so many rejections. I moved in with my dad and his new family, but I never forgot Scarlett. How could I? Each beat of my heart reminded me of the life I stole from my sister."

"Stole?" My voice is merely a whisper. "You didn't steal her life, Roman. You have every right to live."

"I was her twin. Why was my heart healthy, and hers wasn't? Why wasn't my heart the one to fail? I would have given anything, given her my heart if I could." The regret behind his words is unbearable, and I choke back a sob.

He clears his throat, pushing away his tears. "That's why I became a doctor. I wanted to help as many people as I could because each face was Scarlett's. With each person I helped, I gained back my belief that I was worthy of this life."

"Why is it a secret that June is your mother?"

He shakes his head once before sitting beside me. "It's not, but it's not a need to know, either. And besides, I want to be respected for what I've accomplished, of who I am, not because of who my mom is. Up until recently, we didn't even speak."

His lips curve at the corners into a sarcastic smile. "You know what the world is like. Just one slipup and another doctor is waiting in the wings, ready to take my place. This job is sought out by many. I don't want anyone thinking I didn't earn my stripes."

I understand. This world we live in is merciless and cutthroat.

"Once June came to terms with Scarlett's death, she wanted to honor her and her life, and that's why Strawberry Fields exists. I'm sure she's told you all about it. Scarlett would have loved it. Her field is named after John Lennon's memorial in

Central Park."

There is so much to process, but I know we haven't even skimmed the surface. "You said up until recently you didn't speak. What happened for that to change?" I know what happened, I can see it, but I don't understand what I'm seeing.

This entire time, Roman has been lost deep in thought, not making eye contact, but with the slowest of movements, he turns his chin to look at me. I knew he was a beautiful being, but now, his beauty is extraordinary.

My hands sit limply in my lap, but they resurrect when Roman slips his palm over mine. The contact warms every inch of my body. But that warmth pales compared to what he does next. With trusting fingers, he draws my hand upward and places it over his beating heart.

The scar beneath my fingertips is smooth. With a timid touch, I graze over it, but Roman seizes my wrist, as if repulsed that I'm stroking something he finds hideous.

"This is what happened," he replies, letting me go. "Yes, I became a doctor to honor Scarlett, but I also became a doctor to honor me."

My breathing begins a steady climb. "I-I don't understand."

He wets his lips before confessing, "Scarlett and I were twins. What she had, I had too. Mine just lay dormant. I had congenital heart disease, just like Scarlett, but mine was—*is*—a complex, more complicated defect that presented itself for the first time when I turned twenty. Congenital heart defects discovered during adulthood can only be repaired surgically."

The walls close in on me.

"My first surgery"—he absentmindedly rubs over his scar—"was when I was twenty-one. It worked for a little while, but it appears my heart is as stubborn as my head. The second operation was three years later. Open heart surgery to replace my damaged valves. That seemed to work, but I didn't go into this blind. I'm a doctor. I know what my future holds."

"And what's that?" I ask in a mere whisper.

He consoles me, clasping my hand tenderly. "You know what."

No.

This is his secret? His life-changing secret is that he's... dying.

A wave of nausea rolls over me, and I cover my mouth, afraid I'm going to be sick. Nothing comes up, however, because I'm empty inside.

He did all this to save and protect me. Save me from the same fate headed his way, and to protect me from this heartache of knowing that Roman, just like me, has had his life snatched out from under him.

"Why didn't you tell June s-sooner? I know she regrets not being there for you." She told me so herself.

Roman smiles, and it's so bittersweet. "Because my family has had enough heartache. She didn't need another broken heart." He cups my cheek, his thumb wiping away fallen tears I didn't even know I've shed.

Every single memory overcomes me, and I gulp in three deep breaths, desperate to push through and not break down. June's gut-wrenching sobs in the chapel echo loudly in my ears. I now understand who she shed those tears for. She was losing both children. No wonder she showed such interest in Roman's and my affairs. She was making up for lost time, and she had a deadline.

I recall Roman's many comments about not being good enough, or why anyone would want to date him. I now know why. Why start a relationship with somebody when this constant cloud of doom hangs over your head? I know that feeling all too well.

Tamara's comment about him dying a lonely *old* man, and how he had replied with an ambiguous response at the time. But now, it's crystal clear. All of it is.

"Why didn't y-you tell m-me?" My stutter isn't caused by my illness, but rather the fact I'm skating so close to the edge. What happens when I fall? I crumble, that's what.

"You know why," he simply replies.

He pushed me to fight because he understands what it's like to be given an end date. He wants for me what I want for him.

Life.

When you're sick, no one wants to be treated that way. They just want normalcy. Didn't I?

This entire time, I thought he didn't want me because I

was flawed, but in reality, he's the one who saw himself as the biggest imperfection of all.

"You can't give up," I cry, latching on to both hands and pressing them to my cheeks. I need to feel his touch, everywhere, forever. "You taught me to fight."

"There's hope for you, Lola, and that makes me the happiest man alive."

"It still might not work," I press, unable to accept his surrender.

He shakes his head wildly, gripping my cheeks fervently. "Like I once told you, this will work, it has to. I won't accept another outcome. Scarlett dying, my mom being a shell of who she once was, my failing heart, it has to lead to you living. Because what's the point of all this heartache otherwise? Live for me. Live the life I can't live."

Every part of my body aches. "How can I accept being saved? I'm no one special."

Roman pins me with those stormy blue eyes and smiles. "Yes, you are. And aren't I lucky to have something, someone worth saving?"

I throw myself into his arms, holding on so tight I'm certain we've become one.

He brushes over my hair, kissing my thumping pulse. "I pushed you away because how can we be together? How is that fair to you? I didn't mean to fall in love with you. Every time I pushed, you pushed back twice as hard. Every time I tried to stay away, I found myself wanting you more and more. You challenged me, you tested me, and I fell completely and irrevocably under your spell. You have given me something to live for. It may be in vain, but it was nice while it lasted. I shouldn't be here for so many reasons, but I can't stay away from you."

"I don't want you to stay away." I sob into his shoulder. "When I look at you, all I see is hope."

Roman sighs, and I feel an invisible weight lift off his shoulders. He lays gentle kisses under my ear, stoking a fire within. "You thought I was your strength...but the truth is... you were mine."

"Roman." I gasp, unable to stand this turmoil. "There has to be another way."

"There's no cure for me, but there is for you." He presses his lips to my temple. "You're going to heal. You're going to grow strong. You're going to make a beautiful wife and be an amazing mother. That's all I want for you. That's why I pushed you. The greatest gift you can give me is to...live."

A guttural sob takes over my body, and I weep uncontrollably, doubtful I'll ever stop.

We have wasted countless minutes hiding and lying to protect the other from heartache, but if we had been honest from the beginning, then we would have had more time.

Suddenly, time is the enemy, and all I can think about is not wasting another minute—we've wasted enough.

Nothing feels more right than when I press my trembling lips to his. My forwardness catches him off guard, and he freezes, his body growing tense. But he soon relaxes when I meet his eyes, pleading we forget everything but our love.

My tears are long washed away when our lips collide in a union of longing, desperation, and need. Our kisses are fueled by what was just shared, and I suddenly want to climb inside him and never emerge.

I place both hands on his chest, feeling his strong heart beating wildly beneath my palms. The life source is the sound I march to, and I stop overthinking and just let go. I furl my fist over his heart, and with the other, I reach around and begin to unzip my dress.

Our lips never miss a beat as his frenetic fingers draw the straps over my shoulders and down my arms. I maneuver and twist before the dress pools at my waist, leaving us both bare. The moment he scoops me forward and presses us chest to chest, I want more—so much more.

I like that Roman will be my first and last, because no matter what happens, nothing, no one will ever trump this memory we're about to make.

I'm strung tighter than a bow as I toy with the clasp at the front of my lacy bra. Just as it snaps, Roman's hand shoots out, stopping me from disrobing. My eyes pop open, and I pull away in confusion. Why did he stop me?

"You don't want to?" I whisper, unable to hide my fears.

His lips, those soft, luscious lips tip into a sinful smirk. "Of course, I do." The affirmation is confirmed when he hums, his eyes flicking downward. "I just…do you?" He places a tender kiss on my shoulder, circling his tongue, before venturing downward. "Because I want you to know that I didn't tell you this expecting anything."

A besotted moan slips past my lips. He inhales, breathing in my essence. The simple gesture is completely desirable, and I arch backward, allowing him full access as he lays feather-soft kisses against my heated skin.

He continues exploring me, his tongue and lips leaving a roadmap of where he's been. As he kisses lower, over my collarbone, and leading farther down, I know that the answer is yes, I do. I've never been more sure of anything before.

Too afraid to speak, I speak with actions, rather than words. I place my hand over his and gently urge him to let go—physically, emotionally. My bra falls to the sofa, exposing me just as he is. My skin prickles in excitement as he takes a moment to examine every inch of my ripened flesh.

He hums, tonguing his upper lip in utter desire. "You're beautiful. I want you. So much."

"I want you, too." It's the last words spoken as we then speak in a language crafted especially for us.

Our clothes fall to the floor, not a shred left on our skin. We're naked, body and soul, and it's fitting, because all layers have finally been stripped bare. All that remains is pure honesty and love.

Roman lays me down on the sofa, ensuring his weight isn't crushing me, but I want him to. I don't know where to look, and he quietly smiles at my innocence. As we kiss, he curls his hand around the nape of my neck, tightening his hold as we grow more desperate and intense. The other hand slithers to my hip and then inward. My eyes pop open, and I break our connection, a moan escaping me. He takes my bottom lip between his teeth before nudging closer and closer to my heat. I grow slack when his fingers enter me.

For the next untold minutes, he dominates every inch of my body, and I let him. Sweet torment has never felt this good. He punishes me with a grin slathered to his cheeks.

"You're sure?" he breathlessly asks, reaching for a condom from his wallet.

Brushing the fallen hair from his brow, I nod, lifting my quivering lips. He melts into me, kissing me and robbing me of breath. But who needs air when…Roman shifts, and we connect in the most intimate way possible. Who needs air when you've got this.

"Oh." I gasp, never feeling so full.

He stills, waiting and watching for me to soften, always putting my needs first, but I want him to let go. I raise my hips and shudder, losing myself in everything but him. He kisses me tenderly, moving in sync with his measured, rocking movements where we unite.

It hurts, but it hurts *so* good.

It's slow at first as my body learns this very intricate dance for two, but with Roman as my teacher, it doesn't take long to catch up. He pushes, and I pull. We move, breathe, and connect in perfect harmony, and I never want this feeling to end.

As we gallop toward the finish line with Roman sheathed inside, I make a promise to myself that no matter what happens, I will fight until the bitter end. Tears spill from my eyes, and Roman suddenly stills, breathless and panting.

"Have I hurt you?" he asks, touching his fingertip to my tears, fear marring him as he searches every inch of my face.

I shake my head. "No. I've never been happier. Don't stop." I bow my hips, the immense fulfillment unlike anything I've ever felt before.

"I love you," he whispers into my ear, kissing over my frantic pulse, biting my chin.

My eyes roll into the back of my head, the friction and feel of being united this way almost too much.

He watches and protects, ensuring my first time is as perfect as it can be. And it is. With our walls no longer erected, we let go and lose ourselves in the simplicity of this…the simplicity of love.

With my palm pressed over his flouncing heart, I explode with a thunderous pleasure, and he follows soon after. He whispers sweet nothings into my ear, promising never to let go…and I hope he never does.

FOURTEEN

I wake to my second favorite smell in the world—coffee. The first would be the person who is currently clattering around the kitchen.

Stretching like a lazy cat basking in the sun, my body groans, but it's a contented feeling. Last night was incredible. It exceeded anything I ever imagined it to be. I thought I would be tense and timid, but I wasn't. The feel of Roman embedded in my body and soul obliterated all fears, and I lost myself in a union that changed me forever.

Brushing the hair from my brow, I sit up, giggling when I see we somehow ended up on the floor. After our tender lovemaking, Roman held me and we fell into a deep sleep. I woke some hours later to a flutter of kisses. They began over my eyelids, cascading down my cheeks, over my lips, and then down between my breasts. As Roman's tour of my body continued lower and lower, I surrendered and allowed him free rein. We were tangled in each other seconds later, Roman showing me this thing called love comes in many shapes and sizes.

Our first time was tender, getting to know the other's body, but the second and third time, I blush just thinking about all the wicked things we did.

But now that the morning sun has conquered the moon, I focus on the only thing that matters—Roman's survival. I simply cannot accept a world where he doesn't live.

He seems to have accepted his fate. I should know because I was in his shoes not that long ago. But until I've exhausted every possible option, I'm not giving up. I only just found him, and I'll be damned if he gets ripped away from me before we've had a chance to live.

Reaching for my cell off the coffee table, I see that it's after nine a.m. Dialing Dr. Carter's office, I ask his assistant if I may speak with him for a minute. She connects us, and his jovial voice booms across the line seconds later.

"Lola, it's lovely to hear from you. Everything okay for your scan this morning?"

"Yes." I gather the courage to reveal the true reason I called. "I wanted to know…can you recommend any cardiologists?" When he's silent, I quickly add, "It's not for me; it's for a friend."

"I know of a few. I'll have Wilma email over a list. Although

Dr. Archibald is probably the best person to ask."

My heart sinks. I was hoping he wouldn't say that. "Thank you. I'll see you this afternoon." I hang up, feeling a complete and utter failure.

"Mornin'." His smooth voice is like decadent chocolate, and my shoulders instantly sag.

Turning to look at him, I bite my lip, smothering my moan.

The bright sunshine gleaming in from the window highlights everything I admired in the dark of night. His V-muscle is rock-hard, rivaling his washboard abs. His mussed hair sits in rebellious peaks, and that rebellion is challenged by hot nerd status as he's slipped on his dark-rimmed glasses.

He looks like a Calvin Klein model, but all the more wicked.

His scar is his badge of honor, showing the world he was far stronger than whatever tried to beat him. So does his tattoo. He watches me watch him, and consciously scrubs his chest. "Sorry I don't have something nicer to offer you."

Lifting my eyes, I shake my head, pressing the throw I'm swathed in to my chest. "I wouldn't change a thing." His pink lips curve into a sexy smile, and I internally combust.

With two coffees in hand, Roman walks to where I sit on the floor. He stops and appears to weigh up the damage from late last night and early this morning. He seems incredibly pleased with our efforts. Sitting beside me, he offers me a coffee. "Who were you talking to?"

Nothing slips past him.

Savoring my first sip of much-needed caffeine, I cradle the cup and sigh. "Dr. Carter."

Roman's back stiffens. "Are you all right? Do you feel sick?"

I quickly put his mind at ease. "I'm fine. I'm due to see him today. I asked him to take over from..." I leave the sentence hanging.

"Of course, that was a wise thing to do. So you'll stay in Manhattan?"

I raise my shoulders. "I haven't given it much thought. I was, but now..."

"Now, what?" he asks, looking at me over the rim of his glasses.

"Now things have changed."

We're both quiet, sipping our coffees, most likely our minds browsing over the same page. Last night changed everything. Not just the sex, but with Roman's condition, I feel like we're running out of time.

"Last night was—"

"Incredible," he cockily says, interrupting me. I can't help but smile.

"Yes, it really was, but I—" Roman's cup pauses midair, waiting for me to elaborate. "But I, what you told me, how can we change that? There's got to be some other way."

He sighs heavily, finishing his coffee before setting the saucer down on the table. "There isn't. I wish there was." His response is so matter-of-fact. Blinking back my tears, I hold in my sadness, but Roman sees straight through me. "Hey." He cups my cheek, his large hand engulfing my face. "It'll be all right."

"How?" I turn into his touch, addicted to him. "H-how long have you g-got?" I don't want to ask the dreaded question, but I need to know.

"Not long," he softly replies.

My lower lip trembles uncontrollably.

"I didn't tell you this expecting a miracle to happen. I told you because I want to spend whatever time I have left with you. No more wasting time. We've wasted enough. But…"

I swallow nervously, my pulse beginning to rise. "But what?"

"But if it's too much for you, I totally understand. I come with a lot of baggage," he says, sincerely.

"So do I," I reply. "But that didn't stop you."

He smirks, and I melt. "How could I? I was smitten the moment I met you. I didn't stand a chance."

Memories of us pressed together, skin to skin, assault my brain, and an involuntary whimper slips past my lips.

It doesn't go unnoticed by Roman.

His stare instantly drops to my lips, and I bite the inside of my cheek to stop another whimper from escaping. The air crackles around us, and the same budding feeling begins to stir. I remember his lips against my throat as he claimed me with feral possession. I remember never feeling fuller than I did when he moved inside me. He was everywhere, and I liked it.

"Whatever you're thinking, don't stop." He leans over and places a hot kiss beneath my ear. It kicks me in the solar plexus, and I almost topple over.

I arch backward, allowing him full rein of my body. I give, and he takes. The simplest of touches awakens a deep-rooted hunger, and before long, I want more than just his lips on me. But we have an appointment to make.

We get ready, both in a somber mood over what we face today.

Roman said he wanted a bagel, so I don't question where we're going when he leads the way. I'm too lost in my head anyway. However, when I focus on where we are, I feel like I've just stepped out of a time machine and landed in the 1970s.

Snapping my head from left to right, I see luscious undergrowth and weeping, flourishing trees surround us. The greenery serves as the backdrop to the large group of strangers decked out in tie-dyed T-shirts and bell-bottom pants.

A soothing voice accompanied by an acoustic guitar floats on the warm breeze, adding to the slightly hippie vibe. A girl stands next to me, eyes closed, a daisy tucked behind her right ear. She seems hypnotized by the music as she sways and sings along to the words.

I look up, about to ask Roman where we are, but when I see his gaze fixed thoughtfully on the ground, I know the answer lies at our feet. Almost afraid to look, I glance downward, only to become aware of the chorus of the song which I now recognize.

At my feet lays one word.

Imagine.

Roman has led me to Strawberry Fields in Central Park.

I instantly forget about my petty drama and offer him the same support he's constantly giving me. He brought me here because there really was no other place to be. This place brings everything into perspective because we can all imagine.

In the words of Pablo Picasso, "*Everything you can imagine is real.*"

Sighing, I lean my head against Roman's shoulder, closing my eyes and getting lost in the magic that encases this miraculous place. People come here to reflect while others just want a break from the concrete jungle.

I'm not sure how long we stand, entranced by the stillness calming my raging nerves. I can understand why June opted for her own Strawberry Fields. When Roman leads the way toward a bench seat, I follow, no questions asked.

I stay snuggled into his side, and he wraps his arm around me. I wish we could stay this way forever, but being here cements what we both know to be true. "There must be something you can do," I whisper, not even sure if he can hear me.

But he does, loud and clear. "There is." I raise my head,

indicating I'm listening. "I can live whatever time I have left with you and have no regrets."

"It's not enough time." My lip begins to tremble. My emotions are on a roller coaster. I'm not sure how much more I can take.

Roman runs the back of two fingers down my cheek. "Life isn't measured in time, but rather moments, memories."

"I don't want to be a memory." I know I'm being incredibly selfish, seeing as I was the one, weeks ago, accepting the same fate.

"You're the best memory I have."

There is no reasoning with him; he's made up his mind. I would be a complete hypocrite if I argued because I've seen his world from the same side. I let the matter rest, determined not to ruin this moment.

As I'm lost in thought, Roman softly confesses, "Although it is rare, someone who has a life-threatening congenital heart defect can receive a heart transplant. But surgery won't work for me. I have the scars to prove it."

Closing my eyes, I try not to dwell on the finality of his comment. I can't imagine a world without Roman living in it. I would rather imagine a universe where both Roman and I are happy and healthy, where we grow old with our eighteen grandkids surrounding us, retelling the story of when we first met.

Our story isn't conventional, but it's ours.

The moment we walk into Dr. Carter's office, I'm assaulted with memories I wish I could forget. The receptionist, Wilma, smiles when she sees me. "He's running late. Take a seat."

Wilma has been here for as long as I can remember. She probably could have retired years ago, but her admiration for Dr. Carter is clearly evident. He's a good man, and if it weren't for him, I have no doubt I'd be dead.

I half sit in the black leather seat, unable to stay still. Roman doesn't hover. He sits beside me and calmly scrolls through emails on his phone.

When Dr. Carter's office door swings open, I place a quick peck to Roman's lips. "Lola and…" When Roman turns to look up at Dr. Carter, he adds with surprise, "Dr. Archibald. It's nice to see you both." My cheeks flame as I'm certain he saw our not-so-discreet exchange.

"Hello, Dr. Carter. Thank you for seeing me."

"My pleasure. I'm happy to see you again." Dr. Carter is in his late fifties, but time has been kind to him, and he doesn't look a day over forty-five.

Roman stands beside me, extending his hand. "Nice to see you again, Richard."

They shake hands, the mutual respect clearly evident. "You too." The thing I like most about Dr. Carter is that he's not one for small talk. "Shall we? We have to conduct the scan in the other room."

I nod, my heart rate beginning to rise.

"Wilma. I will be back in roughly thirty minutes. Hold all calls until then." She nods and waves goodbye as Roman holds the glass door open for us. We begin walking down the corridor.

"How have you responded to these trials?"

"Good. Better than the first time around."

Dr. Carter nods, placing his hands into his white lab coat. "Have you overseen her trial, Roman?"

He grows rigid beside me. "For the most part, yes, I have."

"Perfect. You can sit with me and monitor the scan so we can discuss the results."

Up until now, I haven't been nervous or anxious. But now, the reality of what I'm about to do hits home, and I feel faint. I march on autopilot, my mind panning over what the next thirty minutes will reveal. It will have either worked, or not. There is no gray. Just black and white.

"Did you ask Dr. Archibald about recommended heart specialists for your friend? I haven't had a chance to email you. I'm sorry."

Roman's head whips my way, and I gingerly focus on the gleaming white floor. "No, Dr. Carter. I haven't." I don't elaborate, but my lackluster response hints it's not a topic I wish to discuss further.

Roman is pissed I went behind his back, but I can deal with

that later. Right now, I have more pressing issues to deal with, like the intimidating machine that greets me when Dr. Carter opens a door. I've been in this machine many times before, but now, there is a sense of urgency surrounding it.

Dr. Carter smiles. "You remember what to do?"

I nod, nervously tugging on my bottom lip. He begins pressing multiple buttons and preparing the MRI machine while I finally meet Roman's eyes.

"Sorry," I whisper, but he shakes his head, gently running his pointer along the length of my neck. I don't have a chance to relish in the touch because it was for a reason. He carefully removes Sadie's necklace—which I recently fixed—into his pocket.

"Are you ready?" he poses, nothing but importance to his question.

"I am." My palms begin to sweat.

"I'll just be out there." He gestures with his chin to where a glass window separates the room.

"Okay."

Whatever the result, we both know it will change our lives forever. If it's worked, it means I get to live, but Roman still dies. And if it hasn't worked…

"See you soon." Bending forward, he places his lips on my forehead.

Once I'm dressed in the hospital gown, I step out from behind the medical screen. Before I boost myself onto the bed,

I look at Roman. He sits, leaned forward, steepling his fingers over his mouth. I hate that he's here because of me. He has enough of his own issues to deal with, yet here he is, forfeiting his health for mine.

"I love you," I mouth, uncaring that Dr. Carter can see.

Roman nods once before placing his palm to the glass, an open invitation that his heart beats for me too.

With that image as my driving force, I lie down, the plastic beneath me cool. I take three steadying breaths, closing my eyes and going to my happy place.

"Okay, we're ready. You can listen to music while inside. This will take approximately twenty minutes."

Roman's pain is flagrant through the glass, but I use that as my strength to calm my nerves and live for us both.

Seconds later, the bed slides into the circular tunnel, cutting me off from the real world. The noise is unbearable, the droning sound cutting into my canals. My scalp begins to smolder, but I know this is a psychological response to why I'm in here.

I squeeze my eyes shut, and I focus on the only thing I can to make all of this go away.

Roman.

After this test finishes, I will know what my future holds, but what about Roman? He said he didn't have long. I swallow past the lump in my throat.

This isn't fair, but I've come to learn that life rarely is. As the machine rattles around me, I plan a course of attack, determined to exhaust every single option for Roman. I won't give up on him. I can't.

Lying here with a possible second chance at life, I come to understand Roman's comment about feeling unworthy of his life. It doesn't seem fair that we're alive, while the ones we love have been taken away, or faced with a grim future ahead.

For the next twenty minutes, I drift off into another plane, neither here nor there. I'm floating above myself, looking down on my life and wondering where I can better things. Roman's life is far more important to me than mine is. I want us to both live, but the reality is, that will not happen. One or both of us will expire, and truth be told, I would rather that person be me.

Tears leak from my eyes and a burning aches in my chest, but I'm brought back to now, realizing the scan is over. The bed slowly retracts, and I'm grateful the twenty minutes felt like two. My pupils take a moment to adjust to the bright light, and I blink, hoping to clear my head.

When I think I can stand, I raise my weary body, but I get the sense that something is horribly, grievously wrong. "Roman?" I whisper, but everything turns cold.

My glasses clear up my vision, but I don't understand what I'm seeing.

"Lola, we will just be a minute." Dr. Carter's voice holds the same grim response it did all those years ago. I'm suddenly transported to when we first met.

Roman stands motionless, hands interlaced atop his head as

his cheeks puff out, exhaling deeply. He looks so lost. I beseech him to tell me what's wrong, but he stares vacantly ahead.

What has happened for him to look like he's dying inside? A plume of disquiet engulfs me, and I lean against the bed for support. I'm certain something has happened to him.

Dr. Carter enters the room, a folder and what appears to be my scan in his left hand. I wait for Roman to enter, but he doesn't. Turning to look back at the window, I no longer see him.

"Dr. Archibald needed a minute."

"A minute for what?" My voice betrays my fears.

"How about we go back to my office, so we can discuss the results?" Why is he stalling? "Would you like to sit?"

"Why are you treating me like I'm sick? I'm fine. What's going on?"

He pulls in his lips, the seriousness of what he is about to reveal weighing heavily on his shoulders. "Your scan results…" He walks over to a board and lights it up, clipping my scan to the top railing. "They have revealed a darkened mass here and here." He reaches into his pocket and produces a small laser light.

I amble over, my feet functioning on autopilot.

"This here"—the red laser circles a black blob—"is your first tumor. And this…" His sentences all mush into one because all I can focus is the word 'first.' First would imply it was here before any others, others which weren't there the last time I checked.

"Where's Roman?" I whisper, cutting Dr. Carter off.

He pauses, the red laser dot stationary on a smaller blob I've not seen before. "Have you heard what I've said?" He speaks in a monotone, like he would to any other patient who has just received the worst news of her life.

"Yes."

"And you understand what it all means?" He peers at me, nothing but sadness reflected on his kind face.

"Not really." I can't accept his news until I know Roman is safe.

Sighing, Dr. Carter gently places his palm to my forearm, requesting my full attention for what he's about to reveal. "Lola. I am so sorry. These drugs, if they worked, would have done so right away. They don't need time to take effect.

"But sadly, now you have two tumors. Your original one has doubled in size. The newer one is still small, but…" His pause leaves me winded. "But it's only a matter of time. It will get bigger. Both will."

"W-what does that mean?" I stutter, my head suddenly weighing a thousand pounds.

"It means it didn't work." The reply doesn't come from Dr. Carter.

Spinning around, I see Roman standing in the doorway, looking beyond broken. His shoulders are slouched, his hands dug deep into his pockets, his downturned face hiding his fears.

"Are you all right?" I ask, unable to stop myself as I run over.

He lifts his chin, and I've never seen him more heartbroken than right now. "Am *I* all right?" he questions, bewildered.

"Yes," I reply, touching his face, ensuring he's real. "Your heart is okay?" On cue, I place my hand over the thundering beat. The frantic rhythm is faster and more irregular than I've ever felt it before.

"Lola, stop it!" Roman shouts, seizing my wrist and clasping it tight. "Stop worrying about me. Worry about yourself!" His outburst has me jarring backward, stunned. "No, my heart is not okay. It's fucking broken! Did you hear what Dr. Carter said?" He drops my wrist, only to clutch at both my upper arms, shaking me fervently. "Why aren't you saying anything? Why aren't you as angry as I am?"

Black consumes his pupils, reflecting what he's feeling within.

"As long as I know you're okay, I can deal with anything I need to." And it's the truth.

This entire time, I was more concerned for Roman's well-being than I was for mine. Is that what sacrifice feels like? Putting the one you love before your needs?

"How is this possible?" Roman lets me go and storms over to Dr. Carter, who is standing blankly in front of the lightened board. "She was getting better."

"Because she wanted to, and at some point, I believe she was," he simply replies. "But the drugs, they were, they are…" I step forward, knowing what he's going to say. "They are simply prolonging the inevitable." He turns to look at me, nothing but regret marring his demeanor. It's the same look he gave me when I told him I quit the first time around.

I've grown to admire Dr. Carter, not only because he's a wonderful doctor, but also because he's a wonderful human being. He gave Georgia hope, and for that, I'll forever be grateful. "Thank you, Dr. Carter. For everything."

He nods, but accepting my gratitude doesn't appear to be an easy thing. "It's been my absolute pleasure."

This is really happening.

Now that the dust has settled, I take in the scan. The two darkened masses look so harmless, but their significance is poisonous. This time there is no miracle pill, but I suppose there never was. This was my fate from the very beginning. The trial bought me some time, time to meet and fall in love with the man who changed my life forever.

"No!" Roman roars, his explosion startling me. I've never seen him this enraged before.

"Roman, it's okay." I try to soothe him, but it's pointless.

"It's not fucking okay! How can it be?" He jabs his finger at the scan, glaring at it like it's his worst enemy and he wants to strangle it with his bare hands. "You're dying! Tell me in what universe can that possibly be okay?"

I open my mouth, but shut it soon after. I understand what he's feeling. I felt it the moment he told me his fate.

"This is bullshit!" He doesn't allow either Dr. Carter or myself time to console him. He storms from the room.

Dr. Carter sighs, running a hand down his weary face. "I'll have Wilma schedule a follow-up appointment."

"Why?"

"There may be something else we can do," he replies, stumped. We both know that we've exhausted my options. It's the end of the line. I'm surprisingly calmer than I thought I would be. But I guess the same news delivered the second time around softens the blow.

"No, I'm done. If there's nothing you think you can do, then I want to live however long I have clearheaded and not doped up."

He nods, understanding my request.

Swallowing, I ask the question we all want to know in a morbid sort of way. "How long?"

I don't envy Dr. Carter. His job would have to be one of the hardest in the world. "I don't know…one month, maybe two."

Wow. I stand with my mouth parted, my mind reeling over everything Dr. Carter has said.

"That's just a guess, judging from the scans. We can always run some tests, but…I really am sorry." Still standing motionless, Dr. Carter does something he's not done before. He hugs me.

I am stunned for so many different reasons, but being embraced by the man who hardly shows any emotion has a tear cascading down my cheek. I have touched someone who has touched me. We go through life hoping to make an impact, and I've managed to accomplish that with a man I respect, admire, and treasure. I can leave this room with a smile on my face.

"I better go find Roman." I sheepishly pull from his embrace. "Thank you again. I really appreciate it. You were so good to Georgia and me. I know she thanks you, too."

Dr. Carter nods, and I bite my cheek. Is this the last time I'll ever see him? He must be able to read my thoughts because he suddenly turns his back, but not before I see a tear catch on his lashes.

I don't make a fuss. I simply grab my clothes and leave.

After changing in the bathroom, I calmly press the call button, peering down at my steady hands. They'll never grow wrinkled, nor will they ever nurture the kin from my womb. This outer shell will be immortalized in time. This is how people will remember me—forever young.

The elevator doors open, and I ride it down to the main foyer. I exit, my steps not wavering, my head held high. I finally feel free. I haven't been delivered a death sentence. I've been given yet another chance to live.

Stepping out of the revolving doors, I see Roman sitting on a park bench, head downturned, legs spread apart. His hands are interlaced low, as if he's praying to whichever god may be listening. I know he will most likely bite my head off, but he needs to know I'm okay with this. I told him I would accept the results, whatever they were. With the good comes the bad, but it's the bad that makes you appreciate and cherish the good.

"I come in peace." Lifting his head, I see the bitter sadness behind his eyes. I stop a few steps away, unsure if he wants me to leave. "May I sit?"

He runs a hand through his snarled hair, so many emotions plaguing him. "You never have to ask permission to be near me."

I wring my hands behind my back. "I know, but you left in a huff. And I'm not sure if you're still huffy." I'm trying to lighten the mood. I can't stand to see him in pain, in pain because of me. I almost holler in delight when he shuffles over to make room.

I don't know how to start a conversation like this one. There is no easy way. Everything has changed, and I don't know what happens now.

"There has to be something more," he says, breaking the silence. I can't help but compare our pleas.

"I went into this knowing the risks. It was never a sure thing."

"How can you be so calm?" he spits, angered.

"I'm pretty sure I asked you the same question."

"That's different," he stubbornly rebukes.

"Why?"

"This wasn't supposed to happen," he declares, shaking his head, his eyes peeled to the ground. "You were supposed to live and…"

His pause has me cocking a brow. "And then what?"

When he exhales and tips his head back, peering into the heavens as if asking for strength, I'm suddenly hit with a menacing weight.

"Tell me," I press.

He shoots up, pacing in front of me, unable to stand still. "And then I was able to go," he confesses with regret.

"*What?*" My gasp leaves me panting for breath. "Go where?" I clench at the seat beneath me.

It takes me a second to realize go means go away for good. So he was planning on leaving all along? But I'm still missing something.

Scanning through every single thing I can remember, I suddenly get slammed with one mystery yet to be solved. I forgot its significance until now. "What's September first?"

When he comes to a halt, I know I've struck a nerve. "Teddy told you?" he asks, jaw clenched.

"No, but you're about to."

"Just leave it. I think we've had enough heartache for the day."

"Tell me." Rising, I grip his bicep, pleading he talk to me.

"No." His tenacious jaw sets.

"No? Are you serious right now?" Now it's my turn to wear

a shade of red. "I thought we were past this. No more secrets, remember? Roman, tell me!"

Finally, he surrenders.

"After your trials…" My feet are cemented to the ground. "Once I knew you were okay…" He's searching for the right words. But I have a feeling there aren't any. "I would go to a small lodge in Niagara my family rented over the summer before Scarlett got sick." His voice is wistful. "So many happy memories are associated with that place. It seems fitting it's one of the first memories I have because it would also be my last. Well, second last."

I don't think I'm breathing.

"The last memory I have will be of you, Lola. The best memory I could ever leave this earth with."

"W-what are you t-talking about?" I swallow, afraid I'm going to faint.

"I won't wait around for this illness to cripple me. When I go, I want it to be on my terms. Teddy knows what to do."

Time stands still.

"Please d-don't tell me you're doing w-what I think you a-are.'" His silence speaks volumes. "Roman, *no*." Tears flash before my eyes. This can't be real. "Why didn't you tell me?"

He sighs, his heavy breath warming my neck. "Because you were the only thing that could change my mind."

"Is that so bad?"

"Yes," he confesses with regret. "I don't want to live this way because I will only grow weaker. I don't want you to remember me that way."

Even though I can relate to his reasoning, I'm still infuriated. "But you made me do the trials."

"Because there's hope for you. There's none for me." Even though that rationale is now obsolete, it made perfect sense at the time.

"There's always hope. You taught me that." I sniff back my tears.

We're now both stuck at a crossroads. What do we do?

"What you're proposing, you're committing suicide." The words feel like acid slipping from my lips.

There is no question of his utter affliction over this entire situation, but his mind is made up. "How is it any different to putting a beloved family pet to sleep? We're showing them compassion; it's the humane thing to do. When there is nothing further one can do, then why prolong it?"

He's so matter-of-fact, it hurts. Surely, things have now changed.

"Then I want to have the same option."

"*What?* No." He recoils, appearing aghast that I would even suggest such a thing.

"Why not? We're both faced with the same predicament now. Why do you get the option, and I don't? Everything you've just told me relates to me too."

His lip curls in pure torment. "And I hate that it does. But this isn't Romeo and Juliet. Once you're gone, you're gone. No one will write a sonnet about us."

I blink, stunned. "You don't think I know that?" I question, angered he thinks so little of me. "I'm not a child." I won't back down. Once upon a time, this may have been a way out for him, but now, it seems like an easy way out—period.

"No, Lola. The answer is no. It will *always* be no. I won't have a part in ending your life," he stubbornly states, jaw clenched.

"But you expect me to sit back and watch you die? Is that it? You get an escape route, while I have to wither away and die! How is that fair?" My calm approach is long gone, and the anger Roman wanted to see from me rears its ugly head.

A surge pulsates through me, and I shove at his chest with all my might. He stumbles backward, surprised by my hostility. This isn't his fault. The fact he wants to be the decider of his fate isn't his fault either. I can relate to his decision. I respect his strength.

But I'm blinded by fury because of how messed up everything is. It wasn't bad enough that one of our lives was coming to a premature end, but now both—what a cruel, sadistic fate we both face. That thought is the fire behind my rage, and I lash out at the only person who understands my pain.

I shove at him again and again, hating that each blow ebbs away at my agony. He accepts the violence, almost as punishment for everything that has transpired between us. My arms grow lax, but I continue fighting, because once I stop, I'll be sure to break down and cry.

"How i-is this f-fair?" I scream, thrashing wildly, my tiny fists not even making a dent.

"None of this is fair!" he exclaims, finally having enough and snaring my wrists.

I try to break free, but it's futile. He's too strong, and I've run out of fight.

He wraps his arms around me, scooping me into his trembling embrace. I want to escape, but he holds on tight. I need time to think.

"Will you change your mind?" I lean my cheek against his chest. The strong thrumming of his heart is a betrayal because it's failing him every single day.

His silence is all the answer I need.

Never thinking I'd ever say these words aloud, I whisper, "Please let me go."

"Lola…"

"No, I need time." He begrudgingly loosens his hold, and I slip free, but I've never felt more trapped.

"Time for what?" he poses, nothing but heartbreak surrounding him.

"Time to think. You throw me this curveball and expect me to accept it. I will not. I especially won't when you won't even negotiate your decision."

He tips his head upward and pushes out an exasperated

breath. "This was never up for negotiation. This is why I didn't tell you. This is *my* life."

I step back, hearing all I needed to hear. "I thought I was part of your life?"

He averts his gaze, as I've obviously struck a nerve.

"I've run out of goodbyes," I declare, holding in my sadness. "You want to leave me, and all I can think about is spending every last minute, every last second I have left holding your hand. But I guess that's the difference between us. I want to fight, even with the odds against us. And you, all you want to do is say goodbye, time and time again."

A single tear slips past the floodgates, but I brush it away. "I'll talk to you later."

"Lola…" He charges forward, but I thrust out my hand.

"No, don't. Please, just give me space."

It's apparent he would rather rip off his own arms, but he nods. "Let me give you money for a cab." He digs into his back pocket, but I shake my head.

"No, I'll walk. The fresh air will do me good." I can see it's taking every ounce of willpower not to protest.

I'm not trying to be difficult. I just need time to get my head around something which makes no sense. He's going away September first so Teddy can inject him with a lethal dose of something to end his battle for good. I never was opposed to euthanasia. How could I be? In some cases, it would have been the humane thing to do. But when we're talking about the man

I love, it's not humane. It's the complete opposite.

Taking one last look at the man who was my shelter, I wonder what happens when he's gone.

FIFTEEN

I thought my head would clear after walking the streets of Manhattan, but it hasn't. There is no way to process all this without wanting to scream, cry, and fight. My results have been furthest away from my thoughts because I've experienced it before. Same prognosis, different time. Not much has changed.

But the bombshell Roman dropped; I don't even know where to start.

I understand his decision, and I respect it. It takes guts to end your life. But it takes the heart of a true champion to live it. Our future is far from ideal, but I'm willing to tackle it head-on.

Dr. Carter said I have one month—four weeks, thirty days—to live. Time is ticking away, and it's time I don't want to waste fighting. But I can't force Roman to live. He may have done so with me, but deep down, I wanted him to. I needed someone to fight for me when I was too scared to.

When June told me about Scarlett, before I knew who she was, I remember thinking how ironic her dying of a hole in the heart because I'm sure June felt that every single day when thinking about her. But now, that's exactly how I feel.

If my day wasn't filled with enough drama, my dad called and said they returned from Europe early. He wanted me to come over for dinner. I could sense the seriousness to his tone, and although I wasn't in any frame of mind, I agreed.

The moment the door opens, I know my father sees it. "Are you all right?" he asks, clearly concerned.

"I'm fine. Just a little dizzy. I didn't sleep well." I quash down my sickness, playing it down, as I don't want to worry him. "Why are you back early?"

My father welcomes me into their palace, while I attempt to block out the bad juju this place has. I attempt to walk, but my legs give out on me, and I go down.

"Lola!" Thankfully, my dad catches me before I hit the hard floor. "You need to lie down."

"I'm fine," I reiterate, but my trembling body says otherwise.

He ignores me and leads me into the living room. It takes five minutes for the room to stop spinning.

"Stop worrying." I smooth out the crinkles between his furrowed brows.

"Impossible." He places a hand to my forehead. "You're

running a fever." He goes to stand, but I snare his wrist.

"I'm okay. I saw Dr. Carter today."

Dad's ears prick. "Dr. Carter? Why are you seeing him?"

"I'm undergoing a new trial," I reply, not having the heart to tell him the truth until after dinner.

"You are?" My father looks at me like he's only just seen me for the first time. "I didn't know, Lola. I'm sorry."

"It's fine. Don't worry about it." I decide to leave out the fact that until I met Roman, I didn't even know I wanted to live.

He has never been one for words, but I just assumed it was because my mom did all the talking. But now that he's not shrouded by her overbearing shadow, it's like I too have just seen him for the first time. "I let you down. I am so sorry for everything. Your mother—"

"Let's not ruin a nice conversation," I butt in, not wanting to hear any excuses for her.

He pulls in his lips, running a hand through his salt and pepper hair. "She loves you. There are things about her…"

I scoff, leaning backward and folding my arms in defiance. My nausea has thankfully passed, replaced with indifference. "It's fine. You don't have to make excuses for me. She is what she is." I refrain from saying what she is—a gigantic, judgmental bitch.

"I think your mother would like to know about these developments."

"I doubt it." My refusal hurts. I can see it, and I instantly feel guilty.

Thoughts of June and Roman's strained relationship play over in my mind. If Roman could forgive his mother, then maybe I should too.

"I'm going to use the bathroom." He reads my need for silence and nods.

Once I'm steady enough to stand, I take a detour to my old room. The bright pink ballerina music box catches my eye. I remember when my mother gave it to me. I was eleven. She wanted to buy me some fancy riches, but all I wanted was that damn music box. The wind-up ballerina inside, snuggled among the pink silk, was the most beautiful thing I'd ever seen. I would sit for hours watching her dance, wishing I could mimic her graceful movements because I had two left feet.

My mom used to brush my hair while I watched the ballerina spin to Tchaikovsky's *Swan Lake*. I reach for the box with trembling hands. It feels so small, but I suppose my hands have grown since the last time I picked it up. Holding it up to eye level, I close one eye, wishing I viewed the world how I once did. Turning it upside down, I wind the small copper handle and run my finger across the ballerina mid-pirouette.

The twirling ballerina is my pendulum, and I'm completely under her spell. If I only knew then what I know now, I would trade places with her in a heartbeat.

"You used to love that music box." I slam the lid shut, almost severing two fingers in the process.

"I used to love a lot of things," I curtly reply, replacing the box on the dresser. Spinning, I cross my arms when I see my mother standing in the doorway. What does she want?

Taking a moment to observe her, I notice something different about her. She looks less...evil. Her white pantsuit might be the reason for her saintly look.

"Your father told me you went to see Dr. Carter. You're doing another trial?" She appears genuinely interested.

I roll my eyes. It's too late for the concerned motherly act. "Yes, I was. But it didn't work. I should be out of your hair in about a month's time."

I'm expecting some sort of reaction like a hip, hip hooray. But for the first time in a long time, I see guilt. It unnerves me to see a human emotion pass across her usual stoic face.

"Lola, may we speak?"

"Speak about what, exactly?"

She clears her throat, evidently uncomfortable with whatever she wishes to say. "I want to clear the air between us.'"

"Excuse me?" I thump my fist to my chest, hoping to dislodge the lump in my throat. When I see that she is serious, I can't help the sarcastic snicker from slipping from my lips. "I'm not sure if you heard me correctly, but I said I have one month to live."

She recoils, wounded that I would imply it would take far longer than that to do what she proposes.

She enters the room, and I instinctively take two steps back.

"You have every right to be angry with me."

"Angry? That's being lenient."

"I don't know the exact moment things fell apart between us." She advances forward, each step leaving me more and more curious to what she wants.

"How about the time you disowned me as your daughter? Or the fact you're ashamed to have an imperfect child?" I throw options her way. Surely, one will fit the profile.

She lowers her eyes, and I feel guilty for snapping. I don't like it. I'm so used to bickering with my mom that I don't know how to handle this side of her—this human side of her.

She sits at the foot of my bed, pensive. "I was never ashamed of you."

"You could have fooled me," I declare, folding my arms across my chest.

"There are so many things I would have done differently. I'm…I'm sorry. I've been an awful mother to you."

My mouth pops open. I have never been more stunned than I am right now. When I regain my composure, I ask, "Why are you telling me this? It's only come about four years too late."

"I know." Who is this person sitting before me? She wears my mother's face, but there is no way this is her.

Lifting her eyes, I gasp when I see they are wet. Does she have something in them because no way are they wet with tears.

"What is the matter with you? Are you dying?" I ask, as that's the only explanation to why she's behaving this way.

She closes her eyes for a second. "If it means you'd live, then I would, happily."

I am actually speechless. I need to sit. Slumping onto the satin settee, I attempt to decipher what the hell is going on.

"You think I'm ashamed of you." I have no choice but to listen to her, as I'm bewitched. "The truth is...I'm ashamed of myself. I failed you."

Something has happened for her to behave this way, and the only thing is that she's been given a second chance.

"What happened?"

She tugs at the pearls around her neck, a sure sign I'm right. I've never seen Camille Van Allen squirm, not until now. "A few days ago, I found a lump...in my breast."

I blink. That was not what I was expecting.

"I thought nothing of it, but I decided to get it checked out. That's why we cut our trip short."

I wait with bated breath.

"I got the results today."

"And?"

She lowers her gaze, her lower lip trembling. "It's all clear. I'm fine."

A winded breath escapes me. I don't understand. "Why do you say that like it's a bad thing?"

She finally meets my confused stare. "Because the entire time, all I was thinking was, how does Lola do this? How has she done this her entire life? I was so scared, but I couldn't remember the last time I saw you scared. You have been burdened for four years, and not once have I heard you say 'why me?'

"That's all I could think when I was sitting there today, waiting for my life to change. I thought about what a strong, brave girl you are, and what a horrible, awful mother I've been to you."

Words escape me. I sit unmoving.

"I was so preoccupied in busying myself because the moment I stopped, all I could think about is how I failed you. I couldn't help you. That's why I wanted to help so many others. What kind of a mother can't help her child? I didn't know what to do. I was so afraid of saying the wrong thing, so I said nothing at all.

"I come from a family that doesn't show emotion. But then I met your father, and he changed that. He showed me it was okay to cry and laugh and love. And we had that. But then you got sick. I didn't know how to act. My only child was sick, and I couldn't do a damn thing to make her better. All the money in the world made no difference. At the end of the day, you were dying, and I had to accept that."

She swallows, while I'm barely breathing.

"I didn't know how to act around you anymore, and I blamed you for that. I am so ashamed of myself. We grew further and further apart, and that was entirely my fault. It hurt to be around you, and I distanced myself because I was—*I am*—a coward."

A tear slides down my cheek, her confession stabbing at my heart.

"This isn't an excuse; this is an explanation, one that has come too late. But today, sitting there in that doctor's office, I came to realize what a truly remarkable woman you are. I have never met anyone more courageous than you, and I am so proud to call you my daughter."

I jump up, unable to sit a moment longer. "I needed you, Mom. But you made me feel like I was never good enough."

She too stands, but I'm thankful she doesn't try to reach out. "I know. I can never apologize enough for letting you down. I don't expect you to forgive me, and regardless of what the results were today with Dr. Carter, I would have told you. I'm not telling you this to unburden my guilt. I'm telling you this because I want you to know that none of this was ever your fault."

A staggered sob breaks free. It's the only thing I've ever wanted to hear. That and…

She places a hand over her mouth, tears I've not seen before slipping free. "I love you, Lola. And I'm so sorry for everything. Please forgive me."

Wrapping my arms around myself, I'm unable to hold back the years of rejection and sadness I've kept bottled away. This does not excuse her behavior, but it's a start. If death has taught me anything, it's that life is too short to hold grudges.

She waits patiently, sniffing back her sorrow. Her entire life, she's been so afraid to be vulnerable, but at this moment, she's never looked stronger. I don't fully understand her reasoning, but the prospect of death makes you do weird things—like voluntary euthanasia.

I could walk from this room and tell her the apology has come too late. But what would that achieve? It takes more effort to hate her than it does to accept that she made a mistake. A huge mistake, but one she seems truly sorry for.

Wiping away my tears, I take a steadying breath. She looks on the verge of breaking down. "I'm glad you're okay."

She blinks twice, not expecting that response. It's the best I can muster. I'm not ready to play happy family just yet, but I'm willing to try.

"Thank you." She smiles, but it's bittersweet. I'm pleased at least one of us received good news today.

So what happens now? It seems too clichéd to give her a hug and pretend all is forgiven. But on the flipside, I don't want her to think I haven't appreciated her honesty, so coming to a compromise, I raise my fist.

She peers down at it, moving her lips from side to side.

Unable to help myself, I playfully mock, "You can do it!"

A lopsided smirk plays at her lips.

She doesn't leave me hanging and softly bumps her fist against mine, shaking her head at my absurdity. A universal fist bump is the first step toward our healing. Who would have thought?

She looks like a weight has been lifted from her shoulders, and in a way, I know how she feels. "I'm going to get ready for dinner. Your father has gone a little overboard. I didn't have the heart to tell him I went to Magnolia Bakery on the way home."

Camille Van Allen is making jokes? Today is truly a strange day.

I'm thankful she doesn't linger, and when she closes the door behind her, I stand in the middle of the room, digesting everything that just happened.

The pink music box catches my eye. Maybe I'm finally free to dance like the ballerina after all.

I can't sleep.

I told Dad about the trials, and he did something I never thought he'd do. He put down his silverware at the dinner table, and he cried. Seeing your father, who you always saw as big, strong, and invincible, sob like a baby, is disconcerting, but it was nice knowing he cared.

My mom shed a tear, but I think she's keeping them locked away, knowing many more are to come.

After stuffing myself fuller than a piñata at a ten-year-old's birthday party, I thanked my parents for dinner and went home. I thought I'd fall into an exhausted heap, considering the events of today, but I didn't. I lie awake, staring up at my ceiling, wondering what happens now.

Undergoing the remainder of the trials seems pointless; as Dr. Carter said, it's just prolonging the inevitable. This decision will result in me crossing the finish line sooner rather than later, but it's what I want.

What I also want is Roman.

I hate the way we left things. I needed time to clear my head, and although it's not any clearer than it was, I do know I don't want to spend my remaining time without him. I don't agree with his decision, but if it's what he wants, then I will try to support him.

Turning onto my back, I huff, annoyed that I'm still wide-awake at three a.m. The harder I try to fall asleep, the more awake I seem to be.

Kicking off the blankets, I give up on the notion of counting sheep and decide to finish writing in the journal Tamara gave me. The entries are plagued with uncertainty, but this entry will be a new chapter.

Just as I press pen to paper, my cell chimes. I pause, peering from left to right, wondering if I'm hearing things. The illuminated screen on my nightstand reveals my hearing isn't failing me just yet. Reaching for my phone, my heart jumps into my throat when I see what the simple message says.

Sunflower.

This word has taken on a whole different meaning. Our SOS.

Jumping from my bed, I skid along the tiles and almost collide with the front door as I open it. However, I do collide into something warm, hard, and delicious smelling when I step out into the hallway.

He catches me, just as I knew he would.

Roman scoops me into his arms and holds me with all his might. "I'm so sorry. I don't know what I was thinking. I'm such a fucking asshole. Please forgive me," he mumbles against my temple.

I close my eyes and bask in his feel, his scent, his warmth. I'm going to miss this so much. "There's nothing to forgive. It's all right. You're here, and that's all that matters."

We stand hugging in the hallway with no sign of letting go. However, when I realize I'm standing in my pajamas in the corridor, I gently pull out from his arms. The dim lights echo his broken stance, and I never want to see that look again.

"Come inside." I'm thankful when he nods.

The moment I close the door, Roman presses his chest to my back and pulls me into his arms once more. There is a lingering urgency to our connection, and I know he feels it too.

"They were supposed to work. This is not how your story ends," he says, tightening his hold around my waist.

"Everyone's story is different."

"I gave you false hope." His guilt is palpable, but he has

nothing to be guilty for.

"Stop it," I press. "Any hope is better than none."

"This is my fault." A tide of his sweetened breath warms the length of my neck. "I was so certain it would work."

"It's nobody's fault. I was so determined to live, and I did. This short amount of time was the best time of my life. I've lived a full life because you love me." My voice wavers, my heart swelling with the immeasurable love I feel for this man.

He nuzzles his nose into my hair, inhaling. "This entire time, our story was supposed to be…you lived, and I died. But alas, plot twist. The writer of our story is one messed up, sadistic bitch."

I can't help but laugh weakly because he's right.

"We're both fighting harder for the other person's life," I say, not fully understanding this irrevocable bond we share.

He's silent, his heavy breathing the only sound betraying his thoughts. "When it comes to accepting your own death…I think we make peace that it's our time. But when faced with the death of someone you love…you'll fight *for* them, *with* them until their last dying breath," he openly confesses.

I gasp because it's exactly how I feel. I just couldn't find the right words.

Roman is forever my protector, but in this circumstance, he has to let go. "You can save people's lives…but you can't save them from life." And that's the god's honest truth.

"You could always do more trials." His pleas are beginning

to fizzle.

"What's the point? You're still dead, and I don't want to live in a world where you don't exist."

"Well, neither do I."

What a crossroad to be stuck at.

"So what do we do now?" And that's the million-dollar question. That's the question I've been asking myself all day.

"Now," he whispers, a mewl slipping from me when he lowers his lips and kisses over my thrumming pulse. "We forget about today and focus on tomorrow."

"I like the sound of that." I barely get the words out as he bites and licks over my sensitive flesh.

It doesn't take long before I'm lax against him, allowing him full rein of my body. His hands and lips are everywhere, taking my breath away with their exigency to engulf me whole. He spins me around, and our lips smash together, desperate to never break apart.

He fists my hair, his ravenous rumbles stirring a burn within my soul. We can no longer wait, as each second is truly precious. He lifts me, and I wrap my legs around his waist, never severing our lips dancing in perfect harmony.

My back hits the sofa and Roman's weight falls on top of me soon after. We're a blur of frenzied hands and hungry tongues as we tug at one another's clothing, the desperation leaving me gasping for breath.

The moment I'm naked beneath him, he cherishes every

inch of my flesh. Losing myself in him, I never want to be found. He milks every last tremor of pleasure from me before he finally comes up for air.

I watch with lust-clouded vision as he reaches over his head and tears off his T-shirt. My eyes zero in on the center of his chest. The soft lighting showcases the scar, bringing home the fact that our time together comes with an expiration date.

I've been brave, but in the partial darkness, I let down my walls. "I'm scared," I whisper, raising my hand and placing a palm to his hammering heart.

"I am too," he confesses. "But everything worth doing starts with being scared."

"It's not the beginning I'm afraid of," I acknowledge, turning my cheek, ashamed.

"Don't be afraid. I'll never stop holding your hand." The importance of his promise comes to a climax when he places his hand over mine. "I'll never give up on you."

And I know he means it.

A single tear falls down my cheek before words will no longer suffice. I reach for his neck, drawing his face back to mine. He presses our foreheads together, staring deeply into my eyes. That single look amounts to a thousand words. I close the distance between us and kiss him like there is no tomorrow.

His pants hit the floor minutes later, and before long, we're moving, breathing, living as one. I will never tire of this feeling. Nothing can ever surmount this.

"I...love you," I gasp, eyes slipping to half-mast in pure ecstasy.

My words inspire him to move faster and harder, linking us so not even a wisp of air can pass between us. "I love you, too."

"Never let me go." With trembling fingers, I trace every curve of his chiseled face, wishing to memorize every single part of him. With an unhurried tempo, he moves, relishing in the feel of us becoming one.

His head falls to my shoulder. He hums, smelling, licking, teasing my slicked flesh. "I promise." He accents his comment with a buck of his hips. I whimper, clutching his sweaty shoulders.

And he stays true to his word. Well, for tonight anyway.

SIXTEEN

Stretching lazily, I partially open one eye.

The sleeping beauty beside me appears contented, a faint smile planted on his pink lips. Today is no clearer than yesterday, but it's okay. With Roman by my side, we can work through anything.

I can't help myself and prop up on an elbow, peering down at the man who has changed my life forever. I never thought I would ever feel this way for another human being, but just meeting Roman has shown me that anything is possible.

Skimming my finger along his forehead, I dip down the slope of his nose, tracing the outline of those sinful lips. I don't waste a minute and lower my mouth to his. A sleepy moan rumbles from his chest.

"Is this my wake-up call? If it is, I think I'm still fast asleep and will be for quite some time. You better try harder." I giggle around his mouth, happy to comply.

I deepen the kiss, my hair falling around us to cloak us from the real world. Our mouths move at a languid pace. We're in no real hurry to leave this room anytime soon. But who says we have to?

I'm still not confident enough to call the shots, but I roll on top of him, dominating him like he would usually dominate me. The move seems to please him, as he groans deeply, the low sound hitting where it hurts.

We're still very naked, and it doesn't take long for something delicious to stir below.

"I'm insatiable when it comes to you," he huskily confesses, biting his bottom lip.

The sight has me mewling.

Going with instinct, I sit upright, straddling Roman's waist. The connection has us both groaning. He raises his hand and runs it down the side of my neck before dipping down and cupping my breasts. I arch my neck backward, losing myself in a feeling comparable to heaven.

However, heaven is about to turn into hell.

"Lola, I hope you don't mind, but we let ourselves in with the spare key—oh, my god!"

I turn over my shoulder so quickly, I'm certain I've pulled a muscle in my neck. But that doesn't compare to the muscle my mother has pulled in her face when her mouth falls open and her eyes bulge from her head. She looks seconds away from passing out.

"I...oh...my...I'm...god...naked...so naked...so sorry!" She fumbles over her words, clutching on to the doorframe, steadying her wavering form.

She has just caught her naked daughter, lying on top of her very naked boyfriend, and I suddenly think it's the funniest thing in the world.

A giggle slips past me as I cross my arms over my chest, while Roman sinks into the sofa, hoping it swallows him whole. "Come back in five minutes."

She nods but doesn't move a muscle. I think she's gone into shock.

"Mom, a little privacy, please."

Roman places his forearm over his eyes, shaking his head in horror. I'm still chuckling.

"Oh god, yes, of course. I'm so sorry." She finally snaps to and slams the front door shut.

When the coast is clear, I snort with laughter, unable to stop.

"This isn't funny," Roman admonishes, only making the situation worse. "I didn't want to meet your mom butt naked."

He gently pushes me off him, jumping from the sofa, on the hunt for his clothes.

I roll onto my side, gasping for breath. "And what a butt it is."

He ignores my outburst, slipping into his jeans and T-shirt. "She's going to kill me, isn't she?"

"No," I reply, catching my breath.

"No?" he questions, pausing midway through combing his fingers through his bed hair.

Jumping from the sofa, I search for some clothes. "Let's do this."

This is a rite of passage as such, as I've never introduced my parents to a boyfriend before. Before I got sick, I dated a few guys, but never anyone serious, never anyone I wanted my parents to meet.

I walk to the front door with Roman dragging his feet every step of the way. "Are you sure I'll leave this house with all parts intact?"

I stifle a laugh behind my hand.

The moment I open the door, my mother pales, while my father smiles, none the wiser. She clearly didn't let on what she walked into. "Hello. Good morning. Hi."

I've never seen my mom bothered. I grin, highly amused. "Good morning. Come in." They do.

Roman clears his throat. "Good morning, Ms. Van Allen. Mr. Van Allen. I'm Roman Archibald, Lola's…"

"He's my boyfriend." I fill in the blanks. I wanted to introduce Roman to my parents another way. But timing doesn't seem to be on my side in all aspects of my life.

My mother gasps, while my father sizes up Roman. He seems happy with what he sees.

"Roman is a doctor," I explain, leaving out the particulars of how we met. They can work out the minor details.

The tension can be cut with a knife until my father says, "Hello, Dr. Archibald."

"Roman is fine," he corrects with a wave.

"Please, call me Dermott then. Are you hungry?" He holds up the bags and coffee tray he's carrying. "We brought breakfast."

"Yes. Thank you."

My mother is still speechless but follows us to the table.

"Up to anything special today?" my dad asks, stirring his coffee.

Roman reaches for a bagel, then places it on my napkin. I look over at him, smiling. "I'm not sure." We probably should discuss what exactly we plan to do.

"There's a color vibe run this weekend, I believe? That sounds like fun." My father must assume Roman works out. His burly build does imply that. "You watched it from your window last year, didn't you, Lola?"

Just as I'm about to change the subject, as I know Roman isn't in any shape to be participating in any runs, he says, "Yes, that's correct. And it is fun. I usually participate every year. But I won't be this year."

Both my mother and father give him their full attention.

He clears his throat. "I actually have a congenital heart defect." My father stops chewing, and my mother's eyes widen for the second time today. "It has gotten progressively worse. My twin sister passed from it many years ago." I instinctively reach out and hold his hand.

My father lowers his coffee. "My condolences to you and your family."

"Thank you. It was a long time ago." Regardless, the pain is still raw.

Roman doesn't need to go into detail. My parents know that the illness will eventually claim his life, too. What they don't know is that he's chosen to beat it the only way he knows how.

"It's okay. Each day is a miracle, one I don't take for granted." I smile at his courage, proud to be his. "I want you to know that I love Lola. Very much," he adds, looking over with nothing but devotion. "I would never hurt her, and I will do everything to protect her."

I cast my eyes downward, understanding the double-edged sword.

"I have a feeling you are the reason Lola participated in the trials," my mother says.

But Roman rebukes her assumption. "No, Ms. Van Allen, *Lola* is the reason because she's a fighter. I may have given her a little push"—he smiles, as that's putting it mildly—"but she's the strongest, most determined person I know. I wish I had her strength."

My father smiles proudly at me. "She gets that from her mother." Once upon a time, that would have utterly offended me, but now, it doesn't seem so bad.

"You're right. You both are," she says with a smile, while my father laughs heartily.

I can't hide my shock. Is she making yet another joke?

We continue eating in silence, everyone absorbing what was shared.

I hate that Roman can no longer participate in events he obviously enjoyed. "Maybe we could check it out?" I suggest, breaking the silence. "There is a shorter leg we can compete in. One mile instead of five."

Roman chews, pensive, but nods. "I'm sure we can manage that." And he's right. With Roman by my side, I can manage anything.

We stopped by Roman's hotel so he could take a shower and grab a change of clothes. It seems silly, him staying in a hotel, but I still don't know what his plans are. September first is not that far away, and if what Dr. Carter said is true, I'll be gone in four, maybe eight weeks if I'm lucky.

The thought of being here without Roman is almost too much to bear. I don't think I can stand by and watch him take his own life. I know he'd never expect me to, but if he still decides to go ahead with it, then I would hold his hand, just as he's holding mine.

Hundreds of thousands of budding competitors crowd the starting line in Brooklyn. Once we arrive at the registration table, I see someone I never thought I'd see again.

"Dr. Archibald?" Erin says. Her surprise is apparent

"Hello, Erin. How have you been?"

She rounds the table and gives him a big hug. "I've been great. What are you doing here?"

"I was hoping we could register."

Erin looks over at me and does a double take when she obviously remembers who I am. "Oh my god. Hi, Lola, right?"

I can't help but smile at her energy. "Yes, that's right. Hi, Erin. It's nice to see you again."

"You too." She looks between us, grinning. She knows something has changed since the last time she saw us together.

"You're cutting it close," she teases, pulling the pencil out from behind her ear. She no longer wears the head scarf I saw her with. She wears her spiky short hair, proudly. "But for you, I can make an exception."

"Dr. Archibald? Are you lost?" teases a middle-aged man as he approaches. He's also in running gear.

Roman laughs, extending his hand. "Hello, Gus. I didn't think they allowed the elderly to compete." Gus explodes into fits of laughter. "It's nice to see you."

"You too. Where have you been hiding?"

"Nowhere, just busy with work."

It's apparent they are good friends. It saddens me that regardless of how well-liked Roman is, he will leave this world alone.

"This is my girlfriend, Lola Van Allen."

I'll never tire of hearing him refer to me that way. I shake Gus's hand; he seems surprised.

"Wow, I'm sorry for staring," he says, still shaking my hand. "But I've known Roman for over ten years, and not once have I ever met any of his girlfriends."

"That's because there was no one to introduce." He wraps his arm around me, pulling me to his side.

I smile proudly, feeling a blush tint my cheeks.

Gus appears beyond elated for Roman, as does Erin. She looks so well. Better than when I saw her last. I'm not resentful that her trials were a success and mine weren't. I'm happy because she's living proof of the lives Roman has touched.

"Come over here, and I'll register you both," Gus says to Roman, gesturing with his head to a table to the left.

"I'll be back in a moment." He kisses my forehead.

I step off to the side, but Erin asks a girl to take over. It's clear she wants to chat.

"I know this is completely out of line," she starts off with. "But I'm so happy Roman has found someone. He has helped the lives of so many people, giving them hope. It only seems fair he's happy, too."

"Thanks, that means a lot to me." Roman has touched so many people. Erin is just one of thousands, I'm sure. I want her to know why Roman introduced us in the first place. "I hope you don't mind, but Roman told me he helped you."

Her smile turns nostalgic. "No, not at all. I'm proud."

"The reason he told me was because…" I pick at my burgundy nail polish, hoping to pay tribute to the next sentence as best I can. "Because I actually have a brain tumor. The same type you had."

Her eyes fill with tears. "Oh, I'm so sorry."

I wave her off, thankful for her compassion. "It's okay, really. I'm so happy things worked out for you."

She lowers her eyes, and I see it. Guilt. The same feeling I felt when given a second chance. "Oh, Lola…" She understands my trial ended differently than hers. "I truly am so sorry."

"Thanks. I didn't tell you to make you feel guilty, but because you're a miracle. You're living proof of Roman's determination and commitment to saving the world." I can't keep the tears away because soon, she will be a rare species.

"I think that every day," she whispers, her lower lip trembling. "If it weren't for Dr. Archibald, I would hate to think where I'd be. I owe him my life."

A lot of people do, I silently reply.

Roman returns, looking at us carefully. We both wipe away our tears.

"Ready to get your ass whipped?" I tease, standing on tippy

toes and wrapping my arms around his neck. Erin smiles before going back to work behind the table.

"I didn't realize this was a race." He smirks, a glimmer in his beautiful blue eyes.

"Let's make things interesting," I reply. "For twenty-four hours, the loser has to do everything the winner says." I am suddenly determined to lose.

Roman hums, the sound resonating all the way to my center. "You know I don't like to lose."

"Well, neither do I," I reply, snaring my bottom lip when a lopsided smirk tugs at his mouth.

"Deal," he finally says. I don't have a chance to respond because he swoops forward and kisses me fiercely.

I clutch at the soft strands of hair curling at the nape of his neck, uncaring that we're making out in front of thousands of people. This is a memory I will never forget.

"Just a taste of what you're in for when I win."

I see stars and smirk. "The utter torture," I taunt. "Bye, Erin." I wave, and she peers up, nodding sentimentally.

Roman appears carefree and relaxed. He shakes out his legs and arms, a true athlete's warmup. I know I have no chance of keeping up with him, but I also know he'll carry me every step of the way.

I turn to him, appreciating every second we're together. "I love you."

His chest inflates proudly. "I love you, too." He leans over, kissing me softly.

The gun suddenly sounds, alerting us that the race has started. But it can't compare to the racing of my heart. Roman breaks our kiss, laughing when I pout. He reaches for my hand, and we commence a slow jog, attempting to keep up with the flow of bodies. Everyone seems to work in unison without pushing or shoving because that's not what this race is about.

The sun is shining down brightly, warming my tired muscles and giving me the strength to continue. We're running at a very slow pace, but it's perfect for Roman and me. I take in the sights of Brooklyn, a truly different world from Manhattan.

I'm enjoying the scenery, unbelieving that I'm here, participating in an event I never thought I would be able to. I've experienced so many firsts with Roman, and each one will forever be etched in my mind.

It also appears Roman has experienced a first with me too.

"So..." I breathlessly pose. "I'm the first girlfriend to be seen in public with you. I'm honored." Roman laughs, his arms swinging as he effortlessly jogs beside me. "So how many non-girlfriends have you had?"

"Too many to count," he mocks, laughing when I turn to glare at him.

"Forget I said anything." I gulp, realizing this is a can of worms I don't wish to open, now or ever.

I pick up the pace, but Roman keeps up with ease. "None of them matter," he says with honesty. "You're the only woman who has ever made me want to live."

I crane my neck to look at him, wondering if he's implying what I think he is. Has he changed his mind?

"And what happens after I go?"

"I go with you," he evenly replies.

"W-what?" I stutter, coming to an abrupt stop. "You've changed your mind? Roman?" I grab his wrist, trapping him to the spot.

He appears saddened, but nods. "Yes. I still intend to go to Niagara, but not until after…" He leaves the sentence hanging, not needing to fill in the blanks.

This is progress. I wish he weren't going to Niagara at all. Although he says he doesn't have long, is there really an expiration date on his life? Could he go in two weeks, or is it more like two years?

"You said you don't have long. How long do you have?" This is the worst place to be asking him this, but when will there ever be a good time.

"Lola," he warns, but I press, squeezing his wrist.

"How long?"

"About six months," he confesses. He knows what I'm about to say before I even have a chance to open my mouth. "But there are no guarantees. I will grow weaker, and my body will fail me. I can't live the rest of my days reminiscing about what I once had, about who I once was. I won't be able to work, and the simplest of chores, which I take for granted now, will be impossible for me to do."

"But six months? So much can happen in that time. A new drug may be released tomorrow."

He shakes his head, incensed. "You don't get it. I have nothing left to live for."

I seal my lips, touched but angered all in the same breath. "Roman…"

But he steps forward, cupping his hands to my cheeks, searching my face. "I made this decision long before I met you. I've made my peace with it. I'm still here because of you, but once you're…" He closes his eyes, pained. "You're not here, then I won't be either. Please respect my wishes."

I want to protest, but how can I? If the tables were turned, would I do the same thing? I know the answer is yes.

A lump forms in my throat because this is really happening. I thought by some miracle he'd change his mind, but that was never an option. He has compromised and stayed true to his word of protecting me until the very end. I just wish I could do the same thing for him.

I can't run away from my fears, but I can run. And that's what I plan on doing. If I stay at a standstill a second longer, I'm sure to break down into tears. I nudge my head, implying let's finish what we started.

Roman reads my inner turmoil, but I don't give him a chance to address it. I take off in a sprint, needing some time to think. We jog in silence, my mind racing. I know I need to accept this, but I can't.

As my mind whips relentlessly, so do my feet. I pick up the pace, not even realizing it. The faster I run, the more confused I feel. I need to find a solution. There must be something I'm missing. A lot can happen in six months, and to think Roman has given up has me wanting to fight twice as hard.

I catalog every scenario, eliminating endless situations because I've gone over them already. As I push my legs harder, my heart beats strongly within my chest. The sound is a hypnotizing pendulum, flaunting my strength and weakness.

The first color station is up ahead, indicating we've managed half a mile. Turning over my shoulder, I see Roman is a few feet behind. His cheeks are a bright red, and it's clear he's struggling to breathe.

This is exactly what he's talking about. A year ago, I have no doubt he'd be close to the finish line. But this year, he'll be lucky to make it a mile.

I push harder and harder, determined to save him. But how? I need a miracle. I need a sign.

People flash past me, and I know I'm running on pure adrenaline, but I'm afraid once I stop, I'll have to face the truth. Roman is dying, and there's not a damn thing I can do about it.

An explosion of color detonates before me, a literal rainbow blazing before my eyes as I plunge past the first color station. Every single color imaginable coats my sweaty skin, transforming something plain into something magical.

My heart trounces inside my chest, uplifting my accomplishment because I thought I could never do it. But that's the problem; Nothing's wrong with my heart. It's my head that's the issue—the perfect oxymoron.

Peering down at my multicolored hands, I flip them over, desperate to uncover how these hands can help heal. There must be something I can do. I can't stand back and watch him take his own life. Until every possible scenario is exhausted, I won't give up. I can't. Roman has never given up on me, and I don't plan on giving up on him.

Thump.

Thump.

Thump.

I'm suddenly hit with a gravity so severe, I stagger backward, gasping for breath as I clutch at my chest. Through the kaleidoscopes of color, I have finally seen the light. I was looking in all the wrong places. The rainbow has led me to the simplest answer, one which has been staring me in the face all along.

Runners push past as I stand unmoving, bleeding colorful tears. I'm crying a rainbow, and it's simply beautiful. I found my pot of gold. I can't believe I didn't think of this sooner.

Turning my hands over and over again, for the first time in a long time, I have hope because…I know how I can save Roman.

I was declared the winner, and I was, just not in the way Roman thinks. We went back to his hotel to shower, after which Roman fell into a deep slumber.

His health is deteriorating. I can understand why he doesn't want to live this way. That fact is the reason I haven't slept a wink. I've researched well into the night, studying something I'm certain will save Roman.

I know without a doubt he'll fight me on this. He'll argue until he's red in the face, so I need to compile a strong, unbending case, then he'll have no other choice but to say yes.

I tell myself that as I'm looking over the billionth webpage on my phone.

There is no way he's going to agree to this. I can see this conversation going down as the worst in history. But I have to try.

Gently rising from the bed, I tiptoe through the room, not wanting to wake Roman. He's been out for the count for hours, and it doesn't look like he'll be waking anytime soon. I lock myself in the bathroom, staring at my cell.

Once I make this call, it'll be official. There'll be no turning back. Leaning against the door, I gaze at myself in the mirror. I recall every single memory that has led me here. My friends dying, me dying, it all can't be in vain.

Roman once said to me that if I died, what was the point to all this heartache? That sentence has resonated with me since I first heard it because I now know what all this means.

My fingers tremble as I scroll through my contact list. It's just after five a.m., but I can't wait. I'm afraid I'll chicken out if I do. I plan to leave a message, so I'm surprised when Dr. Carter answers the phone.

"Lola?" His croaky voice is a sure sign I've woken him. I instantly feel awful for disturbing him. "Is everything all right?"

"I'm so sorry, Dr. Carter. I didn't mean to wake you. I can call back…" I make a face, embarrassed I woke him.

"No, no, it's okay. I'm awake now. What can I do for you?" I hear a rustle and soft footsteps.

"I was wondering if I could come to see you today. I wanted to ask you something." I bite my lip, nervous he'll refuse.

"Of course. Come see me around midday."

I exhale in relief. "Thank you so much."

"Will Dr. Archibald be coming with you?"

Peering at my reflection, I tell myself this is the right thing to do. Roman has his entire life to be angry with me. "No, just me. If you wouldn't mind, can you not mention this to anyone?"

He's silent, most likely wondering why. "Of course. I'll see you this afternoon."

I hang up, one step closer to achieving what I know will work. Roman will hate me—of this I'm sure—but this is the only way.

I leave a letter telling Roman I will be back later, ready to claim my prize.

I know this most likely will be the last time I see Dr. Carter. After today, my life will change forever.

This waiting room with its flawless exterior only covers what's hiding beneath. These walls have seen immeasurable pain, but I'm hoping to be in the minority where things are sometimes just how they should be.

Wilma peers at me from over her marbled counter, focusing on my foot, which is bouncing uncontrollably. "Sorry," I mouth, lost in my own world.

She smiles. I've always liked her. She has been good to Georgia and me. The thought of my friend has me pulling back my shoulders. I know she would be proud of what I've decided.

"Lola." Dr. Carter opens his office door, smiling when he sees me.

I press the folder with the mountain of printouts to my chest as I stand. "Hi, Dr. Carter."

He gives me all the time I need as I limp to his door. I know today is just one of many to come.

Once I've crossed the threshold, I slump on the leather seat, taking a deep breath. This is it. The point of no return.

Dr. Carter reads my desperation and places formalities

aside. "What can I do for you?"

My heart begins to beat madly. Although I'm terrified, the sound is comforting. It encourages me to continue. Leaning forward, I pass him the folder. Everything I need to say is in there.

He accepts it, his confusion apparent. Nonetheless, he slips on his silver-framed glasses and opens what I hope to be Roman's future. Dr. Carter is an intelligent man, and it doesn't take him long to figure out why I'm here. The note I've written him is the first thing he reads.

"Is this true?" he asks, shaking his head, stunned.

I nod, toying with the locket around my neck. "Yes."

He leans back in his seat, blowing out a heavy breath. I give him all the time he needs because it's a lot to take in. "Lola... this is..."

"I know." He doesn't need to complete the sentence. I know what he's thinking.

"Are you sure this is what you want to do?"

"Yes." I don't need time to think because it's the only thing that makes sense.

He steeples his fingers, pondering. He can't say no. He's the only person I know who can help me.

"Please...help me help *him*. He's the only thing that matters."

Dr. Carter has seen my tears before, but something in this plea touches him. Whether it's my honesty or what I'm proposing, I'll never know, but when he nods, time stands still. "Okay."

I remain seated, too afraid to move. This is really happening. "T-thank you."

He sighs, picking up his phone. "Wilma?" She replies a second later. "Please clear my schedule. And can you bring in two black coffees?"

I shuffle in my seat, a ball of nervous energy. This is the first step, and I've never been more curious to see how it ends.

Peering at my reflection in the mirrored elevator wall, I touch up my plum lipstick and straighten out my black dress. Everything has to be perfect. The doors open, and I hesitate. I've never been more scared. Once I step out of this car, everything will change. The scary part is, I don't know if that change will be for the better.

I can do this.

I thank my mom for her stupid catchphrase as I walk toward Roman's door. When it opens, all my fears and worries disappear. I'm doing this for the man I love. I know he'll see reason—eventually.

"Wow," Roman exclaims, examining me from head to toe. "You look amazing."

"This old thing?" I tease, attempting to hide my

embarrassment.

He smirks while I remind myself to breathe. "Come in." I step forward, only for him to pull me into his arms.

Peering up at him from under my mascara-clad lashes, I hope he doesn't note my nerves. If he looks hard enough, I know he'll be able to see.

"I missed you," he huskily declares.

"I-I missed you too." My heart begins to beat faster and faster.

"You're shaking. What's the matter?" With the gentlest of touches, he brushes the hair from my cheek.

"I...I need to talk to you."

He arches a brow. "About what?" His voice is swimming with suspicion and alarm.

"Let's go inside." I reach for his hand and guide him inside. He follows, but his body is suddenly wound tight.

I wanted to lead in a little more subtly, but I should have known he'd see right through me. Nevertheless, I lead us over to the couch, but I don't think I can sit still.

"What's going on?" He folds his arms over his chest, waiting for me to explain my bizarre behavior.

"I, just...can you sit?" I rub my forehead, unhappy with how this has started. His lips pull into a thin, angry line, but he eventually complies.

The mood is set for a romantic evening; pillar candles flicker warmly around the room, and a bottle of wine is on the table. But that will have to wait.

I stand in front of him, wondering how to start this conversation. I've practiced what to say a million times in my head, but my mouth has unexpectedly been struck mute.

Roman leans forward, legs spread, his stance ready to pounce. "Lola?"

"I...I..." I need to move. I begin pacing, scolding myself for getting stage fright at the worst possible time. The words sit like a heavy lump in my throat.

Exhaling, I decide to show, rather than tell, because each second wasted is edging Roman closer to the edge. Reaching into my bag, I retrieve the folder I showed Dr. Carter. It's grown since today. He's given me everything I need, and my pitch is now flawless. The choice is now Roman's.

Passing him the folder, I snatch it back quickly when he reaches for it. "Promise me something."

He huffs, annoyed. "Okay." He gives me his full attention.

"Promise me you will read through everything before you say a word."

"Lola," he warns.

"Promise me," I press. "Promise me you'll read this with an open mind."

His brows knit together, and he shakes his head, utterly baffled, but then he finally nods. He knows he has no choice but to agree if he wants to see what's inside because my unyielding stance is final.

Satisfied, I loosen my hold and pray that this doesn't backfire.

Before he opens it, I add, "And remember our wager. You have to do everything I say starting from now." I need to lighten the mood.

He frowns, not amused.

This is it. I will my racing heart to calm down. It *is* the reason I'm here.

Roman skims his palm across the front, deep in thought. Does he know the contents could change his life forever?

"Whatever happens, remember I love you more than life itself. Everything I do…I do for you."

He peers up at me; he looks as lost as I feel. He nods before opening what I can only hope is his future.

I can't bear to watch, but I also can't bear to look away. His expression is stoic. I know this is just the beginning of what's to come. He reads the first page, his brows scrunching in confusion. It's a lot to take in, and I know it'll take a while to sink in.

When he turns the next page and then the next, the color drains from his face, and he gasps. His eyes arrow upward, searching my face, begging me to tell him this is a joke. But it's not.

"W-what is this?" he demands heatedly, waving the papers in the air.

"You know what it is," I reply softly, my body trembling.

"No, I really don't, because what I'm reading makes no fucking sense!" He jumps up, completely livid. "Please tell me you're joking."

I bite my lip but stand my ground. "No. I'm not."

"Have you gone mad?"

"Roman, just listen…" I advance but quickly retreat.

"No!" he shouts, hurling the papers onto the floor, unable to stomach the sight of them. "I will not. That"—he points at the fallen paperwork strewn all over the white carpet—"is not happening. Ever!" He curls his lip, appalled.

"You promised you would read it with an open mind."

He sniggers. "I made that promise not knowing I was going to read the most horrifying thing you could ever propose. How can you think I would agree to that?"

"Because it makes sense. It will work." I'm trying to keep cool because he's just gone from zero to ten billion in five seconds.

"No, it doesn't, and it won't!" He treads forward, on the warpath. "None of this makes any sense."

I don't back down. "I've done the research. I've consulted with Dr. Carter and the finest doctors in New York. They all said it will work. Please"—I crouch down, picking up the paperwork—"just read the rest." I offer a fistful. He recoils as if I've just asked him to commit the ultimate sin.

"No. Get that away from me!" He waves his hand, turning his head, unable to look my way.

"Roman. Please. This will work." I'm on my knees, begging for him to see reason, but he doesn't.

"You don't get it!" He throws his arms out to the side. "I don't care what the results say. It may work, we may be a match, but I won't do it. How can I? How can you expect me to?"

Tears sting my eyes. This has gone much worse than I expected.

"B-because I want you to live," I cry, gathering the folder and its contents, needing to do something other than look at the mess I've made.

"Lola...I can't." The fire in his tone abates. "I would do anything for you...*anything*...but there is no fucking way I would *ever* agree to that."

My fingers fumble, and tears cloud my vision. This was my final plea. This was the only way I knew how to save him. But he doesn't want it. A strangled sob escapes me, but I cover my mouth, not wanting to break down. I failed. I can't believe how terribly so.

"Please don't cry. I'm sorry, but I can't do this."

"Can't or won't?" I press, still on my knees.

He's silent, the anger slowly subsiding. But the undercurrent still has the capacity to drag us under. "Look at me."

But I can't. I'm afraid of what I'll say or do.

"Please." He lowers himself before me on both knees.

I lift my eyes, a tear sliding down my cheek. He wipes it away, stroking my jaw.

"This isn't a solution. It's a tragedy. How can I do this? How can I walk around every day knowing what I did?" His voice breaks.

Surrendering, I declare the only thing that makes any sense. In this tumultuous blackness, this is the only light I can find. Placing my hand over his strong heart, I lose myself in the rhythm.

"Because…you gave me your heart…and now…it's time I gave you mine." And I mean that in every literal sense.

Roman closes his eyes, shaking his head, pained.

The paperwork confronting Roman was notes detailing that I was a suitable donor. My heart would beat inside him. It would give him life. By ending my life, I could breathe new life into him. I did the tests, and my heart is healthy. The medication has left it unscathed.

"This is the only way."

He hisses, the truth burning him. "This is where you were today?"

"Yes," I whisper.

"Why didn't you come to me?"

"Because I knew you'd react this way! You gave me no other choice. You said that this was the only way. That a heart transplant would save your life." Reaching for his hand, I place it over my chest. "Well, I have a heart. Take mine. I don't need it." Searching his face, I beg him to see reason. "It's breaking every day anyway, knowing that you're dying. I can do something to help save you. Please. Take it."

He pulls his palm away, shaking it frantically. "I can't! Don't you see why I can't?"

"No. All I see is your pigheadedness standing in the way." We're silent, both glaring at the other.

"Even if I did this, how could I live with myself? How could I live knowing I'm alive because you're dead? I can't." The fight in him begins to fizzle, and all that's left is utter grief.

"If the tables were turned, would you do the same for me?"

His jaw clenches. "That's not the same thing."

"Answer me," I demand. "Would you?" When he turns his cheek, I force him to look at me by gripping his chin.

"Lola…" His blue-gray eyes swarm with grief.

"Tell me!"

"Yes!" he roars, his anger laced with devotion. "Of course, I would. I would happily end my life to save yours! I will fight for your life with my last dying breath." He shoots up, pacing, yanking at his hair. The hard resolve of his stance reveals that regardless of what he confessed, it doesn't make a lick of difference.

"So that's it then? You won't even discuss this with me?"

"No. There's nothing to discuss. I'm furious at you! How could you even think I'd be okay with this? And not only that, you went behind my back." He continues pacing, resembling a caged tiger.

"No one but Dr. Carter knows it's you."

"That's not the point!" I've never seen him this angry. It's evident he wants some time alone as he turns his back. "No. The answer is no."

Standing, I whisper, "If this is goodbye, then you say it first." My voice trembles. I can't believe it has come to this.

The scattered paperwork strewn on the floor is like a ticker tape parade highlighting my failure.

"It'll never be goodbye," he declares hollowly.

Holding back my tears, I turn to leave but then stop. "You're a hypocrite, Dr. Archibald. You were so adamant that I was to live, but the truth is...you're so afraid of living." I close the door behind me.

Only when I enter the elevator do I allow the tears to fall. I sob ugly tears, and I'm not sure I'll ever be able to stop. I went behind Roman's back, knowing full well that it would end this way. But I had to try.

It's better to be scared while dying instead of being scared of trying.

I catch a cab home.

Slipping off my ballet flats, I stagger to my room, silent sobs robbing me of breath. I want to shake sense into Roman. He's so angry because he knows I'm right. He knows this is the only way, but to gain back his life, I have to lose mine.

Slumping onto the end of my bed, I cradle my face, sobbing into my palms. A small part of me thought that maybe, just maybe Roman would see reason, and although it's not something I expected him to accept right away, he'd eventually come around.

But I thought wrong.

Three Days Later

I slept a lot, unable to face the world because Roman hasn't called.

By suggesting what I did, I never expected to push him away. In some naïve way, I thought it would bring us closer together.

It's now daylight; I know this because my mother has just given me my marching orders to get out of bed and shower. I really need to revoke her spare key.

After I'm showered and dressed, I feel semi-human, but a gaping hole has been punched through my chest. I miss Roman. So much. Even though I stand by my convictions, I never wanted things to turn out this way.

"Lola? Can you come out here?" my mom calls from outside my bedroom door.

Applying a coat of ChapStick, I don't bother with shoes as I hobble down the hallway.

My condition seems exacerbated since my fight with Roman. Could it be he was my magical potion all along?

Once I turn the corner, I take a moment to catch my breath, but that breath is taken in vain.

"Roman?" I wheeze. Surely, my vision has failed me. Actually, I'm certain it has.

I rub my eyes under my lenses, expecting that when I remove them, this will all be my imagination playing a cruel trick.

But it's not. Here he stands, in my living room looking worse than I do. His beard is full, his hair is snarled, and I'm certain he looks skinnier than when I saw him last.

"W-what are you doing here?" I clutch on to the top of the sofa, afraid I'm going to fall on my face.

"I called him," my mother says, carrying a silver tray as she enters the room. The smell of coffee follows her.

"Why?"

Roman winces, clearly hurt, but screw him.

"Because I think it's time you spoke." She is so matter-of-fact. I can see where I get my stubbornness from.

I purse my lips, purposely avoiding looking at him. "The last time we spoke, he didn't have much to say."

"Because you did all the talking," he counters lightly.

"Well, I call it as I see it, and all I see"—I finally make eye contact, quashing down the happiness at seeing him here—"is someone giving up. And I don't like quitters. A quality you apparently liked about me, Dr. Archibald."

Roman sighs, fisting his hair in frustration.

"Oh, Lola, stop it. You know you're happy to see him." I turn to look at my mom, making big eyes her way. Just whose side is she on?

He smirks, and just like that, I can breathe again.

"I'll leave you two alone. Go easy."

"I will," Roman says, nodding his gratitude at my mom.

But she shakes her head. "No, I was talking to my daughter."

I roll my eyes. "Goodbye, Mother."

She exits with a smile. Damn her meddling, but I can't deny she's done good this time.

An uncomfortable silence fills the room. Not a common occurrence between Roman and I, but I guess things change.

"Do you want any coffee?"

"No, I'm okay."

Silence.

Well, this isn't at all awkward.

He stands by the mantel, watching me. I tug at my skirt, suddenly feeling like I'm on show.

"Lola…" I wait, using the couch as my barricade. "I'm so sorry about the other day. I overreacted."

"You think?" I scoff.

"I'm trying here," he exclaims, obviously expecting a better reunion.

Roman annoys the bejesus out of me because we're both headstrong and stubborn, especially when it comes to the well-being of the other.

"Did you think this was going to be easy? If you did, you thought wrong."

"No," he sighs. "Nothing is ever easy with you."

"I don't make apologies for who I am."

"And I don't want you to. I love that about you."

The L-bomb. It's nice to know he still cares. But the question is, does he care enough?

He digs his hands into his pockets, his hair shrouding his face as he lowers his chin. "I read over the paperwork. Impressive. You'd make a good attorney."

"Maybe in another lifetime," I reply, waiting for him to continue.

"You're right"—he meets my gaze—"this would work. But…I just can't. It's all I've thought about these past few days, but I just…I can't. I would feel…"

"Undeserving? Guilty?" I offer when he pauses.

"Yes."

I know those feelings well. Wasn't I the one who expressed the same concerns when Roman presented me with the opportunity to live again? I'm angry, disappointed, but most of all, I understand how he feels.

On paper, this works, but morally, Roman couldn't live with himself. "Put yourself in my shoes. How would you feel if I proposed what you are?"

Would I rather die than live the rest of my days with Roman's heart beating soundly within my chest? Each beat a constant reminder of all that I've lost. A blanket of hopelessness swathes me, and I suddenly can't breathe.

"I know it's not what you wanted to hear, but…"

I can't listen to another word.

"Excuse me." I make my way to my room.

My world is turned upside down, because this is it. No matter how much I hate what Roman has decided, I understand. To save his life, I'd have to forfeit mine. Of course, I would wait until nature takes its course, but that doesn't make a difference. At the end of the day, Roman would be alive and I wouldn't. He can't live with the guilt.

"May I come in?"

"I can't stop you," I reply despondently from the foot of my bed.

Roman enters, closing the door behind him. He stands in the middle of the room, arms linked behind his back. "I don't want to fight with you. *I love you.* I love that you would be willing to do this for me. You literally are offering me your heart." He steps forward, kneeling at my feet. "Thank you. That's what I should have said to you. Thank you for offering me life."

I gaze down at him, too afraid to speak. His stance is defeated. Before me kneels a broken man. "You're w-welcome," I whisper.

With a tremor to his touch, he gently cups both hands around my calves. The moment he makes contact, goose bumps break out across my flesh. I've missed him so much. "I will stay with you for as long as I can."

His promise cements our fate. We're both going to die. I never fully accepted that truth until now. My last shred of hope floats on the wind, leaving us raw and naked. There are no second chances. All that's left to do is…live.

I shut out the uncertainties we face and instead, focus on his touch. The tenderness of his caresses brings tears to my eyes. I will miss him…so much. How can someone bury themselves so deep within your core, you almost forget what it felt like before you met them? The answer is, before Roman, I was only half alive.

Roman continues his strokes, appearing just as desperate for touch as I am.

"I may be dying," I whisper, my eyes slipping to half-mast. "But I'll die with a smile on my face because I loved, and I was loved in return."

"You will be loved until your last dying breath. That I promise you."

I blink past my sorrow, not wanting this moment to be a memory coated in tears. That's all Roman and I have left— moments to make into memories. And I plan on making memories every second I have left.

Reaching for the scruff of his shirt, I yank him upward, smashing my lips to his. He kisses me without a second thought, this deed between us as natural as the sun setting. This kiss isn't gentle; it's filled with desperation and longing.

I taste salty kisses before long, but I don't know if they're my tears or Roman's, but it doesn't matter. My pain is his. He cups my neck, robbing me of breath as he dominates my mouth in the way only he knows how.

His tongue explores every inch of me, igniting a fire deep within. With *Carpe Diem* as my motto, I crawl backward, falling onto the mattress and taking Roman with me. We're frenzied, ripping at one another's clothes, desperate to peel back all the layers, leaving us exposed and bare.

Once I'm naked beneath him, Roman sits back on his heels, studying every inch of me. I would once shy away, but not today. There is nothing but complete worship behind his gaze, and I feel like the luckiest woman alive.

He slides his hand in the valley of my chest, before circling over my galloping heart. No words are needed. I understand. I shudder when he cups one breast, then the other, awakening every inch of my flesh.

His lips chase after his touch. He's everywhere. His tongue swirls over my pearled buds, dipping downward to leave a wet trail along my quivering stomach. I arch upward, needing more. My legs fall open, welcoming him home.

He worships not only my body, but my soul. He tells me how much he loves me, and that I'm his forever. We both know that our forever is timeless because our memories will never fade.

He enters me slowly, savoring each second, each touch,

because each moment is precious. I will never tire of feeling him rooted so deeply. Being connected as one is the closest I'll get to our hearts beating as one.

We move in harmony, his yang to my yin. We are connected, and death won't change that. "I love you." I gasp, threading my hands through his hair.

"And I you," he pants, dominating my body with his powerful strokes.

My release is close, it always is, but something about this feels different. We've finally accepted that this is our future. No matter how short it may be, we will never let go. I would rather live a day being loved by Roman, than live a lifetime without him by my side.

That thought is my undoing, and I explode with an earth-shattering scream.

He moves deeply within me, whispering into my ear. "You're the best thing that has ever happened to me. Know that my heart will forever be yours."

I squeeze my eyes shut, sobbing from pleasure and pain.

Quickening his pace, he follows suit soon after, speaking tragically beautiful words.

We lie in one another's arms for hours, naked and spent. Nothing has ever been more perfect.

Just as I'm on the cusp of sleep, Roman settles beneath the covers, tucking me into his chest. "What is one thing you've always wanted to do?"

"Sleep," I groggily reply.

He chuckles, his breath warming my cheeks. "I plan on making you the happiest girl alive."

"You already have."

As we're both about to fall into a peaceful slumber, I realize this is really happening, and I'm ready for whatever life throws my way. Whatever is coming, I will never give up. And I mean that in every way possible.

SEVENTEEN

Six Weeks Later

I've beaten all odds, but there really is no surprise there. Each day I grow weaker, but funnily enough, that doesn't make me sad. I know I don't have long, but each day spent with Roman over these past few weeks has made me appreciate life in ways I never thought possible.

We traveled, we laughed, we loved, and we cried. Nothing stood in our way. Nothing was too far or too much. We embraced life with both hands.

My health has not only deteriorated but so has Roman's. He struggles to do simple chores such as climbing a staircase or taking Freud for a walk. I know he hates it, but we're locked in a silent agreement not to discuss "it." He's still stubborn, headstrong, and as infuriating as usual about the subject, but so am I.

I let it rest, though, because I wanted to live out our final days in peace. And we have. No talk of dying or doom or gloom has been allowed.

But that's about to change.

I believe everything happens for a reason, so my return to Strawberry Fields was inevitable. If miracles can happen, then tonight is the night. It seems fitting it ends where it all started because Roman has no idea what's about to happen.

June has organized a party for the kids and their families. It's quite a lavish affair. But there's a reason we're all here.

I knew once I left here, I would be a changed woman, but I just never knew how much. I've grown into the woman I've always wanted to become, and I've achieved everything I've wanted, regardless of the fact I had a deadline. We all want more time, but I wouldn't give up my life, even as it is.

"Sit still," Zoe admonishes playfully, tugging at a curl in my hair.

Clutching at the locket between my breasts, I meet Zoe's gaze in the mirror in her room. "Thank you." And I mean that in every literal way.

She nods, a nostalgic smile tugging at her lips.

Facing death hasn't turned me into some superhero. It's made me human. I never knew the reason I was drawn here, but now I do.

"Ready?" Zoe asks, placing her hands on my shoulder.

She knows me too well. I will never give up on Roman. I will fight for him with my last dying breath.

"Yes. I was born ready."

She laughs, and the sound is one I will truly miss.

It takes me three attempts, but I eventually stand.

"You look so beautiful." Zoe brushes a curl behind my ear.

Taking one last look at myself in the mirror, I come to appreciate that I don't look beautiful; I look alive, which is an oxymoron, considering I'm embracing the end of my days. I've opted for contacts, and my eyes are swathed in a gray shimmer. My mascara lashes are long and full, and my cheeks are tinted with a rosy glow. One could almost mistake me for healthy—almost.

She offers me her arm, always my pillar of strength.

My jeweled flats scuff along the carpet, but Zoe doesn't rush me. She is with me every slow step of the way.

It takes about twenty minutes, but we eventually arrive at the outdoor pavilion. An eighties love song catches on the cool breeze, and a flurry of butterflies suddenly fills my belly.

"I'm nervous," I confess, wiping my hands on my ballooned dress.

"Don't be." Zoe is right. What I have planned will make all this worthwhile.

Taking a deep breath, I appreciate the glorious sight before us. The night sky glows bright with hundreds of tea light candles sprinkled around the grounds. Tables as far as the eye can see are scattered around the lawn.

I make out many familiar faces, most of whom I invited. Teddy and Dr. Carter are sitting by the small bar. Dr. Carter's hoarse voice booms loudly, no doubt subjected to Teddy's infamous charm.

Tamara and my peers sit at a table, chatting and smiling happily. She must feel me watching her because she turns and meets my eyes. There are no hard feelings between us. For her to move on, Roman told her everything. His actions were explained, and she soon realized it wasn't her. If things were different, she would be a perfect mate, but life doesn't work that way. I should know.

She nods, a knowing smile passing over her lips. I'll miss her.

My parents are on the makeshift dance floor, embraced tight as they whisper sweet nothings to each other. They look happy. My mother's health scare changed both their lives for the better. Sometimes, we need to lose something to appreciate its worth.

I observe the sea of familiar faces, thankful I got the chance to meet them.

Suddenly, someone with a head of luscious long brown hair catches my eye. I blink, certain I'm seeing things, but when she turns, I know I'm not.

My Georgia wouldn't miss this for the world.

She stops twirling around the dance floor, standing still. There was always an air of tranquility surrounding her, and now is no exception. She looks healthy. She looks happy. She's welcoming me home.

She raises her hand in a still wave, a gentle gesture that she's ready whenever I am. I raise my hand, feeling her familiar warmth against my skin. The world is spinning around her, but time would stand still to save her.

"Who are you waving to?" Zoe asks, peering overhead to catch a glimpse of who has captured my attention. But she won't see anyone.

"No one," I reply dreamily.

Georgia nods with a conscious smile. She knows it's not time, not yet anyway. Her feet glide along the floor, ghost-like, as she sways to the haunting music. She's weightless. She dances to the beat of her own drum. She always has.

My fatigued legs tremble, begging for a reprieve, but we're not done yet. There is only one person my heart seeks out. It will, until the end of time, always search for him in a crowd.

The low hanging branches of a tall tree shadow my Prince Charming. But eternal darkness can never shun his light. His tuxedo sets off his true masculine beauty; he looks rugged, and commanding, and he's all mine.

A lopsided smirk tugs at his lips as he curls his finger, beckoning me over to the dark side. I don't stand a chance.

I begin my slow descent down the star-sprinkled carpet, stopping beneath the arch and admiring its splendor. Tresses of diamonds fall from the summit, and small stars hang from the ends. It truly feels like I'm dancing under the stars.

Roman watches me with nothing but patience as he waits for me. No one, nothing exists but us. I keep my eyes locked on his, unbelieving this man is truly mine. He has taught me so many things, but most of all, we've taught one another how to live.

He steps out from under the tree, the full moon illuminating his radiance. Nothing has been more perfect. It gives me the strength to continue.

We come to a stop a few feet away, both appreciating the sight before us. His hair is slicked back, and his beard is full. He looks nothing like when we first met, but I suppose I don't either. We've both grown and learned, and those life lessons have turned us into the people we were always destined to become.

My heart instantly recognizes him and begins the familiar dance of wanting to become one. But Roman has another dance in mind.

"May I have this dance?" He extends his hand, and just like that, I'm in heaven.

I slip my palm into his and allow him to escort me to the dance floor. My gown trails behind me, leaving footprints of magic in its wake. My parents beam as Roman draws me into his arms, appearing happy I've finally found my forever.

I melt into his arms, resting my head against his chest as we sway gently to the music. Our bodies move in sync. I'm engulfed in his fragrance and his warmth, and I only wish it could always be this way between us. But this moment, the memories we've made are more than enough. I will never forget.

"Are you having fun?" he whispers into my ear.

"Yes." I snuggle closer, not wanting to talk because I'm afraid of what I'll say. Roman's life is about to change in minutes. Keeping this a secret from him wasn't an easy thing to do.

I wanted to tell him so many times, but that unspoken promise stood in the way. I've held off for as long as I could, but time isn't on our side, and I can no longer wait. I hope this doesn't backfire. I hope he understands why I've done what I have.

I allow one final heartbeat of comfort before I seek out my prize.

Erin stands by a table, waiting for my cue. I nod with a gentle smile.

She tosses back her beer, appearing to need the Dutch courage. I know the feeling too well. She steps out onto the dance floor, headed our way. I clutch Roman tighter, imprinting him to memory, but my memories will always pale compared to the real thing.

"May I cut in?" Erin asks. Roman doesn't hide his surprise at seeing her here. I answer for him as I step from his arms. He frowns, missing the connection. I can't help but love him even more.

I kiss his cheek, wondering if he knows what's coming. I don't look back.

I seek out Zoe, who is chatting with Tamara. Everything is where it should be.

"Are you sure you want to do this?" Zoe asks, her eyes focused on Erin and Roman, watching my plan unfold.

"Yes."

"He's going to be so mad," Tamara says, a touch of humor to her tone.

I shrug, playfully. "That's nothing new."

She chuckles but turns serious. "Do you think it'll work?"

Watching the change in Roman's bearing due to Erin's tears, I know the answer is yes. It has to. "It will work. I've made sure of it."

Both girls are quiet, not questioning my confidence because they know I never give up on what I want.

Tonight is about Roman. It always has been. I may not have spoken about the unspoken, but that doesn't mean I wasn't plotting. I didn't want to taint our last moments with sadness, but now, I've got nothing left to lose.

Looking at the guest list, they all have one thing in common—Roman. Each person was touched by him, or they saw how he touched me. This entire time, Roman doubted his worth. I'm here to show him just how valuable he truly is.

The song ends, and Erin wipes away her tears. She kisses Roman on the cheek before leaving the dance floor, needing a moment alone. Teddy is next in line. Just as Roman makes a move to where I'm standing, Teddy grabs him by the arm and leads him toward the bar. Dr. Carter and Gus are also there.

For the next forty-five minutes, they talk to Roman, detailing how he not only touched their lives but also changed the lives of so many others. His work as a doctor has saved countless lives. If he leaves this world, then who will fill his shoes?

Teddy turns serious before pulling Roman in for a hug. And that's my next cue.

The kids Roman cared for circle him, all sharing their personal experiences with him. He slumps onto the barstool, running a hand down his face. I stand in clear view, not wanting to hide.

Tamara strokes my shoulder before joining the band of advocates.

I know she loves Roman, and although nothing is worse than loving someone who doesn't feel that way in return, she still wants to help save him because he's someone worth saving.

Both she and Roman sit huddled, her sobbing into his chest. He comforts her, his face in tatters with each word she speaks. Zoe is next. She speaks on behalf of Sadie. My parents take over from her when she's done.

They didn't detail what they planned to tell Roman, but I

know they respect and accept my decision. It took them a while because coming to terms with the fact their daughter wants to donate her heart to the man she loves isn't something you hear every day. But they've seen the change in me, and if that change is thanks to Roman, then they were more than happy to help save his life.

As my parents leave, the long list of people I found who were more than happy to vouch for Roman's kindness step up to the plate—doctors, nurses, patients, volunteers, old teachers, and strangers he met for a mere moment…the list is endless.

Roman has touched so many lives, and the thought that he will end his is a reality I will never accept. I know he said no, but I'm a Van Allen. I don't take no for an answer.

My mother's tears are ugly as she turns over her shoulder, her love for me swimming in her gaze. I have no idea what she said to him, but whatever it is, he finally lifts his heavy eyes and meets mine.

This entire time, he's kept his cards close to his chest. I have no doubt he's furious with me, but deep down, I know he's amazed that I did all this for him. He may not be able to see his worth, but I can. I always have.

The world needs Roman. He just needs to see why.

I hold back my tears as I see it—a glimmer of hope. Beneath the layers of anger and stubbornness is a smidgeon of acceptance. He arches a brow, extending his arms out, asking if this was my doing. I shake my head slowly and gesture to the people around us—it was ours.

Each person who leaves Roman has tears in their eyes. They've unburdened their souls, and I can only hope he's done the same.

A gentle touch has me smiling. She's my ace in a hole. She's the reason I was able to pull this off. "I'm pretty sure I can hear him curse your name from here."

"That's nothing new, June." I turn to look at her with a smile.

When I informed her of my plan, she wanted nothing to do with it at first. Her relationship with Roman was still strained.

But her support shone through when it mattered the most. She can never make up for the years lost, but she can reset their history and try again.

"I knew you came here for a reason," she confesses. Now that I know she and Roman are mother and son, I can't help but compare the compassion they share. "You came here to save my son. And you came here to save me. Thank you, Lola." She wraps her arms around me, kissing my cheek. "I'll never be able to thank you enough."

Hugging her tightly, I whisper, "You already have. Look after him," I cry into her shoulder, knowing that it's almost time. "Please give it to him once I'm gone."

"I will." She promises to deliver my last parting gift to Roman.

We break apart. She wipes away my tears. With one final smile, she turns and walks toward her son. The moment she simply enfolds him into her arms and he goes willingly, I know he's going to be okay. I can go now.

Taking one final look around me, I catalog every moment I spent here and file it deep within my heart. I now understand why I came here. And that was to live.

My exit isn't grand or memorable. I merely slip into the darkness; every part of me filled with love. I hobble to the only place I belong.

"I'm proud of you, kiddo."

Closing my eyes, I walk on autopilot, my body slowing down. "Thanks, G. I c-couldn't h-have done i-it without you."

The sweet smell guides me. It's not far now. *"No, that's where you're wrong. You were always the strong one. You just needed to see that yourself."*

I smile, happy that I've finally uncovered why I'm here.

"I'll be waiting. Whenever you're ready, know that I'm here. We all are."

I burst into happy tears, my shoulders shuddering with bittersweet bliss. I come to a stop, slowly opening my eyes.

The perpetual rows of roses have always taken my breath away, and now is no exception. I feel at peace here. Like I belong. I slump to the ground, my beautiful dress pooling around me, blanketed in the dirt.

I fist the ground, the energy vibrating up my arm. Everything is heightened. This is not the end...it's only the beginning. I once wished I was somebody else, but not anymore. I'm proud to be me. How can I not? Look at all I've experienced. Look at the amazing, extraordinary life I've led.

I may have only known Roman for a minuscule space in time, but I wouldn't change that for the world. I can wish I was somebody else, but if I were, I would never have met Roman, and I'd rather die with his memory than live without it.

"You know I'm not okay with this."

His voice breaks through the silence and warms my trembling form. "I k-know."

"And you know I would rather give up my life to save yours."

"I know." There is nothing more I can say.

He stands above me, his bow tie unraveled, and his top button undone. "But you're going to make me do this, aren't you?"

"Yes." I risk meeting his eyes, hoping his fight has gone.

"You are the most infuriating woman I have ever met." He begins pacing, tearing at his hair.

"Thank you."

He turns on his heel, pointing an accusing finger my way. "When did you plan all this?" He's trying to make sense of how he missed it. "How?"

"When you weren't looking," I reply, not having the energy to go into detail.

"I told you how I felt." His comment holds bite.

"And I told you I don't give up," I rebuke, just as stubbornly. "Just because I wasn't talking about it, didn't mean I wasn't thinking about it. I can't force you to live, but I wanted you to see the impact your decision would have on so many people. You're a good man, Roman. The world needs you."

"I should be furious at you, but that doesn't seem to make a difference."

I give him the time he needs to process this because I know it's a lot.

"Be mad at me all you want, but don't punish yourself. You know this is the end of the line for me. You know this is the right thing to do."

He hisses, pouncing forward. "Don't...don't you say it. There is no right in this situation. There never will be."

I avert my gaze, suddenly fearful that tonight won't make a lick of difference. "Life isn't fair; we both know that. But one of us has a chance at living. *Live.*" It's a plea, my last appeal. The fight ebbs from my bones. "You can't run away from life. I won't let you."

He exhales, interlacing his hands behind his neck. "How can I accept this? How can I deal with you...dying?" It's the first time he's said it. The first time he's accepted this.

Everything begins to grow sluggish, but I push on. "By doing this, you're honoring my life."

He turns his cheek, pained. "You were supposed to live."

"I have."

"You're twenty-five!" he cries, shaking his head. "Your life has only just begun."

I'm so tired, so gravely tired. "My life started the day I met you…and it'll live on in you."

Roman's chest shudders, holding back his tears. "I just…I want more time."

His pleas are my undoing, and a string of sniffs escapes me. "I *was* given more time…more time to meet you. And it was enough because meeting you was timeless. This was my destiny all along. I don't want to go…but I have to."

Roman takes a moment, peering up into the star-filled sky. "I'm stealing yet another life."

His guilt stabs at my very core. "No, Roman, you're not." I know he's talking about Scarlett. "You told me you would have given her your heart if you could." He lowers his chin, the moonlight reflecting his sadness. "Well, I feel the same. You *are* worthy of this life. You're worth so much more."

It takes him seconds to process what I said before he falls to his knees, defeated and overcome.

This was the final piece—me.

Placing my palm over his chest, I commit to memory this moment because it's why I'm here. "Don't break my heart," I whisper, blinking past my tears. "Look after it. Take it. It's yours. It belongs to you. It always has."

His heart pounds beneath my hand. It gives me strength knowing that soon, my heart will beat for him. He closes his eyes, shaking his head, utterly broken.

"Lola," he cries, crushing me in his arms. The moment he

surrenders, I smile. He may not know it yet, but I know that I've won—we both have.

We stay hugging for minutes, Roman never wanting to let go. "I'm not making any promises. For the moment, I'm… undecided."

"Undecided is better than hell to the fuck no."

He chuckles at my choice of words.

"I'm still angry with you, but thank you for tonight. Seeing the way the world, the way *you* see me is just…indescribable. You never cease to amaze me."

Things grow quiet.

"I didn't tell you how beautiful you look. How beautiful you are," he adds, kissing over my pulse. "Will you dance with me?"

Although I'm thankful for the change of pace, I pull back gently, my brows knitted. "Here?"

He nods, his poignant eyes hopeful.

"But there's no music."

"Let's make our own," he whispers, laying a gentle kiss against my lips, before standing and scooping me into his arms. I snuggle against him, wrapping my arms around his neck.

He begins swaying to an invisible beat, but it's the perfect tempo, the perfect song. He's holding me tightly, carrying me as though I'm his most cherished prize. We dance through a soundtrack crafted especially for us. Roman never lets me go. I stay huddled against him, my final dance the best one of my life.

The full moon is our only beacon of light, and under the

stars, I get lost in every single memory that led me here. Roman has given me so much to remember, and these memories will tell my story long after I'm gone. I collect each one and fold them deep inside my heart, so whenever Roman is lonesome, he can unlock each one, remembering the impact our love had on the world.

"Are you scared?" His voice floats across the still night, giving me comfort for what's ahead.

"Not right now," I reply, closing my eyes and burying my face into his neck.

"Why?" He continues swaying, the movement lulling me into a comfortable state.

"Because…you're holding my hand."

A pained breath escapes him. He's biding his time. "I promise…I'll never let go. No matter where you go…I'll find you. I love you. So much."

"I know," I whisper, the darkness beginning to conquer the light. But I'm not scared. I have saved the man I love, so I am finally free. With shallow breath, my parting words are my final bow. "Lead with your heart…and you'll find me. Always."

There is no more pain or uncertainty. All that is left is love…

EPILOGUE

"Chase me!" The sparkle of a child's carefree laughter reminds us of the simplicity to life. I sometimes forget what that feels like.

"Owen, go play with your sister!" Owen crosses his chubby arms across his chest, pouting. So stubborn, just like his father. He complies a second later, however, chasing after his younger sister.

The sun is balmy against my aged skin, but I lost the ability to stay warm long ago.

My weary body creaks as I lower myself to the rich soil, but I ignore the ache, the memories overriding any pain. This garden has provided me endless hours of comfort. Coming here is like coming home.

Strawberry Fields has never looked more beautiful. The sweet perfume of roses transports me back in time, and I close my eyes, revisiting my favorite memory of all.

"Lead with your heart…and you'll find me. Always."

And she was right. She always was.

We danced the night away with her tucked snugly in my arms. If I dig deep enough, I can almost taste, feel, smell her—I long to feel her just one more time. That miraculous evening was the last night we spent together.

After I took her home, we made love one final time. The next morning, she slipped into a deep coma, which she succumbed to three days later. Her dying wish was for me to take her heart, but the thought was too heinous to even comprehend.

I knew she would go when she was ready. Lola never did anything she didn't want to do. So I sat with her, holding her hand. I promised never to let go, and I didn't. Seeing the person you love more than life itself slip away before your eyes does something to you. I didn't see the point in living if the person who made your life worth living was gone.

I tried to grapple with the reality that I would live once she was gone, thanks to her. But I didn't want to be here without her. So with my mind made up, I waited, waited to be reunited with my one true love.

But in true Lola Van Allen fashion, she fought until the bitter end, speaking to me on the cusp of death. My mother knew my decision, and she didn't push, but she said Lola wanted me to have something, hoping that I would make the right choice.

When she handed me Lola's journal and Sadie's necklace, I knew that even from beyond the grave, she wouldn't let this go. That journal was my savior. It felt like Lola was reading me her words. A lost, scared woman wrote the first entry, but each page detailed her strength, her growth.

I laughed; I cried. I never felt more loved than I did when reading how I appeared through Lola's eyes.

The last page I read on the very last day. I was holding off, knowing that whatever was scrawled upon that page had the ability to change my mind in a heartbeat…and it did.

I watched Lola's life begin to fade away, and before it was too late, I opened the book, realizing the ending was only the beginning.

Who knew one simple word could change a person's life forever. But in our case, that word was forever ours.

Live.

It may not have been poetic, but that one word changed my mind. I would do this for her. I would live in her honor, her heart becoming ours.

"Dad, are you all right?" My son's voice brings me back to the present, reminding me that I stayed true to Lola's words—I lived.

The transplant was a success. Her heart now drummed within my chest. Each strong beat was a reminder of everything I not only lost but also what I gained. I didn't need a photograph to remember Lola because she gave me so much to remember.

My arthritic hand closes a fist over my heart—she's within there—always.

Once I was well enough, I did everything I knew she'd want me to do. I lived.

I took a vacation with Teddy, and we went to the jazz festival in Birmingham, Alabama. She mentioned this to him when she was being her usual nosy self. I ran in the color vibe, honoring her with each step I took. Her face was on every billboard I could find. We raised over ten million dollars to research the disease which claimed her young life.

I stopped hiding behind my fears, speaking to people who were just like Lola and me. Camille helped any way she could; she was the master of speeches, after all. I never hid the fact that the woman I loved saved my life. I was determined for the world to know just who Lola Van Allen was.

My talks around the country gained the attention of a publishing house in New York. They offered me a deal I couldn't refuse. Two years later, Lola's beautiful face was on every bestselling list, worldwide. The story entailed her struggle and mine. It was the hardest thing I've ever had to do, but knowing my Lola would never be forgotten was worth the pain.

Readers from across the globe wrote me, saying how much

our story touched them. They would never forget Lola. My soul mate was forever immortalized.

The money I made funded medication trials and groundbreaking procedures to cure brain tumors and heart defects. I ran the biggest cancer research center in the US. Every person who participated in the trials was Lola. I visited them as not only a friend but as their doctor.

Lola has helped save so many lives. Her death was never in vain.

Years passed, and although I never forgot my love for her, I fell in love with someone I know she would approve of. At first, I felt like I was betraying Lola, but her journal, the one I kept tucked away in my bedside table, was proof she wanted me to move on.

I married a fellow doctor who had lost her partner to leukemia years ago. We were both broken, but somehow together, we fit. Her name was Ivy, and we had three wonderful children.

Once June passed, I was the official owner of Strawberry Fields. Ivy understood why I wanted to hold on to it, and we did. We continued my mother's vision, opening the doors to anyone who needed this magical place as their sanctuary.

These walls have seen so much pain and sorrow, but they've also provided a haven for people just like Lola. And just like Scarlett. This place is for them—it's for every single soul who found their way home.

"I'm fine, son. I'll be in, in just a minute." My eldest, Peter, is just like his mother. Forever caring and ensuring the well-being of others.

He hesitates, but when my grandson, Owen, and his twin sister, Olivia, demand ice cream, he knows he better comply.

Peter, Addison, and Lachlan are my children, all of whom I am so proud of. They work here at Strawberry Fields, as my tired body can no longer keep up. Ivy passed five years ago, so now, it's just me.

I have my kids and grandkids, but they have their own lives to live, and I want them to. Everyone is deserving of this gift called life. Each beat of my heart is confirmation of that.

Opening my eyes, I peer upward, gazing upon the towering giant above me. I made her a promise, and I honor it every day. In life, Lola Van Allen stood out from a crowd…so it only seems fitting that she does the same in death.

A commanding yellow sunflower shoots into the heavens, soaring high above the roses it is planted among. My weathered hands, hands which miss her touch every day, fist the dirt around its roots, feeling the life source shoot through my veins.

This is in honor of her—of the woman whose heart gave me life, not only physically, but emotionally as well. I miss her so much. I was only half living until I met her, and even though I have lived the most extraordinary life thanks to her, I'm ready to see her again.

She will forever be young and beautiful, and I will always

remember that girl. I will always remember the way she made me feel. And I want to feel that way again.

I will look back on this life with nothing but happiness, and that thought has my heart, *our* heart slowing down, finally allowing me to slip back into the past and become lost forever with her.

Laying my aged body against the soil, I wait for her to come. The sun peeks out from behind the yellow sunflower petals, suddenly warming my wintry frame.

"Lola?" I hardly recognize my voice anymore.

Lub-dub…

Lub-dub…

Lub…. dub…

Our heart sings for her, begging her to save me this one final time.

Reaching into my pocket, I retrieve the one picture I've allowed myself to keep. My shaky hands have memorized the folds, and over the years, I've had to handle this keepsake with care. It's yellowed, aged, and faded, but it's clearer than any other photo taken after it.

Opening it tenderly, I strain my poor eyesight to see two people who look like mere strangers, but my cherished memories of that day at the baseball game confirm that my old senile mind isn't lost just yet. My eyes slip shut, a smile marked on my face.

I remember the softness of her skin, the tender touch of

her lips. The rain pelted down around us, but she didn't care. As long as we were together, the world could fall into place around us.

And it still can.

"Hello, Dr. Archibald."

I'm suddenly transported back in time.

My eyes pop open, and I blink twice. I can see clearly. Waving my hand out in front of me, I gasp when the weathered planes are no longer visible. What's going on?

Sitting upright, I'm surprised I can move without pain. But that surprise is quickly forgotten when I see who is standing feet away.

"Lola?"

When she smiles, my heart stills…I've come home.

"I missed you." Her voice…it sings to my soul.

I can hardly believe it. This is surely a dream. "I…I missed you too."

She looks exactly how I remember her, but when I take a closer look, she looks different—she looks healthy and alive. Sadie's necklace sits around her neck.

When she drops to both knees, her signature fragrance assaults my senses, and memory upon memory collides into me. I don't dare breathe when she reaches out and gently runs her fingers down my cheek. I can feel her. I smother my moan.

"Are you ready?"

"Ready for what?" My mind is ricocheting, unable to keep up.

She smirks that brazen smile I've missed so much. "Ready to live."

My heart kick-starts again, strong, vibrant, and alive.

Placing my hand against her chest, a sense of peace surrounds me because her heart beats strongly too. It's all I've ever wished since she left.

"Yes. I'm ready."

And I am.

I don't give her a chance to catch her breath as I smash my lips to hers, unable to wait a second longer. But where we're going, we don't need air—she's the only air I breathe.

The moment we connect, everything falls into place, and the long lost years of missing her seem like mere minutes. Nothing else matters but this. She has always been my destiny, my forever and a day.

As we clutch on to each other, both crying happy tears, I realize that I tried so desperately to save her, but truth be told, in the end, she saved me.

And even now, in death, she's saved me once again.

ACKNOWLEDGEMENTS

My author family: Elle Kennedy and Vi Keeland—I love you both very much.

My ever-supporting parents. You guys are the best. I am who I am because of you. I love you. RIP Papa. Gone but never forgotten. You're in my heart. Always.

My agent, Kimberly Brower from Brower Literary & Management. Thank you for your patience and thank you for being an amazing human being.

My editor, Jenny Sims. What can I say other than I LOVE YOU! Thank you for everything. You go above and beyond for me.

My proofreader—My Brother's Editor, YOU ROCK!

Sommer Stein, you NAILED this cover! Thank you for being so patient and making the process so fun. I'm sorry for annoying you constantly.

My publicist—Danielle Sanchez from Wildfire Marketing Solutions. Thank you for all your help.

A special shout-out to: Bombay Sapphire Gin, Kell Donaldson, L.J. Shen, Christina Lauren, Natasha Madison, Willow Winters, K. Webster, Giana Darling, S.M. Soto, Devney Perry, Penelope Ward, Tillie Cole, Lisa Edward, Cheri Grand Anderman, Lauren Rosa, Louise, Nichole Strauss, Toni

Rakstraw, Kimberly Whalen, Ben Ellis—Tall Story Designs, Nasha Lama, Natasha Tomic, Heyne, Random House, Kinneret Zmora, Hugo & Cie, Planeta, MxM Bookmark, Art Eternal, Carbaccio, Fischer, Sieben Verlag, Bookouture, Egmont Bulgaria, Brilliance Publishing, Audible, Hope Editions, Buzzfeed, BookBub, PopSugar, Hugues De Saint Vincent, Paris, New York, Sarah Sentz (you're my cover go-to queen!) Jessica—PeaceLoveBooks.

To the endless blogs that have supported me since day one—You guys rock my world.

My bookstagrammers—This book has allowed me to meet SO many of you. Your creativity astounds me. The effort you go to is just amazing. Thank you for the posts, the teasers, the support, the messages, the love, the EVERYTHING! I see what you do, and I am so, so thankful.

My ARC TEAM—You guys are THE BEST! Thanks for all the support.

My reader group—sending you all a big kiss.

My beautiful family—Daniel, Mum, Papa, Fran, Matt, Samantha, Amelia, Gayle, Peter, Luke, Leah, Jimmy, Jack, Shirley, Michael, Rob, Elisa, Evan, Alex, Francesca, and my aunties, uncles, and cousins—I am the luckiest person alive to know each and every one of you. You brighten up my world in ways I honestly cannot express.

Samantha and Amelia— I love you both so very much.

To my family in Holland and Italy, and abroad. Sending

you guys much love and kisses.

Papa, Zio Nello, Zio Frank, Zia Rosetta, and Zia Giuseppina—you are in our hearts. Always.

My fur babies— mamma loves you so much! Buckwheat, you are my best buddy. Dacca, I will always protect you from the big bad Bellie. Mitch, refer to Dacca's comment. Jag, you're a wombat in disguise. Bellie, your singing voice is so beautiful. And Ninja, thanks for watching over me. To the newest addition, Wabbit; I love your apricot face.

To anyone I have missed, I'm sorry. It wasn't intentional!

Last but certainly not least, I want to thank YOU! Thank you for welcoming me into your hearts and homes. My readers are the BEST readers in this entire universe! Love you all!

ABOUT THE AUTHOR

Monica James spent her youth devouring the works of Anne Rice, William Shakespeare, and Emily Dickinson.

When she is not writing, Monica is busy running her own business, but she always finds a balance between the two. She enjoys writing honest, heartfelt, and turbulent stories, hoping to leave an imprint on her readers. She draws her inspiration from life.

She is a bestselling author in the U.S.A., Australia, Canada, France, Germany, Israel, and The U.K.

Monica James resides in Melbourne, Australia, with her wonderful family, and menagerie of animals. She is slightly obsessed with cats, chucks, and lip gloss, and secretly wishes she was a ninja on the weekends.

CONNECT WITH
MONICA JAMES

Facebook: facebook.com/authormonicajames
Twitter: twitter.com/monicajames81
Goodreads: goodreads.com/MonicaJames
Instagram: instagram.com/authormonicajames
Website: authormonicajames.com
Pinterest: pinterest.com/monicajames81
BookBub: bookbub.com/authors/monica-james
Amazon: https://amzn.to/2EWZSyS
Join my Reader Group: http://bit.ly/2nUaRyi

CPSIA information can be obtained
at www.ICGtesting.com
Printed in the USA
LVHW020706300121
677807LV00005B/567